The Path That Turns Toward Spring

The Path That Turns Toward Spring

***

by Melanie Lageschulte

The Path That Turns Toward Spring

by Melanie Lageschulte
Fremont Creek Press

Paperback: 978-1-952066-45-0
Hardcover: 978-1-952066-46-7
Kindle: 978-1-952066-39-9
Large print paperback: 978-1-952066-44-3

Web: fremontcreekpress.com

Also by Melanie Lageschulte

MAILBOX MYSTERIES SERIES

The Route That Takes You Home
The Road to Golden Days
The Lane That Leads to Christmas
The Path That Turns Toward Spring

GROWING SEASON SERIES

Growing Season
Harvest Season
The Peaceful Season
Waiting Season
Songbird Season
The Bright Season
Turning Season
The Blessed Season
Daffodil Season
Firefly Season

SHORT FICTION

A Tin Train Christmas

* 1 *

Kate sighed as she tugged her knit stocking cap lower over her ears. Maybe this wasn't the best way to spend part of her Sunday afternoon. After all, there was laundry to do, and the bathroom needed a scrub ...

A big, fluffy feline paw on the leg of her insulated jeans caught her attention. Kate's layers of outerwear made her a bit slower to reach down and pick up Scout, but she got the job done.

"I'm not the only one with cabin fever, huh? Hazel has it, too. I mean, look at her."

While some small drifts continued to resist the recent thaw, last year's dead brown grass was now visible across most of the lawn. Hazel had first made a manic sprint around the brick farmhouse's foundation, and now turned her attention to what was apparently her favorite part of a mid-March farmyard: the mud.

Kate Duncan groaned as her dog gleefully launched herself into one mucky puddle after another.

Slop soon covered Hazel's feet, and a good portion of her legs. Eager to get a deep sniff of the ground, she plopped her snout into the gravel driveway's deepest crater, then raised it with a triumphant "woof!"

Kate marveled at how Scout's white paws stayed mostly

pristine, even as his long black coat shed its winter layers all over her chore parka.

"You know better than to get that dirty, don't you? It's just as well that I haven't mopped the kitchen floor yet. Hazel's going to need a toweling-down, and then some. She'll have to wait, though, since we're off to check out the pasture. Maggie, are you coming?"

The petite gray-tabby cat planted her feet on the damp sidewalk behind the back porch, and wrapped her tail around her paws.

"That's a no, then. As for Jerry, who knows where he went? It looks like it's just the three of us. Hazel, come on!"

The far side of the yard wasn't much better than the area up by the house. Soft ground was everywhere, along with small, shallow puddles and clumps of dirty snow. The only pops of color came from the row of evergreen trees along the pasture fence, and the scattering of overgrown juniper bushes next to the chicken house. Those were in desperate need of pruning, one of the countless chores Kate would have to tackle when spring finally arrived.

As for when that might happen, she knew better than to rely on the calendar. It claimed spring was just days away; but in northern Iowa, vicious snowstorms were possible well into April. Kate couldn't be sure if the moisture in the air today was only due to the thawing earth, or if the heavy clouds would bring more snow by tomorrow.

Her bright-yellow galoshes kept Kate's toes dry as she picked her way through the slush. What if ...

"Hazel, how about I get you some boots, too?"

The German Shepherd mix barely looked up from whatever she was sniffing in the sodden, snow-flecked grass. Probably the trail of a squirrel or a rabbit, if not something larger. Because the metal-grid pasture fence wasn't that high, and more useful for corralling sheep or goats than cows or horses. The local deer population likely cleared it with ease.

Back here, away from the shelter of the outbuildings and trees, the north wind whipped Kate's strawberry-blonde hair around her face and pinched her cheeks. Scout was growing restless in her arms, and she was careful to set him down in a patch of brown grass rather than in the mud. She leaned over the gate, which was just a cattle panel on hinges, and tried to get a better look at the pasture.

When she'd purchased this place in late summer, the small field had been overrun by scraggly grasses and weeds. A few thistles had been easy to spot near the fence, and Kate hadn't dared to explore this back section of her land when she had no idea what else had taken root there. Stinging nettle? Poison ivy? But now, when the vegetation was still dormant and had been flattened by snow drifts and howling winter winds, the land could be easily navigated.

Kate had heard there was a pocket of native prairie plants tucked in the back of this pasture. And just this morning, as she banked the incinerator with some of last week's garbage, she was sure she'd noticed something new back by the creek: a spot of green.

"It may not be anything. But what if it is? We have to find out."

Hazel whined in anticipation as Kate removed one of her thick-padded gloves to work the padlock and chain that kept the gate closed. She knew the combination, but it was of no use. The great March meltdown might be underway, but the lock was still encrusted with ice.

"I can't get it." She sighed in frustration. "Stupid thing! Well, there's another way in."

Kate toed her way up and over the gates' metal bars, which were still coated with frost, as Hazel whimpered in disappointment. "Yeah, sorry, I can't take you along. You'll have to wait where you are."

Scout, of course, gracefully slipped through the fence. The terrain turned rough as they picked their way through the pasture, and the ground carried more ice than Kate had anticipated. Why was she out here, anyway?

Because if even one green thing was poking its head out of this sodden, waterlogged dirt, maybe spring wasn't far away, after all.

"It should be right over there." Kate pointed to the left, as if Scout cared in the least. He was too busy sniffing the ground. "I'm sure I saw something. That's it!"

Sheltered by a chunk of packed ice and a clump of dead weeds, three green leaves had poked their way through last year's brown vegetation. But they were too small for Kate to have any idea what they were, or what they might become.

Scout sniffed the tiny plant, and his curious nose was almost too much for the fragile stem to bear. Kate removed a glove long enough to touch one of the tiny leaves, and marveled at how something so small could be so brave as to appear in this pasture at this time of year.

"What do you think? A crocus, maybe? Some sort of wildflower?"

Whatever it was, it probably wouldn't make it. But maybe it would.

There was always hope, Kate decided as she pulled her glove back on, picked up Scout, and straightened her parka hood over her knit hat. And then, she laughed.

"It's probably just a weed. A thistle, even, one of many that will be eager to take over this pasture. I need to find a foolproof way to get rid of the toxic things, yet keep the good ones."

As Kate picked her way back toward the fence, she realized that concept also applied to so many aspects of her life in the past year.

Chicago, Ben, their soured marriage ... those were all gone. But she still had her family and her house cat, Charlie, as well as all the good things that had arrived: a move back to Eagle River, her new coworkers at this post office. This little acreage, Hazel and the Three Mouseketeers, new friends.

And someone else, too. Before Kate could unwrap all her winter layers on the enclosed back porch, her phone chimed in her pocket. Despite the gloom outside, her face broke into a smile as she read Alex's text.

I've been thinking about you all day.

"Just a second," she told Hazel, who was eager to be wiped down with her personal towel before she was allowed into the house. "I'll answer him, then we can get to work."

Same here. Looking forward to tonight!

Kate barely had Hazel's left front paw marginally clean when her phone beeped again.

It's my only night off this week, and I want to spend it with you.

There hadn't been anyone since Ben. Well, that was true if Kate ignored one well-meant but ill-advised night with an old friend not long after Ben had moved out. But was she ready to really move on? Apparently so.

Can't wait. Kate carefully reviewed her emoji options. A heart seemed to be a little too much. But a face with a wink? Perfect.

* * *

Kate was pleased to find a parking spot just half a block from The Eagle's Nest, her hometown's only sports bar. "Good thing we decided to meet early. It'll be packed before the game starts, I'm sure."

She cut the engine and checked her reflection in the visor's mirror. Not bad. Had she actually styled her hair? Put a little thought into her makeup?

The Eagle's Nest was rather upscale compared to Paul's Place, the town's only other bar, but it was still just a cozy hangout in a small town. And it wasn't the hometown crowd, or even Alex Walsh, that Kate wanted to impress tonight. She'd shined up just for herself.

After she'd moved home, there'd been few opportunities for anything that even hinted at a special social outing, much less a date, until things began to heat up with Alex. Kate had almost forgotten how much fun it could be to get ready for a night out.

When she spotted Alex waiting for her in a booth, she had to laugh at the sight of him hanging out at the establishment that was his bar's only competition.

His brown eyes sparkled with mirth as she started his way. "What?"

Despite his question, Kate suspected he knew what she was thinking. Alex was one of the most perceptive people she had ever known. Next to herself, of course.

"Taking a trip to the dark side, huh?" She glanced around at the colorful sports memorabilia on the soft green walls, and noted how the warm lights lit up the honey-oak floors and booths. "Or more like, the bright side. Are you sure you're comfortable here? I mean, you can see all the way across the room."

"We do have electricity at my bar. But I like to keep expenses in check." Alex swiped a finger over the top of the table, and nodded his approval. "My place is just as clean. I come here quite frequently, you know. And Leo's not above dropping in at my little dive on occasion."

Leo Deegan, the head bartender, waved to Kate and Alex as he filled a row of pint glasses with beer.

"You two have a good-enough view?" Leo called over the din of the bar, which was already three-quarters full, then dipped his head to the left. "There's a free spot closer to the other TVs."

"We're good," Alex promised before he turned back to Kate. "You know, a change of scenery is good for the soul." His eyes roamed over her from top to bottom, and she couldn't help but tingle from head to toe. "You look great, by the way."

Then he chuckled. “It shouldn’t matter. I shouldn’t say stuff that ...”

“Yes, you should.” Kate grinned as she settled into the other side of the booth. “I spent a full thirty minutes getting ready, you know. After I took a shower and washed my hair.”

Alex’s wistful expression made Kate glance at the clock on the wall. How long would this basketball game last? Two hours, or more.

Like everyone else, Kate was eager to see if the Hawkeyes would move ahead in the national tournament, but she wasn’t sure if she and Alex would still be at the bar by the time the basketball game was over.

They had been spending a great deal of their free time together over the past two months. It wasn’t always much, hour wise, considering she had to be at the post office by seven in the morning and he was very much a night owl, but they both seemed eager to make this work. And make the most of it.

Maybe she was rushing into things; maybe they both were. But that was over and done with weeks ago, already.

A waitress clad in black and gold, rather than the Eagle River school district’s traditional blue and white, dropped off two menus. “What’ll it be to start?”

They settled on their beers, and Kate opened her menu with a sigh of contentment. She loved her shabby-chic farmhouse, and spending most evenings curled up with Charlie and Hazel, along with a good book or a great show.

But here she was, on a random Sunday night, dining out with who had to be the best-looking guy in Eagle River (she was rapidly becoming biased, of course), wearing one of her nicest sweaters, and taking her pick from a wide range of dinner options she wouldn’t have to cook herself.

“You know,” Alex deadpanned as he studied his menu, “I think I might get a burger.”

Kate gave him an incredulous look. The food options at

Paul's Place didn't even merit menus. Burgers, fries, and coleslaw were all it offered; that was tradition. "Oh, really?"

He laughed. "Absolutely not. No, I'm gonna go crazy and get the lasagna." Alex leaned over the table. "Leo has a new line cook. She's really shaking things up around here, going way beyond the sandwiches, salads and apps. I hear her Friday fish special is out of this world."

Kate raised her eyebrows. "Henry and Eloise better watch out, then." The Peabodys ran the only other sit-down restaurant in town, which was a family style place. "Are you thinking of hiring her away?"

"Nope. We'll stick with what works for us."

More patrons began to fill the bar, most of them sporting Hawkeye spirit gear. Just as Kate tucked into her chicken-strips basket, someone tapped her on the arm. It was Postmaster Schupp.

"Hey, Roberta." Kate gave Oliver, Roberta's husband, a friendly nod. "Looks like the game's about to start."

"We got here just in time." Oliver looked around. "I think I'll grab that spot over there. That OK, honey?"

"Sure, sounds good." Roberta seemed distracted, and Kate had a good idea why.

A few of Kate's friends knew she was seeing Alex, but she had done her best to keep this romantic development off the post office's gossip radar. Bev Stewart was the only one of the carriers who knew, and she was known for her discretion.

Roberta gazed across the table at Alex. "Well, I sure like what you have there."

For a second, Kate thought the boss was making a cheeky comment about her date. But before she could think of a quip and a distraction, Roberta clarified things. "That lasagna looks fabulous. Is there any left?"

Alex shrugged. "Half a pan, I think. But that was maybe ten minutes ago. You'd better hurry."

"Let's hope the Hawks can pull it off tonight," Roberta

said as she nudged Kate and gave her a sly wink. Then she leaned in and whispered, "I think you have a winner here."

While Alex appeared to be distracted by his phone, he was likely eavesdropping. Kate tried to keep a straight face. "Thanks. I'll see you tomorrow."

By the time the underdog Hawks tipped off against their higher-seeded opponent, the bar was standing-room only. Even in Alex and Kate's booth along the far wall, it was nearly impossible to hold a conversation over all the whoops and cheers. The game was close from the start; and when the Hawks built a sizable lead after halftime, the energy inside the bar reached a feverish pitch.

"Can you believe it?" Alex shouted to Kate. "They just might pull this off yet."

"This is one of the best games they've played all year!" Kate was a University of Wisconsin graduate, but she'd been a Hawkeye all her life. Her dad and brother had seen to that. "If they can advance to the next round, this whole state is going to be in a frenzy all week."

Leo could hardly keep up behind the bar, and more than once Kate saw a patron lean over and nudge him when cheering for the Hawks delayed his pouring duties. The servers edged through the crowd as best they could, their trays held high and mostly out of the way. Kate wondered what the vibe was like at Paul's Place, and Alex said word was that his regulars were packed around the two screens there.

A few minutes later, Kate's ears picked up on a nearby conversation that didn't seem to have anything to do with the game.

"I knew it!" It was a man's voice, so full of disgust and anger that Kate couldn't help but try to find the source. "You're selling us out, huh?"

"It's not up to me!" another man answered. "Even so, at the end of the day, it doesn't concern you."

Alex's curiosity was piqued, too. He frowned at Kate, then

scanned the crowd. Kate heard a loud clunk as a heavy glass landed on a table.

"The hell it doesn't! I've given almost ten years to that place. I'm not the first in my family to do it, either. My grandpa worked there for decades. And it's not just my job that's on the line. What about everyone else?"

A woman standing close to Kate and Alex's booth had also noticed the argument. "What's going on?" she asked Kate. "I think someone's had too many beers."

Kate leaned out of the booth and spotted a man who, given his defensive posture, was on the receiving end of the vitriol.

"That's Dylan Wheeler!" Dylan had been a year ahead of Kate in school. "His family owns the auction barn." She blinked in surprise; were the Wheelers planning to sell their company? "I can't imagine they'd be looking for a buyer."

Dylan was trying to back away from the red-faced guy who wore a heavy beard along with a black-and-gold jersey, but could only gain a few inches inside this packed-house bar.

"Do you think I don't care?" Dylan tried another tactic with the angry man. "We're on the same side here, Chuck. I work there, too."

Chuck moved in closer. "Yeah, but so what? You're loaded! Your whole family's been raking in the cash for, what, over a hundred years? You're not like the rest of us. You'll land on your feet if you sell the auction barn!"

Gasps echoed through their section of the bar as more people turned away from the basketball game and tuned in to the showdown happening just a few feet away. Kate wasn't sure if that was due to Chuck's aggressive behavior, or the last sentence he'd uttered.

Wheeler Auction Company had been a fixture of Eagle River since the late 1800s. Between its livestock sales and the estate auctions it managed on the side, the business was well known throughout the region and beyond. It was also one of the largest employers in and around Eagle River, with probably three dozen full-time employees and many more part-timers on hand from spring until fall.

Chuck stood his ground, fists clenched. The fury in his eyes demanded some sort of response. Dylan's patience seemed to be wearing thin, and he put a protective arm around the woman next to him. Kate couldn't remember who Dylan had married, but she was another local.

"You're the loaded one, man," he told Chuck. "I think you've had enough tonight. And you're supposed to clock in at seven tomorrow. I think it's time for you to go home and sleep it off."

Dylan's suggestion only fueled Chuck's anger.

"See, he didn't deny it!" Chuck shouted to the people around him, confident he'd drawn a crowd that was now hanging on every word of this confrontation. "Sam, you're a witness to this," he told his friend. "It's true; it has to be!"

Sam elbowed his way between Dylan and Chuck. "If it's not going to happen," Sam said to Dylan, "what are all the closed-door meetings about, huh? Your dad and your uncle were holed up in the main office for over two hours yesterday with that spiffed-up dude. He was wearing a pressed shirt, on a Saturday," Sam explained to the crowd. "He doesn't work there. I've never seen him before in my life!"

Then Sam laughed. "How stupid are you people, anyway? Did you think no one would find out what's going on?"

Dylan opened his mouth as if to speak, but Chuck only shook his head in derision.

"No, no, don't even try to deny it. It's too late to lie." He took two quick steps and got right in Dylan's face. "Something's up, that's for sure! If you sell out, you'll take this town with you, you son-of-a ..."

Leo had noticed the commotion, and he gave Alex a nod as he tossed his towel on the bar and ran out from behind it. In seconds, Alex was edging toward the feud.

"Hey! Let's dial it back a notch, OK? This isn't the place."

"The hell it's not!" Chuck momentarily turned his fury on Alex, but Alex remained calm. Chuck then pointed at Dylan.

"He won't 'fess up, but he'd better! Everyone here deserves to know the truth."

The crowd grew restless, the basketball game nearly forgotten despite the bracket-busting upset playing out on the screens. Leo and Alex now hovered next to Sam, and two other men quickly placed themselves between Dylan and Chuck and urged everyone to take a step back.

"I have nothing more to say." Dylan's jaw was tight with anger as he stared Chuck down. "Except maybe one thing. I'll remind both of you there's a code of conduct written into your employment agreement. Don't talk yourself out of a job."

"We'll work this out later!" Chuck's tone carried a new level of menace. "I'll remind *you* to hide in your office and count your money; don't you dare step foot onto our turf. Stay out of the stockyards, rich boy, or you'll be very, very sorry."

"That's a threat." Alex's tone was low and cold. "Harassment. Now's the time to quit, Chuck."

"I've called it in," Leo told Chuck and Sam. "You can hang out until the cops show up; or you can leave, right now."

With a few more mumbles and glares sent Dylan's way, the angry men snatched up their coats and charged out of the bar. Dylan thanked Leo, Alex, and the other men for their assistance, then he and his wife returned to their table of friends.

A three-pointer by the Hawkeyes quickly brought the crowd's attention back to the game, and the unrest that had rolled through the bar only minutes ago evaporated as quickly as it had arrived.

While Leo and Alex compared notes, Kate pondered what she'd just seen and heard. Was the auction barn really up for sale? A change in ownership would indeed be big news in little Eagle River.

Even so, Chuck's worries didn't quite make sense. Anyone who took over the business would still need employees; Chuck and his friends wouldn't necessarily lose their jobs.

So, who might buy the auction barn?

Kate couldn't think of a similar business within sixty miles, or even a hundred. It wasn't a common industry; the Wheelers had no serious competition anywhere close by.

What if the Wheelers were ready to hang it up, but weren't able to find the right buyer?

Maybe that was what Chuck was really worried about. Could an institution that had been part of Eagle River for over a hundred and thirty years be on the brink of closure?

Cheers erupted throughout the bar as the Hawkeyes started another scoring run. It looked like they were well on their way to victory; even so, Kate no longer cared.

"Well, that pretty much ruined the evening, huh?" Alex sighed and ran a hand through his thick brown hair. Despite her worries, Kate suddenly wanted to do the same. "Nothing like a bar fight to put a damper on what looks to be a historic night for the Hawks."

Kate nodded. "True, but it's still early." The lilt in her voice caused Alex to smile.

"I gave Leo the rundown from my perspective. He'll fill out the report when the cops arrive." Alex leaned in until no one else could hear. "How about we get out of here? Go somewhere quiet, where it's just us?"

"I'd like that." Kate calculated her bill and reached for her purse. When they both had left cash on the table, Alex flagged down their server.

"Keep the change," he told her, then turned back to Kate. "How about my place? Because there's someone there that I know you want to meet."

* * *

Alex's house was on the east side of town, not far from his bar. An older bungalow with narrow-clapboard siding faded to a light gray, with a front porch whose steps were just about level. He'd purchased it about five years ago, after he'd bought Paul's Place, and it had been a work in progress ever since.

Despite the property's challenges, Kate thought Alex had made a great bargain. Of course she'd checked the county assessor's site to see exactly how much he'd paid.

"He got it cheap, so it was a smart money move," Kate reminded herself as she parked behind Alex's truck. The single-stall garage didn't slant as much as it used to, but it was packed with construction tools. "Even so, it looks better in the dark."

The place did have potential. Alex saw it, right away; and, after an enthusiasm-filled tour on her first visit two months ago, Kate could, too. And this relationship, if Kate named it as such, might have a promising future as well. Even so, she was keeping her expectations in check.

A porch light flipped on down the street, then a dog barked, but Kate didn't care who saw her pick her way up these frosty front steps. The neighborhood was filled with weathered tract houses in various states of modernization and decay, and most of the residents were probably too busy trying to get by to wonder which local lady had just appeared in Alex Walsh's driveway.

Besides, Kate knew she was the only one coming over these days. That was the one thing she'd insisted on before she and Alex had become so ... entangled.

And then he opened the front door, and Kate promised herself she'd stay right in this moment.

"He's in the kitchen." Alex grinned as he turned off his own porch light. "Go on back and say hello!"

Kate shed her parka and dropped it on the couch as she moved through the living area, then passed the dining room's built-in buffet on her way into the compact kitchen. It was the heart of this house, even though it was in the rear, and Alex had tried to brighten its old plaster walls with blue-gray paint while he waited for enough time and money to rip out the remains of past remodels and start fresh.

But it wasn't the speckled laminate counters, or the faux-wood paneling trying to pass as wainscoting, that slowed Kate's steps. The brown-tabby cat in the corner by the back door was simply huge.

"Oh, my! Look at you!" She crouched down next to the tomcat, who looked up from his food bowl with a glint of confidence in his topaz eyes. "I bet you weigh well over fifteen pounds. Even Scout is small by comparison."

"And that's why he's now known as Moose." Alex beamed with affection as he leaned against the counter's edge. "I got the food you suggested. I think he likes it."

"I bet he does." She held out one hand, and the big cat leaned over for a cautious sniff. Kate was thrilled when he lifted his tail in greeting, and brushed his substantial flank against her palm. "It's good stuff. Definitely way better than whatever he was fishing out of the Dumpster behind the bar."

Alex pulled a bottle of beer from the rumbling refrigerator, and showed it to Kate. When she nodded, he reached in for one more. "He's been here five days as of tomorrow, and hasn't asked once to go outside. Not even to meet the squirrels he spies on through the window above the sink."

"I think he's made his choice." Kate turned away from the massive cat long enough to put a hand on Alex's forearm, and give him a quick kiss. "Congratulations, Alex Walsh! The cat distribution system has chosen you. You're officially a cat dad! They have tee shirts for that, you know."

"Oh, he's alright, I guess." But the way Alex topped off Moose's nearly full kibble bowl and carefully scrubbed the water dish before refilling it told Kate all she needed to know:

Alex was over the moon about his new buddy. "I mean, I couldn't just leave him out there."

Kate laughed as she opened her beer. "From what you told me, I don't think you had much say in the matter."

The big brown cat had shown up behind Paul's Place a few weeks ago. Alex didn't know if someone had dumped the furry guy out, or if he was a stray from the river bottoms that backed the bar's property. But the cat had obviously decided the aroma of leftover hamburger bites wafting from the bar's trash meant it was a good place to camp.

The cat wouldn't come near anyone, at first. But he meowed and howled from a safe perch atop the Dumpster's lid whenever employees took a seat at the old picnic table that served as the staff's outdoor break zone. They started feeding him fresh chunks of cooked hamburger, straight from the kitchen, and the hungry cat would also pounce on bits of bun and cheese if those were offered.

When the kitchen guy reported the brazen cat had snatched a French fry right out of his hand and ran off with it into the woods, Alex had decided to offer more-nutritious grub. Food and water bowls appeared by the picnic table the next day. The cat finally let Alex pet him but continued to refuse to go inside, despite repeated overtures of friendship and warnings that winter was far from over.

Then one night last week, after Alex locked up the bar in the wee hours, he came out to find the big brown cat waiting on the hood of his truck. When the cab's door was opened, the feline had jumped down, climbed in, and settled himself on the passenger side of the seat. He'd then stared at Alex as if to say, "well, are we going home, or what?"

Only a few hours later, while the cat was curled up under Alex's bed, a winter storm had arrived with howling winds and nine inches of snow.

Alex now beamed with pride at how quickly Moose warmed up to Kate. But then he gave the back porch door a worried glance that made her giggle.

"I don't think you have to worry about him taking off," Kate told him. "I'd bet he's not going anywhere ever again. Except maybe out to patrol the back yard's perimeter, now and then. With this kind of buffet, soft places to perch, and a super-cool roommate, why would he ever leave?"

"You're right." Alex relaxed and took a gulp of his beer, then motioned for Kate to turn the corner into the house's only bathroom. "Want to see the latest updates?"

Alex suspected the bathroom was created long ago by someone framing in a section of the back porch. Houses in this part of town were so old, indoor facilities hadn't been the norm when they were constructed. But thanks to Alex's capable hands, the space was being transformed.

"Wow, this looks amazing!" Kate edged into the tiny space. "New subway tiles, halfway up the wall; all the white goes great with the hexagon floor. Nicely done!"

The tiny white-and-black floor tiles were likely original to the bathroom's construction, and Alex had wanted to preserve them if he could.

By contrast, the only bathroom at Kate's house was more kitschy than historic. "Mine's still stuck in salmon-pink mode. You know I want to fix that, as well as turn the kitchen pantry into a powder room."

Alex shrugged. "I could help."

"Really?" His renovation skills were up to par, but Kate still wasn't sure. "You think we can create a bathroom from scratch and not end up in a shouting match, or several? And there's not one square corner in my century-old farmhouse. Much less a level floor, in the pantry or elsewhere."

"It's the same here. I've had to become a bit of an expert in making do." Alex leaned toward the oval mirror above the old sink, and wiped away a stray fleck of toothpaste with his finger. His house might be old, but it was immaculately clean. "Where there's a will, there's a way."

Moose soon appeared in the narrow doorway, and meowed some sort of directive.

"I've never been owned by a cat before," Alex said, "so this is all new for me. Including *this*. Moose needs to use the facilities, and he likes his privacy."

Once Kate and Alex sidled out of the bathroom, the big cat sauntered his way in. Alex reached back to pull the door partially closed. "I suppose this is a big step up from doing your business in the woods, especially when the ground is frozen."

"Cats can feel vulnerable when they're using the litter box," Kate explained as they returned to the kitchen. "Maybe once the two of you get more acclimated, you can be in there at the same time."

"Do you think I could get him to use the toilet?" Alex wondered. "I've seen videos online, people have done it. It's tight quarters in there. I have to step around the litter box to get to the shower."

"You could try, I guess. But cats tend to do what they want to do. No more, no less. I really like what you've done with the bathroom so far. It makes me want to go home, find a sledgehammer, and get started."

Alex slipped his arms around her. She did the same before they bumped into the side of the refrigerator. To be fair, it was only a few steps away.

"I'd like you to hold off on that," he said huskily. "I'd rather you stay here with me, at least for a little while."

"Do you?" Kate kissed him again, this time for much longer. "We could go into the living room, turn on the game, and see what the score is." But she didn't really mean that, and Alex knew it.

"I think there's somewhere else I'd rather go," he whispered as he took her hand. Before they could start toward the bedroom, he kissed her ear. "Like here." Then, it was her neck. "Or, maybe here."

* 2 *

The sky was just starting to turn blue when Kate left home Tuesday morning, and her spirits climbed along with the rising sun. The temperature was supposed to soar to fifty degrees that afternoon, and she hoped the warmth would help dry out the gravel roads.

"I bet you do, too." She patted Bertha's dash as they reached the county blacktop. Grandpa Wayne Burberry, who'd worked at the area's post offices his entire career, had brokered Kate's purchase of this trusty mail car from a retiring carrier. "I'd like to give you a bath, but I think it's useless until things really improve."

Eagle River was a town of just over a thousand people, but it still offered two car washes: a dual-bay setup on the back property of the town's auto body shop; and a second, larger facility at the lone convenience store at the south edge of town. Given her line of work, Kate frequently visited both businesses.

"It's a good thing you're beige," she told Bertha as they reached the edge of town. "You blend right in, don't you?"

Despite the sunshine, Kate was struck by how dull and tired Eagle River looked this morning. The holiday decorations were long gone, and dirty clumps of snow clung to the streets' curbs. Her work boots mucked their way through the parking lot's slush to reach the post office's back door.

While she usually tried to take a bemused approach to the waves of gossip that flowed through this post office, as well as around Eagle River in general, Kate was in a much different frame of mind this morning. She'd been at home all day yesterday, so she hadn't heard anything more about the possible sale of the auction barn.

It was likely that Roberta and Oliver had still been at the bar Sunday night when the confrontation occurred. And, while Kate hadn't noticed any of her other co-workers in attendance that night, many of them had probably heard about it. Maybe someone would have a hint about what might happen next.

But something else looked like it might be the biggest topic of discussion this morning.

When Kate opened the back door, she found four pairs of boots clustered along one wall of the tiny vestibule. And a new sign taped to the interior door.

NO OUTSIDE SHOES! Unless you plan to mop the floor yourself.

Kate chuckled as she removed her work boots. "Well, that's one way to handle things, Roberta. I wonder if that directive works at home, too?"

Mud being tracked in from outside was certainly a nuisance this time of year, but what spring weather did to the gravel roads was a serious problem.

As the temperatures surged high and plummeted down, the unpaved roadbeds heaved up in some places and became scarred by deep tire ruts in others. The best bet was to find vehicle tracks that weren't too deep, and follow their natural drift to the right when they approached the crest of a hill. Rural crossroads were often the worst, as some of those tracks became curved grooves in the mushy gravel.

Kate's navy wool socks had a bit of wear along their toes,

but there wasn't much time to ponder the sad state of part of her work uniform. Because only moments after she stepped into the bustling back room, Bev shoved a pair of slip-on rubber sandals in her face.

"You'll need these, since this concrete's too smooth for safety reasons." Then Bev chuckled. "Just be glad these neutral brown ones will fit your feet."

Jack O'Brien, one of the senior carriers, was modeling his new footwear for the crew. But his sour expression was the opposite of his bright-hued sandals.

"I can't believe I ended up with pink!" he called over to Roberta, who was on the phone at her corner desk. "Are you serious?"

A smirk pulled at the corner of the postmaster's mouth.

"I like mine." Randy VanBuren wiggled his toes inside his gray socks, which were in much better shape than Kate's. "This light blue is really, I don't know ... it makes me think of being on a beach, somewhere. The footbeds are comfy, too."

"I have several pairs of these at home." Marge Koenig showed off her lime-green footwear. "I don't walk around the house without them on, most of the time. My knees love these things. And they have an excellent grip on the bottom."

Marge pointed at Jack's cutesy pair. "I know Roberta got them at a good discount. But she had to take some of the 'louder' colors, if you will, whatever was on sale in our sizes. We're only wearing them here in the shop, so who cares?"

"I do," Jack muttered as he picked up his coffee thermos.

"You know, these will be really comfy when we're working the counter." Randy's eyes twinkled with mischief when Jack stopped in his tracks. "Hey, aren't you on the schedule for tomorrow afternoon? People are going to love yours."

Jack muttered something under his breath as he turned away. His pink sandals tapped out a disgruntled rhythm as he started for the break room.

Bev let out a hoot. "Ten bucks says he gets online as fast

as he can and shells out a little cash for a 'manly' pair in his size. How soon do you think they can get here?"

Kate set her purse and lunch tote on the counter. "Overnight air costs a fortune. Of course, if he can find some at ... well, you know, our competitor, they might be here sooner than you think."

She didn't need to say more. The global commerce e-retailer with the navy cargo vans had taken a significant share of shipping business away from the post office, as well as the brown-truck company people had relied on for decades.

"He's looking at maybe forty-five bucks," Randy was quick to report as he checked his phone. Bev raised an eyebrow.

"Well, it's a free country!" Randy said. "I shop there. So do you."

"Of course. Who doesn't?" Bev shrugged as she peeked over Randy's arm. "Good. They have black and navy in stock. One of those should stop his complaining."

After Roberta completed her call, she came over to where the carriers were congregated. Aaron Thatcher and Allison Carmichael had just walked in, and Jack was soon back from the break room.

"We'll talk more details at our staff meeting tomorrow afternoon," Roberta told the crew, "but there's one sign of spring that I'm really excited about. I can hardly believe it's time to set up the bird nursery again. How time flies!"

Roberta's half-hearted attempt at a joke at this early hour drew a few chuckles and smirks. Even so, chick delivery was a serious business.

While the babies' eggshells provided them with all the nutrition they needed when they first pecked their way out at the hatchery, they had to reach their local post office, and then be settled under their new home's heat lamps with food and water, within seventy-two hours. Kate's parents had acquired baby chicks through the mail before, but it had been several years since their last order.

Eagle River's post office would soon be filled with chirps and peeps as dozens of just-hatched chickens passed through on their way to area residents' farms. There might be a few shipments of baby ducks and geese, too.

Bev eagerly volunteered. "I'm happy to get started on the nursery this afternoon." As the crew's only part-timer, she had the most flexible schedule of all the carriers. "Clyde and I have our own shipment coming, but we're holding off until April."

"We're doing the same," Randy told Bev. He and his wife had farmed for years and still lived just outside town. "You never know how cold it will be for how long. It's safer to wait." He looked at Kate. "Are you placing an order?"

"Not this year." She turned toward Roberta. "How early do you open for people to pick up their chicks?"

"Well, that's the not-so-fun part of all of this. The babies usually arrive before six, so I'll set up an early rotation and we'll all take turns. Usually, people are almost breaking the door down to pick them up. But occasionally, we end up delivering them along with the rest of our stuff."

"Front-door service?" Now that part, Kate didn't remember. "I'm sure the farmers love it. But I'd bet that makes for some interesting routes."

Kate loved animals, outside of an angry bull or other such threat. But the idea of navigating Bertha down muddy gravel roads with an aerated cardboard box full of peeping birds in the back was something she hadn't considered. Old towels might not be enough to protect Bertha's worn-but-clean back seat; a plastic tarp could be needed.

"You're not in Chicago, anymore." Jack hooted before he sipped his coffee. "But really, Duncan, it's kind of fun." Then he laughed harder. "Just leave Hazel at home on those days."

"We don't get that many requests for to-the-coop drop offs," Roberta explained. "The hatcheries and our customers are good about letting us know which days there's a special shipment coming, but the transition doesn't always go as smoothly as we'd like."

"Which is why we need the nursery." Bev looked like she couldn't wait to get started. "Heat lamps, waterers, food, crates; we like to keep them comfy while they wait."

Some of the supplies were stored in the shed behind the post office. The others were brought in by Roberta or the other carriers.

Marge smiled as she reached for her stack of still-unsorted mail. "It'll really start to feel like spring when the babies arrive. But they can just about drive you crazy with all that peeping."

Between preparing for chick shipments and discussing their new in-office footwear, the crew's thoughts were definitely not focused on the auction barn this morning.

Kate's route today was through the rural area south of town that included the tiny hamlet of Mapleville, and she decided her stop at that co-op was her best chance to hear any gossip regarding the Wheelers' plans.

"I expect to wrap up before three," she told Bev as she packed her mail case. "I told Roberta I'd take the counter when she steps out early for an appointment."

"I should be hard at work in the break room by then." Bev had a tall stack of parcels to sort first, but her spirits were as bright as the morning's sunshine. "Setting up the chicks' corner will be the perfect excuse to give this place a bit of spring cleaning."

* * *

Bev had the break room scrubbed and polished by the time Kate finished her rounds. Even the old refrigerator's white metal shell and chrome trim gleamed in the glow of the ceiling's lone light fixture.

Kate nodded her approval as she rinsed her coffee

thermos at the sink. "The chicks are going to think they're bunking at a five-star hotel by the time you're done. Where do the heat lamps go?"

Bev pointed to a series of small hooks jutting out from the back wall and down from the ceiling. All of them were painted to blend into their immediate surroundings.

Kate had never noticed them before, and wondered what other curiosities this old building had to share. Grandpa Wayne had worked there for years, and Kate used to visit him often after school, but maybe she needed to give this place a closer look.

"I'll get the crates set up tomorrow, if not yet today." Bev went to the break room's open doorway to get a glimpse of the small windows in the far wall of the post office's main space. "What's it doing out there? Is it warm enough to wash the crates outside?"

"Barely. Bertha's dash said forty degrees just now. It's clouded over, but there aren't any sprinkles yet."

Bev filled two buckets with hot water at the sink, added disinfectant to one of them, and started for the back door. Roberta was reaching for her purse and coat as Kate exited the break room. "Has it been busy?" Kate asked the boss.

Roberta shook her head. "Not really, but still busy enough to make a mess of the lobby floor. Be careful if you have to come out from behind the counter. I set out the 'caution' signs."

The next hour passed slowly for Kate, as there were just a handful of package drop offs and a few stamp-packet sales. The post office's newest design featured flowers, and Kate yearned for warmer weather as she made change and swiped credit cards.

When the stream of customers trickled to a halt, she decided to pull the wheeled mop bucket out of the corner and take another run at that messy floor. If they could keep ahead of the dirt and mud, that would be something.

She was halfway across the lobby's tile when an older pickup pulled up out front. It was navy in color, and its crusted-over underside told Kate it spent most of its time in the country. She paused, mop in hand, and watched an elderly man carefully lower himself from the cab.

"Ugh! I bet his boots are as dirty as that truck. Yep, look at that. And it's really thick. I hope that's not ..."

But it was. The unmistakable scent of barnyard blew in the door with the old man, whose irate expression quickly diverted Kate's attention from the clumps of manure falling off his boots.

"I need to talk to someone!" His lined face was blotchy and red; given the frustration in his raspy voice, she suspected that wasn't only from the wind. "This is an abomination! I can't believe it!"

"Just tell me what's going on." Kate set the mop in the bucket and rolled it away with one foot. She instinctively stepped toward the elderly man, but then stopped herself.

"Yeah, I know," he said, "my boots are awful. My wife told me to change my clothes before coming to town, but this can't wait." He gestured at the clock. "You're closing soon, and this has to be handled *today*."

He reached into one pocket of his faded canvas chore coat, pulled out a folded envelope, and handed it to Kate. "We got this notice, just this afternoon. Our carrier dropped it in our mailbox a few hours ago."

Kate opened the already unsealed flap, and pulled out a letter. "Some sort of business correspondence?" She knitted her eyebrows and gave the old man a quizzical look. "It looks to have the correct postage attached. I don't ..."

"Read it." He pulled off his frayed stocking hat and stuffed it in his other coat pocket. "Oh, I can't believe this is happening!"

Discretion was a large part of any mail carrier's role, so it was second nature for Kate to hesitate. But the man so obviously wanted her to read the letter that she complied.

"Wheeler Auction Company" was emblazoned across the top of the stationery. And as she scanned the sternly worded message, Kate stifled a gasp of surprise.

The letter noted a review of the company's finances indicated John Grant's account was delinquent, and the outstanding balance had to be paid immediately. If the issue wasn't settled within thirty days from the date of the notice, the matter would be sent to a collection agency.

The amount due was significant, as Mr. Grant allegedly owed the auction barn exactly $1,829.42. Given the worry on John's lined face and the shabby state of his truck, Kate suspected it was far beyond what the elderly man could afford.

"Oh, my! That's quite a bit of money." Kate was so shocked, she didn't know what else to say.

"You're telling me! But that's not the real problem. We paid that bill, fair and square, over two years ago. I mailed them a check for those hogs the very-next day after the sale. We keep all our bank statements, and it clearly shows the check went through."

He was as anxious as he was outraged. "They got their money. I don't understand why they're coming after us now!"

John Grant seemed like an honest man. Years of interacting with people from all walks of life told Kate he was telling her the truth. She wasn't sure when, or how, this mix-up had occurred, but the motivation for the auction barn to review its records seemed clear enough. If the company was indeed being put up for sale, it would be imperative to have its finances in order.

Kate's route that day hadn't netted her any gossip on the matter; not even the manager of the Mapleville co-op had mentioned it. Which had made her start to wonder if the auction barn's possible sale was only the drunken ramblings of a bitter employee. But now, she had to admit that Chuck's rant at the bar might have some basis in factual information.

How might Eagle River be affected if one of its landmark businesses changed hands? Kate hated to think about that, and it was just as well. Because John Grant was desperate for any suggestions anyone might offer.

"Well, I guess I'm surprised they even would take a check after the fact. Is that common?" Kate could hardly believe such an old-school practice still happened in the digital age. "I mean, don't they require people to pay the day of the sale, before they take their livestock home?"

"Well, normally, yes. But I'd forgotten the check book that day. I was running late. Mary had used it last, and it was still in her purse." He shrugged. "I don't know how you ladies keep track of anything in there! It's a black hole. It's much easier to just carry a wallet in your back pocket, you know?"

Kate smothered a laugh. "Yeah, you guys have it easy."

"And there's no way I'd carry that kind of cash with me, especially to a sale. I don't like credit cards; we have only one, just for emergencies, and that was at home, too."

John tossed up his hands in a helpless gesture. "It was already late afternoon, and they didn't want the hassle of keeping the pigs overnight. Pete Wheeler and I settled it with a handshake. I loaded up the pigs and took them home. And mailed in the check the next day, as promised."

Kate could see why the auction barn wouldn't want to house and feed the pigs any longer than necessary, but she was still surprised that Dylan's dad had let John take his newly purchased livestock off the property without even asking for a deposit.

A handshake and a promise? Fifty years ago or more, that might have been the norm. But today? While such an agreement made the transaction feel like one between old friends, Kate thought it also sounded like a recipe for financial disaster. One that had nothing to do with the post office.

"Maybe you need to check with the auction barn," she said kindly. "I'm sure their office is open until five. I'm sorry, but I'm not sure how we can help you out."

"I need you to pull up a scan of my payment envelope," John insisted. "Everything runs through a computer nowadays, I'm sure. I looked back in our records. That sale would've been on February 25, two years ago, as that's when I brought the pigs home. So I mailed the check on February 26. It would've been postmarked here on the twenty-seventh, at the latest."

John's complete confidence in the postal system made Kate's heart sink. It was true that the fronts of items were scanned, but those were only temporary files. And even if the images were stored long term in a vast database somewhere, a screenshot of an envelope would never prove what was inside.

Judging by the hopeful, desperate look on John's face, he'd put his faith in the post office delivering what he needed. Kate wasn't sure of the best way to break the bad news to him, but someone else might know.

"Let me run to the back for just a bit," she said with an understanding smile. "I'll see if there's anyone around who can help us."

She hurried into the break room, where Bev was hanging the last of the heat lamps in the corner, and explained John's predicament. Bev's eyes widened with shock, then she wiped her hands on her jeans.

"Oh, the poor man! I'll come up and see what's what."

Kate was relieved when Bev met a familiar face at the counter. Like Bev and Clyde, John and his wife were members of Panther Junction Christian Church.

"Well, hello!" Bev's eager smile tried to brighten John's dreary afternoon. "Kate says you're in a bit of a pickle."

John's shoulders relaxed a bit. But then, his hands began to tremble as Bev explained the situation.

"You're telling me there's no way you can prove I mailed them that check?"

"No, and I'm so sorry."

"They say they want their money." John handed the letter to Bev, as if hoping she could find an answer to his predicament within its paragraphs. "And that we have only thirty days! We barely had the cash the first time."

He raised his chin. "We paid our bill, as we always do. But we can't pay it a second time."

"And you shouldn't have to," Kate assured him. "Have you talked to your bank? They should have a copy of the check, if you don't."

"I've been there already." He pointed down the street and gave a sarcastic laugh. "You know what that little gal at the counter told me? She said they couldn't find it in the system! What's the point of them taking pictures of those checks if they just lose them?"

Kate didn't have to ask John where he and his wife had their accounts; Eagle River Savings Bank was the only option in town. And given what Kate had heard about that place, she wasn't too surprised to hear their digital records weren't as reliable as they should be.

"Are you sure you don't have the canceled check somewhere at home?"

"We'll look again. We'll tear the house apart, if we have to, to find it. And we'd better. If the bank can't help us, and the post office can't help us ... I don't know what's going to happen. No one's going to take the word of an old farmer like myself. A collection agency! Never thought I'd see the day I had to tussle with the likes of those."

Bev lifted the hatch in the front counter to join John on the customers' side. Despite the grubbiness of his chore coat, she patted him on the arm.

"I'd say you've done all you can, for now. Why don't you call your son, let him handle it? Maybe Liam can talk some sense into the folks in the auction company's office."

John nodded, but it was more a gesture of resignation than agreement. "We'll give that a go, maybe he can do something. Well, tell Clyde I said hello. See you Sunday."

The bell above the lobby's door noted John's departure. In the silence that followed, Bev and Kate exchanged concerned looks.

"Twenty-eight hundred dollars." Kate shook her head in awe. "And change! They have a record of the transaction's balance right down to the penny, yet they can't find the money? And the payment's been unaccounted for for two whole years already! Who's doing the books up there? How did this even happen?"

Bev picked up the broom, and began to tackle the now-dry barnyard gunk that had hitched a ride on the bottom of John's work boots. Until most of it was removed, it would be a disaster to reach for a mop.

"Judy Martin is the head of the business office. She's been in that role for the past, oh, fifteen years, I'd say. And she's worked there much longer than that. I'd assume she manages the accounts, but I don't know for sure. I can't imagine Judy letting something like that go from one month to the next, much less this long."

"Doesn't Allison's sister work there?" Kate began to straighten the counter and get everything ready for tomorrow morning. "It's Betsy, right?"

"Sister-in-law, but yes. Clyde said he'd heard something yesterday about the auction barn going up for sale. That would explain a review of the books. Do you think it's true?"

"It could be."

Kate almost shared what she'd witnessed at The Eagle's Nest on Sunday night, but stopped. Roberta had been there as well, and apparently had said very little, if anything, about what had happened. There was still the possibility an impending sale was nothing more than speculation. If her boss hadn't spread that story around, maybe Kate shouldn't, either.

But if someone like John Grant had received such an ominous notice, he probably wasn't the only one. And the idea of a local business handing several local residents' accounts over to a collection agency was even more stunning than the possibility of a potential sale.

How big was the problem, anyway? How many people might find themselves ensnared in this drama before it was resolved?

Bev came back behind the counter. "Well, I'm sure we'll hear more on this soon. A place like that changing hands would be a big change for this town. If it's indeed in the works, it won't stay quiet for long."

She paused by the door into the back room. "The horses are going to be mighty cross if I'm late with their supper, not to mention the barn cats. I'd better get that nursery finished."

✻ 3 ✻

The evening breeze carried a hint of winter's chill, but Kate was energized by the fact that the sun was still shining right into her eyes as she headed west into town. A few weeks ago, it would have been dark by now.

Even better? She had a co-pilot in the backseat.

"It stays light a little longer every day, doesn't it?" Hazel's only response was a high-pitched whine of excitement. She loved to ride in the car, whether making a mail run with Bertha or taking a trip in Kate's personal vehicle, as she was tonight.

"Eventually, it'll get warm and stay that way. Just think of all the fun you and the Three Mouseketeers are going to have when it does."

There was only one stoplight in Eagle River, just south of the Main Street bridge, and Kate gave the town an evaluating glance as she waited for her light to turn green.

Friday night always meant a few more cars in the business district.

Many of them were in front of The Eagle's Nest, and there were more down by The Daily Grind, the town's coffee shop. Kate was certain the parking lot at Peabody's, on the north end of town, was filling up, too. It was finally the weekend, and residents from Eagle River and the surrounding rural areas were eager for a chance to celebrate.

Kate was doing the same, but she wasn't headed to any restaurant. Friday nights often meant homemade pizza at her parents' farm. Bryan and Anna would be there, of course, although they might not show the next time around. Their little boy was due any day now, and Kate's sister-in-law was trying to take it easy.

Even better, Grandpa and Grandma Duncan were back for the weekend. They had moved to Fort Dodge after they'd retired from farming, to be closer to Aunt Elaine and her family. But their friends' fiftieth wedding anniversary celebration was tomorrow, so they were camping out in Bryan's old room for a few nights. Kate suspected Grandpa was also eager for in-person accounts from her dad and Bryan as they geared up for spring planting.

"Grandma Lillian is definitely enjoying retirement," Kate reported to Hazel as they left Eagle River behind. "But I bet Grandpa James is spinning his wheels these days, sitting around at a senior-living community while Bryan and Dad make their plans."

With additional faces around the family's table, tonight's pizza party was going to be extra special. But as Kate turned south off the blacktop toward her parents' place, her mind kept returning to her own, significantly smaller farm.

She couldn't prove it, but she was certain she had a visitor. Something, not someone; which was a relief. Even so, it made her a bit uneasy.

Throughout the winter, she hadn't exactly lingered outside during her morning and evening chore runs to the cats' customized machine shed. Visits to the garbage incinerator had been hurried affairs, as well. But now, with the positive changes in the weather, she'd been inclined to spend more time outside, playing with the barn cats and tossing sticks for Hazel.

"Maybe that's all it is. Maybe nothing is different; I'm just more in tune with the status quo out there." But then, she shook her head. "No, no. Something has changed. I'm being watched; I can feel it."

Kate looked in the rearview mirror. "What do you think, Hazel-girl? Scout and the gang don't seem fazed by it, whatever it is, but I'd like to get to the bottom of it. I'm putting you in charge of the investigation."

Whatever was observing her, Kate had decided, often seemed to linger in the windbreak along the north edge of the yard. But tonight, she'd sensed that the "something" was much closer, in the shrubs behind the chicken house.

Other than that, Kate had nothing to go on. The opening in the front wall of the machine shed was just the right size to let the cats in, but keep most wildlife out.

Their dishes weren't being disturbed; there were no flipped kibble pans, no splashed-empty water bowls smeared with muddy paw prints.

So, what might it be? Raccoons were always roaming around Kate's little farm, that wasn't anything new. They liked to paw through the compost pile, and more than once she'd caught them in the middle of past-prime veggie theft. But they were confident and nosy, not shy enough to hide whenever Kate appeared in the yard.

What about a fox? They were the opposite: stealthy and silent, and too wily to visit the main areas of the lawn when any human was about. Owls and eagles were sharp observers of their surroundings, as well, but Kate was certain this visitor was on the ground, not up in the trees.

"Maybe I'll call Gwen and get her opinion on this mystery. I wonder if she's noticed anything unusual at her place?"

This would be the perfect excuse to check in with her closest neighbor, and the idea of that made Kate smile. And then she laughed, because Hazel started to bark the second she spotted her doggie friend, Waylon.

"Yeah, he's excited to see you, too!" Kate pulled in by her

parents' farmhouse and cut the engine. "And there's the rest of the welcoming committee."

A handful of barn cats had gathered around the Duncans' dog, and Kate paused to hand out several pets before she let Hazel out of the backseat. "Be nice, now. Not all of these kitties love you the way Scout and his crew do. No chasing, OK? My goodness, it's as windy out here as it is east of town!"

Kate reached back into the car for the pumpkin pie she'd brought along, and sheltered the dessert with her arms as she made her way toward the steps.

"Quite the gale, huh?" her mom called from the back porch door. "Here, let me take that. Bryan and Anna will be here in a few minutes."

The farmhouse kitchen enveloped Kate with warmth as soon as she went inside, and her cheeks momentarily flared at the change in temperature. The pizzas were already in the oven, and their aroma reminded Kate just how hungry she was. And how wonderful it was to be back in Eagle River to stay, to enjoy regular meals with her family.

Grandpa and Grandma Duncan were in the midst of a spirited conversation with Kate's dad in the next room. Kate popped in long enough to wave hello, then returned to the kitchen and added her coat to the hooks just inside the door. There would be plenty of time for visiting later. Right now, there was work to be done.

"What do you need help with?" she asked Charlotte. "Should I start the garlic bread?"

"Of course! I was saving that for you." Kate's mom pointed to the far end of the counter. "It's ready for your special secret spice blend."

Just like the plaid curtains over the sink's window and the floral wallpaper border right under the ceiling, Kate's role in this Friday-night tradition hadn't changed in over a decade. As for her "secret" recipe, the herb mixture she whipped into the softened butter changed slightly every time she made it.

The tradition had started years ago, before the family sat down to a spaghetti dinner, then soon expanded to encompass pizza nights, too. After all, there was no such thing as too many carbs on a Friday night.

"There you are!" Grandma Lillian's eyes lit up with joy as she crossed the kitchen toward Kate. "I need my hug."

Once she'd received it, Grandma glanced around, then peered through the kitchen door's half window into the enclosed back porch. "Where is your friend? Is he getting something from the car?"

"My friend?" Kate frowned as she reached for the dried oregano and chives. "I didn't ..."

Charlotte looked a little guilty.

"Oh, I get it." Kate gave her mom a pointed look, and the garlic flakes a generous shake. "Grandma, I think you've been given some, um, erroneous information. Alex, if that's who you are referring to, is at his bar. Or at least, I think that's where he is right now."

Kate gave a small shrug as she added more herbs to the bowl of butter. "I don't keep close tabs on him, most of the time, and I hadn't invited him to join us tonight."

"I see." But Grandma Lillian's tone indicated she didn't.

"We're not serious." Kate made sure her gaze included her mom as well as her grandmother. "I wouldn't expect him to show up here anytime soon."

Charlotte reached for a potholder, then turned away. "I'll just check the pizzas. Maybe they need to swap racks before we pop in the garlic bread."

After Grandma refreshed her coffee and returned to the dining room, Kate sighed. "What exactly did you tell her?"

"Not much." Charlotte was defensive. "But then, there's not much to tell since there's not much I know."

Kate bit back another sigh as she evenly sliced the Italian loaf, being careful to not cut all the way to the bottom.

This was one of the drawbacks of being so geographically

close to her family again. Everyone could be overly invested in your personal business if they wanted to. Or, more like, if you let them.

"It's not a big deal, really." She tried to keep her tone cheerful as she buttered the slices. "We're just ... hanging out, that's all."

Charlotte's smirked, but Kate didn't give her mom a chance to say anything more. "If things get serious, I promise to let all of you know. In the meantime ..."

"Not my business, I get it." Charlotte held up one oven-mittened hand in a quick salute. "You're a grownup, an adult. Both of my kids are." She shook her head, but then she smiled; there was a grandbaby on the way. "I'll await further details. Or not."

"Thank you." Kate added a smear of herb butter to the top of the loaf, because why not? Then she motioned toward the oven. "Can you get the door? This won't take long, and I'm glad. I'm starving!"

Bryan and Anna's arrival allowed Kate to step out of the spotlight. And then, conversation around the Duncans' table came to a near-standstill as serious dents were made in the pizza, garlic bread, and salad. Once second helpings had made their way around the table, Grandpa James looked up from his plate with a satisfied smile.

"How good it is to be back home!" He reached over and squeezed Grandma Lillian's hand. "And I'm so excited to be a great grandpa again. We have two so far, but ..."

"Three." Lillian gently corrected her husband. "Christine had her little girl just two weeks ago, remember?"

Grandpa James gave a halfhearted shrug and tried for a laugh. "See what I mean? So many of them, I can barely keep up."

It was a simple error, but Kate wondered if Grandpa James was starting to have memory issues. From the worry etched on Grandma Lillian's face, it seemed possible.

"But anyway," Grandpa hurried on, "a new little one is always exciting. And he will be the sixth generation to farm around here. The Duncan dynasty continues!"

Anna blushed. "Oh, 'dynasty' might be a little too much. But yes, it's good to be so close to family." She gave Kate a warm look. "With my parents just outside of Swanton, everyone is right here."

Anna was a teacher's associate at Eagle River's elementary school, along with helping with the livestock and the crops. With a little one joining the family, she planned to go part time starting in the fall. Bryan had been farming with his parents even before he'd finished his agriculture studies at Iowa State University.

When Grandma and Grandpa Duncan had retired, they'd sold their land to Bryan at a deeply discounted rate. Since those acres also contained the Duncans' original homestead, it had been a priority to keep them in the family.

"Farming is a tough business to break into," Bryan reminded his relatives. "We never could have made a start without everyone's help."

"How many years has it been, exactly?" Kate asked. "Grandpa, when did your grandparents buy those initial acres? Was it a hundred years ago?"

"Almost; that was in 1928." When it came to the past, Grandpa's mind was as sharp as ever. "Oh, sure, our family has been around Eagle River much longer than that. But they'd sold their place north of town that fall, and bought the land Bryan and Anna now live on."

Grandma shook her head in wonder. "So it won't be long, and we'll have a century farm. How exciting!" She leaned toward Bryan. "You'll be able to apply for one of those certificates, get a sign put up at the end of the driveway."

"Wow, I hadn't thought that far ahead." Bryan took a sip of his iced tea. "We'll certainly have to look into that when the time comes."

"Absolutely." Anna pushed back from the table. "But right now, I think it's time for dessert."

She had brought a blueberry pie to pair with Kate's pumpkin. By the time they returned with the pies and a bucket of ice cream, the conversation had turned to the gossip swirling around the auction barn.

Grandpa James was surprised to hear the Wheelers might be putting their business up for sale.

And he was flabbergasted when Bryan shared that, like so many other area residents, the Duncans had received a notice regarding an outstanding bill with the company.

"Don't worry, it's an error." Curtis helped himself to a slice of pumpkin pie as Kate's fork froze over her own dessert. "We paid it, and we have proof that we paid it. But it was a surprise, for sure."

"How much?" Kate thought of John Grant, and his obvious distress the other day at the post office. Her dad and brother, however, didn't seem too concerned.

"Fifty-two dollars and thirteen cents," Bryan recited as he rolled his eyes.

"For three chickens we bought at a Saturday sale last year. I swiped my card, and I got a receipt, of course. The whole thing is just strange, if you ask me."

"Marvin always ran a tight ship, back in the day," James said of Dylan's grandfather, then shook his head. "I wish I could say the same about Pete. He means well, but he'd rather be down by the ring, chatting with everyone, than minding the office."

Pete had gradually taken over the company as his parents aged. His sister, Betty, was a stay-at-home grandma, but her husband, Bill Kirkland, still worked for the auction service. As did Betty and Bill's son, Nate.

Grandma Lillian apparently shared her husband's assessment of Pete Wheeler's lacking business skills.

"Maybe it was just a matter of time before something like

this happened. It makes you wonder how many discrepancies they've found."

Charlotte reached for the ice cream. "We know of at least fifteen people who've received the same sort of correspondence. Word is, the total is in the dozens, at the very least. And everyone claims they don't owe the auction barn a dime."

Grandpa looked at Kate, and then Bryan. "I know you went to school with Dylan. Now, there's a born leader if I ever saw one." He tucked into his blueberry pie with the conviction of a man who'd just made up his mind.

"I say, given what's happened, it's time for Pete to step down. Let Dylan and Nate take the reins. The younger generation could save that place, if they were given the chance. I'm sure of it."

Kate enjoyed her pie and ice cream, but her mind kept returning to the Wheelers' dilemma as well as her own family's history. If she remembered right, Dylan and Nate were the sixth generation to run the auction barn.

As she looked around the table, and took in the smiling faces and laughter of her own family members, she couldn't imagine how heartbreaking it would be to see all of those decades of effort unravel ... much less come to an end.

❄ 4 ❄

"Oh, I need coffee." Kate closed her eyes for a moment after she cut Bertha's engine in Peabody's parking lot. Monday morning had come early, as it always seemed to do; but that was especially true since Kate began spending most of her Sunday nights with Alex.

While the restaurant was packed, the mood was rather subdued. At first, Kate assumed that was because many of the diners were having a tough time shifting back into the workweek grind.

But she overheard several urgent whispers as she passed through the dining room, and found Grandpa Wayne and his friends looking rather glum at their usual table.

"Hello there." Grandpa Wayne raised a hand in greeting, but his smile was short and quick. He reached for the coffee pot. "You ready for a cup?"

"Yes, definitely." Kate yawned, and looked around the table. "What's up?"

Chris Everton, who operated Eagle River's pharmacy, raised his eyebrows in surprise.

"Let me guess." Kate picked up her menu. "You've heard of several people who've received one of those delinquent-account letters from the auction barn."

She turned toward Harvey Watson, who was a retired

farmer. "Or received one, yourself."

"I sure did." Harvey picked up his fork. Their little community was in turmoil, but his scrambled eggs wouldn't stay hot for long. "It came on Friday. The nerve! I've never left a bill unpaid in my life!"

Joan Murray leaned down the table toward Harvey. "I'm sure yours was a misunderstanding, just like the others. No one is saying you did anything wrong."

"But *they* are! The auction barn, I mean." Harvey chewed for a moment, then held up his coffee cup in a sort-of pledge. "I swear I paid for that sheep buck, fair and square. I'd never short anyone two hundred dollars on anything."

"Two hundred?" Max Sherwood, the retired mayor, was shocked. "What kind of ram were you able to get that cheap?"

Then he chuckled. "He probably didn't have his papers, huh?"

"Oh, he certainly did. And he was a good one, too; not as mean as some of them. But, see, I bought him over fifteen years ago."

Kate had been barely listening to the conversation, too focused on getting her sleep-deprived mind to choose between an omelet and a breakfast platter. But this was an interesting twist, and the others noticed it, too.

"That long ago?" She frowned at Harvey. "My dad's notice was from last year."

Ward Benson, Eagle River's current mayor, looked as weary as Kate felt. "Looks like the Wheelers' plan to sell the auction barn has uncovered a hornets' nest of bad bookkeeping. Who knows how far back it goes?"

"And how much they are short." Max had always said that dealing with drama was the worst part of holding public office in a town this small. Kate was sure he was more relieved than ever that he'd passed the mayoral baton to Ward a few years ago. "I doubt we'll ever get a firm number, but I'm hearing it's in the tens of thousands."

Forks fell to plates all around the table. Kate, who'd just given their waitress her order, noted the anxious expression on Ward's face. "So you're thinking it might be, well ... not accidental?"

She had almost uttered the word "criminal," but stopped herself just in time. Rumors were already flying around, as it was. She'd let that distinction be made by someone more in the loop than herself.

"Is it theft?" Grandpa Wayne leaned in. "Do you mean ..."

Chris was shocked. "They think someone's embezzling?"

Harvey already had a theory. "It's gotta be an inside job. Someone with easy access to the computer system. The office staff ..."

"Nope, it's one of the Wheelers, for sure." Max was just as confident about his guess. "The buck stops with them, after all."

Ward rapped lightly on the table with his knuckles. "OK, hold up. It's too soon to play judge and jury."

Chris rubbed his forehead, then poured himself more coffee. "Makes you wonder if they'll even be able to sell the business with something like this hanging over it."

"Can't imagine they could," Kate said. "You're right; who would want to take over such a mess?"

"And that's what I'm most worried about," Ward admitted. "What if this puts them out of business? I mean, they're already looking to let it go. And now, with this ... What happens to Eagle River if there's no auction barn, at all?"

"This is quite the doomsday discussion for a bright spring morning," Harvey told his friends. "We're getting ahead of ourselves here. Surely this will sort itself out, one way or another."

"But it could happen." Max reached for another package of jam. "And that would be a terrible loss."

"And not just in terms of employment," Chris added. "If more people have to leave town for work, they're more likely to shop away from here, too."

Kate knew Chris was right. It would be too easy to stop somewhere in Charles City or Swanton, or wherever else someone spent most of their work week, than make an effort to frequent Chris and Janet's business on Eagle River's Main Street.

The post office wasn't likely to be affected, but what about other places around Eagle River? The auction barn had a small lunch stand known for its beefburgers, homemade pies, and oversized cinnamon rolls; but sale days also brought crowds across the street to Peabody's for sit-down meals.

Like the hearty breakfast that had just arrived for Kate. But suddenly, she wasn't so hungry. Given the concern visible on Joan's face, the older woman was likely thinking the same thing.

"I need this part-time job." Joan's voice was barely above a whisper. A retired nurse, she waited tables at Peabody's a few days a week. "If there's less foot traffic in here, Henry and Eloise might have to cut back on some of our shifts."

Kate tried to find something encouraging to say as she worked through her omelet.

"Harvey is right; we don't know how bad this is yet. If letters went out to that many people, I'd say someone is getting to the bottom of this right now."

Even as she spoke, Kate tried to remember who she knew that worked for the Wheelers these days. It was a good part-time job for teenagers, especially through the busier summer months; Bryan had worked there for a while in high school. Beyond that, and more important to this discussion, was figuring out who was part of the full-time staff.

There was Chuck and Sam from the bar, of course; but Kate had no idea who else worked in the stockyards. Ben Dvorak, the volunteer chief for Eagle River's fire and emergency crews, was head of maintenance at the auction barn. And then, Allison's sister-in-law worked in the office ...

Oh, no. Kate wasn't sure what Betsy Carmichael's duties entailed, but it was likely she had something to do with the business side of things. Jack was going to have a field day with this, and he and Allison were often at odds, as it was.

"I hope we'll hear more this week," Ward was saying. "Maybe the Wheelers will come out with something, anything, that will ease everyone's worries."

He looked at Chris, and then Joan.

"You're not the first people to express concerns about our local economy. I think most folks around town, and the whole region, recognize that Wheeler Auction Company is a cornerstone of this community."

"And now, it sounds like their foundation is crumbling." Grandpa Wayne shook his head. "Man, I can hardly believe it. Tens of thousands of dollars!"

Chris checked the wall clock, then turned back to his pancakes. Like Kate, he had to get to work. "How would someone get away with something like that? I mean, in the modern age. Gone are the days when someone could snitch cash from the safe, or whatever. Everything's electronic, there's a paper trail for everything."

"You've obviously given this a great deal of thought," Harvey said. "You think Janet's been skimming off the top, too?" Harvey's attempt at humor apparently succeeded, as his friend laughed.

"Well, she keeps saying she wants a real vacation this summer, maybe a trip out West. I guess if I suddenly hear she's booked us a luxury suite on the Las Vegas strip, I'd better give the books a closer look, huh?"

Chris' attention quickly turned to the restaurant's newest customer. "Hey, there's someone who might be able to tell us more." He nudged Ward, and the mayor waved the man in their direction.

Kate thought the guy looked familiar. He was maybe in his late forties, sandy-blond hair touched with gray, the start of a rounded belly beneath his faded polo shirt. But she couldn't place him, until Ward got out of his chair to good-naturedly slap the man on the back. "Ray, it's good to see you! Won't you join us?"

Police Chief Raymond Calcott grinned as he requisitioned a chair from a nearby empty table. "Don't mind if I do, Mayor."

While he poured his first cup of coffee, Chief Calcott studied the faces around this table. When his gaze momentarily paused on Kate, Ward stepped in.

"Oh, of course! You know everyone here, I think, except for Kate Duncan." Ward beamed at her from across the way. "Eagle River mail carrier extraordinaire, and Wayne's granddaughter, to boot."

"A legacy hire, then."

Did a hint of a smirk just cross the police chief's face? Kate couldn't be sure. No one else seemed to notice. But then, no one else at this table was dating the chief's cousin.

"Oh, that's right! I heard she was back from Chicago." Ray's tone was nothing other than jovial and friendly, but Kate had to wonder exactly what the chief had heard about her.

She knew Alex was close to his Aunt Helen, Ray's mom. But how well did he get along with his cousin, and the rest of his family here in town?

Kate now realized she had no idea. Ray's wife worked somewhere, but Kate couldn't recall the details. And they had a few young kids ...

What else did she know about Chief Calcott? Hardly anything, other than Roberta and Bev had both offered lukewarm opinions of him, at best. Kate wasn't sure why.

But given the self-satisfied demeanor the chief projected this morning, Kate wondered exactly where he'd served previously, and if he was merely coasting toward retirement in a town as small as Eagle River.

She noticed several heads had turned in the police chief's direction, and suspected many diners were eager to pepper Calcott with questions.

But since he was out of uniform this morning, she wondered if some folks would hold back.

Grandpa Wayne, of course, couldn't help himself.

"We were just talking about the auction barn. What's the latest?"

Henry Peabody had just appeared in the doorway between the dining room and kitchen to ask if Ray wanted his usual breakfast. The police chief seized the opportunity to ignore Grandpa Wayne's question for a few moments.

"That'll be great, thanks!" Ray told Henry before turning back to the table, which was hanging on his every word. Kate sensed Ray liked it that way, truth be told.

Chief Calcott glanced around the table again while he added sugar to his coffee, as if weighing how much he should say.

"Ah, yes; the case of the missing money. There does appear to be a ... let's say, a sizable amount of funds currently unaccounted for at one of our fine local businesses."

"How much?" Harvey was losing patience with the police chief.

Calcott shrugged. "I don't know the exact amount. I'm going to let the financial experts figure that one out." He turned to Mayor Benson with a self-deprecating frown. "As you know, Ward, budgets and such are my least-favorite part of the gig."

He's stalling, Kate decided. *He thinks if he makes enough jokes, Grandpa and his friends will give up and not ask any more questions.*

Well, Kate needed to get to work. And she was as eager for answers as everyone else.

"Do you think there's a chance this is just a massive misunderstanding?" She reached for her purse, and handed

Grandpa enough cash for her meal and a generous tip. "Or is something criminal going on here?"

Grandpa gave her a proud nod from across the table.

"I will say that there's an ongoing investigation." Chief Calcott's good humor had quickly disappeared. "You can take that to mean whatever you like."

As in: *Leave it alone. Let me do my job.*

Joan sensed the chief's hint of derision, and jumped into the conversation. "Let's just say that something fishy is going on. How would your department get to the bottom of that? I mean, financial crimes must be very complicated."

"Oh, for sure; they are one of the toughest nuts to crack." The police chief shook his head.

"Especially these days, with all the online accounts, credit-card transactions, and such. We'll need to bring in outside investigators to work on this."

Ward let out a barely audible sigh. Kate could imagine him wondering what that was going to cost.

In contrast to Ward's dejected reaction, Chief Calcott seemed rather excited about that prospect. Perhaps he was secretly eager to rub elbows with officers from outside this little corner of the world. It was the sort of case that could draw a lot of attention. Kate wondered if that was going to be helpful, or the opposite.

Ray turned his attention to the pancakes and sausage that had appeared before him. Henry himself had just brought them out from the kitchen.

And then, the police chief laughed.

"You know, it's like I was telling my crew last night: It's too bad we don't just have a murder to deal with. Homicides have their own challenges, sure. But a dead body? We could handle that on our own. It'd be so much easier."

The restaurant fell into an awkward silence. Ward seemed too stunned to speak. But Max wasn't.

"It's been decades since there's been a murder around

here." The retired mayor glared at the police chief from across the table. Kate decided Calcott was lucky he answered to Ward, and not Max. "I'd say that's a good thing."

Calcott merely nodded. "Joan, would you be a dear and pass me the butter packets? Thanks."

Joan did, then gave Kate a knowing glance before she spoke. "I'm sure we'll all be eager to hear more, when we can. The auction barn has been an important part of this community for over a hundred years. What happens now affects everyone in Eagle River."

"And the whole area, really," Chris added.

Ray smiled. "Well, hopefully we can put all of this behind us as soon as possible."

He tucked into his breakfast while the others exchanged worried looks.

"Give Roberta my regards," Grandpa Wayne told Kate before she started for the door. His gaze landed briefly on Calcott.

"I've been retired from the post office for several years now, but I know how important it is to have competent, compassionate folks serving the community."

* * *

The more Kate thought about the police chief's remarks, the more frustrated she became. By the time she reached the post office's back lot, which was only a handful of blocks from Peabody's, she was fuming.

"What an idiot! I can't believe he'd prefer to tackle a homicide, much less admit it. I guess if your time is normally spent pulling over drunk drivers, and parking next to the bridge to make sure no one crosses it at twenty-*seven* miles an hour, any big case might feel like more than you can handle."

She gathered up her work gear, and punched Bertha's key fob with more force than was necessary.

"But to say it out loud? And in front of both the current and former mayors, and in a room full of people with ears as big as their pancakes? That's just stupid."

Some of Kate's coworkers were also in less-than-cheerful moods that morning. She could hear the arguing even before she had her work boots unlaced and dumped on the mat in the vestibule.

She couldn't make out the words until she opened the door into the back room, but the voices were easy to identify: Jack and Allison were really going at it.

"I can't believe you just said that!" Allison dropped a stack of letters on the counter before tossing up her hands in frustration. "Betsy would never, ever, be involved in something like this!"

Jack's casual shrug seemed to only fuel Allison's anger. "Well, someone is guilty of embezzlement."

He pointed north, in the general direction of the auction barn. "Mark my words, the thief works in the office. They have to, since those folks handle all the accounts."

"My sister-in-law is as honest as the day is long," Allison spat out. "She's on the steering committee for Prosper's community center; she delivers meals to shut-ins twice a month. Hell, she's a Sunday school teacher, for God's sake!"

The irony of Allison's last statement wasn't lost on Kate. Randy, who'd positioned himself as a sort-of-referee between the two feuding carriers, bit back a chuckle as he held up a hand. "Now, come on, that's enough. No one knows what's going on yet."

Jack and Allison both paused to take a deep breath as Randy continued.

"I'm sure the proper authorities know the real deal by now, and they're on it. Let's let them figure it out, OK?"

Kate grunted with exasperation as she opened her locker. Bev, who was at her own cubbyhole, gave her a curious look. Kate just rolled her eyes.

"Fine." Allison seemed ready to let things go for now. "Innocent until proven guilty, right?"

"Well, usually. But someone's guilty, and they've been at it for a long time, from what I hear." Jack softened his stance, if just a bit. "Betsy's only been there, what, six years or so? Maybe she's not involved."

"Thank you." Allison arched an eyebrow and returned to her stack of mail. "See, it's not so hard to admit you're wrong, is it?"

Jack wouldn't let it go. "But it has to be someone else working for the company; unless one of the Wheelers themselves is the thief." He frowned for a second, then turned to Randy. "Who's been in that office a long time? Judy Martin's worked there for decades, I believe."

"Yeah, it's been twenty-five years, if not more," Randy said. "It seems like she's the head bookkeeper."

Marge paused on her way past the sorting counter, her hand cart stacked with parcels. "Judy wouldn't do that, either."

Aaron gave the idea some thought. "I don't know Judy, and I barely know Betsy. But I swear I saw something online a while back ... maybe a scandal in some small town, somewhere? A bunch of money went missing; a school district, I think. Turns out, one of the women in the office took it."

"I read that, too." Jack was quick to chime in. "Or, maybe it was a different one that I saw? A municipal employee who had her hand in the city's cookie jar?"

Jared Larsen was out that day, which meant the men were definitely outnumbered by the ladies. The back room turned ominously quiet as the guys continued to speculate about potential suspects.

"I heard about that." Randy nodded. "Same kinda deal, I think. She was making up invoices, or some such nonsense; then padding other ones with a few bucks here and there.

Took them years to catch her at it, too."

Jack laughed. "Well, it may not be Betsy or Judy. But women tend to hold those sorts of jobs, no matter where you go. That means it was probably ..."

The door from the lobby flew open, and Roberta stomped through.

"That's enough!" She pointed at Jack and Randy and then Aaron, who opened his mouth as if he were about to plead his innocence.

"I know what you were going to say," the boss told Jack, "and I don't want to hear it."

"But ..."

"One more word," Roberta told him, "and you'll be scrubbing these floors for a month. With a toothbrush."

That did it. Jack reached for his still-unorganized mail carton, and ambled over to the adjoining table. With his back turned, he settled down to his pre-route tasks as Marge and Allison openly laughed at his being bested.

With Roberta now at her desk in the corner, alternately glancing at her computer monitor and giving Jack the side-eye, Kate took stock of the room. Everyone on shift today was within earshot, which meant the break room was currently empty.

"I need to fill my thermos," she told Bev, then jerked her head in that general direction.

Bev didn't hesitate for even a second. "Me, too."

Once they were alone, Kate turned to her friend. "I wasn't going to spread this around. But at least a dozen other people heard every word of it, and I'm sure they'll be sharing it far and wide. You won't believe what happened at breakfast this morning."

Bev gasped when Kate relayed Chief Calcott's statement, but then shook her head. "Well, I guess I shouldn't be surprised."

Kate added more grounds to the coffee maker. "Is our

lead law enforcement officer prone to putting his foot in his mouth like that? I hadn't met him yet, I realized this morning; so I don't know what he's like."

But he certainly knew who I was, Kate thought but didn't say. And, she realized, that made her uncomfortable.

The fact that Kate was dating Alex wasn't exactly a secret, but it was nice to have some privacy in a town this tiny. Or was it because Kate wasn't sure exactly what sort of "relationship" they had, at least not yet?

She yawned and turned her reeling thoughts back toward Bev, who had started a rundown regarding Police Chief Ray Calcott that was most noteworthy for its middle-of-the road mentality.

After all, most people's opinions of their local leaders landed clearly in the "yes" or "no" camp.

"He seems nice enough, I guess. You know, it's interesting: For someone who holds such an important role in our community, it seems like we don't see that much of him. Off duty, I mean. Look at Ward; or Max, before him. They are always out and about, interacting with people."

"Or Ben Dvorak." The coffee maker chirped, and Kate reached for her thermos. "He's the volunteer leader of the fire and EMS crew, and you see him all over the place: school sporting events, church socials ... not to mention I've run into him several times at the Evertons' store, stocking up on the essentials."

Ray Calcott was hired as Eagle River's police chief about seven years ago, Bev said, after Wade Friese retired.

Friese was the police chief Kate remembered from her growing-up years. He had been a fatherly presence, eager to chat with the teenagers gathered in the high school's parking lot before class, or help an elderly resident carry groceries to their car.

Bev couldn't remember where Ray Calcott had served before he arrived in Eagle River ... wasn't that a bit odd, when everyone around here always seemed to know everyone else's business?

"But who knows? I suppose since Clyde and I live in the country, I haven't paid all that much attention to Calcott." Bev frowned.

"But given his attitude this morning, I'm afraid you're probably right: He's in over his head with this one. And worst of all, he doesn't seem that concerned."

Kate had already been worried about the possible sale of the auction barn, and what that might do to her hometown. But the financial crimes that apparently had been occurring there, and for so many years, were even more troubling.

And the fact that the law-enforcement official ultimately in charge of the case didn't seem to be taking it too seriously? That was something she couldn't set aside.

"I wonder what Ben's heard," Bev mused as she filled her thermos. "He's head of maintenance, and he's also probably more in the loop with Calcott than anyone else in town. I can't imagine Calcott's attitude is sitting well with him."

"Are you going to try to find out?" Kate asked. "Seems like Ben's dad and Clyde go way back. Weren't they neighbors as kids?"

"Well done!" Bev's grin stretched from ear to ear. "Since your return, you've gotten really good at cataloging all the connections around Eagle River."

"I have a massive whiteboard at home," Kate quipped. "Every night, Hazel and Charlie and I diagram the latest details: who's related to whom; who are best friends; which person hasn't spoken to this other person in years, and why."

Bev hooted. "I bet that's something to see! I doubt there's much blank space left on it. But seriously, it's good to keep those connections in mind. Especially in our line of work." Then she turned serious.

"Here's what I really want to know: Do you think Calcott, even with the state's help, is capable of managing this case?"

"No." Kate didn't hesitate for even a second. And the more she mulled over her friend's question, the more certain she was about her answer.

"Absolutely not. If this fell under Sheriff Preston's jurisdiction, I'd feel differently."

"Maybe it still could." Bev sounded hopeful. "I mean, even indirectly. Who knows who's involved? Sure, the auction barn is here in town, but most of its customers live in the rural areas of the county, and beyond. There are lots of possibilities."

Kate smirked. "Jack has it solved already, remember? Or he's close, at least."

"Yeah, right." Bev considered the situation for a moment. "But you know who might be able to crack it?"

"Who?" Laughing, Kate played along. That was one question she knew the answer to.

"Hmm, let's see. I think there are two ladies at the Eagle River post office who are amassing quite the track record when it comes to local crimes. Missing persons, theft, arson ... their skills just might be in demand here."

"I think you're right." Kate checked the break room's clock. "Perhaps they'll turn up some clues today."

Bev shook her head. "Here's the thing, though: This is going to be incredibly difficult. And not just because the incidents of embezzlement go back years. We're talking about ... intangibles, if you will. There is nothing concrete to see, no actual items to find."

She waved her hands in the air. "Money changes hands electronically these days, has for years."

"You're right. There's no magic vault somewhere, stuffed with stacks of bills. Well, I suppose someone could have a hidden stash. But even if you could find that, how could you ever prove where the money came from?"

As much as Kate hated to admit it, maybe Chief Calcott wasn't as lazy as he'd seemed this morning. It was going to take a whole team of financial technology wizards, working every angle they could possibly find, to track this criminal down.

Even so ...

"Gossip." Bev nodded with determination. "Yes, gathering gossip is our only choice here. While they go high tech, we'll go old school. It might not always be accurate, and it certainly will never be enough to prove a case. But it's about the only option we have to help solve this string of crimes."

Kate agreed. "And maybe, we can help save one of Eagle River's oldest businesses from going under. I was kidding about that whiteboard at home; but I may need to start one before this is over."

* 5 *

Kate had Jared's route that day, which took her out into the country. By the time she turned Bertha toward home late that afternoon, Kate wasn't any closer to figuring out who'd been swiping money from the auction barn. She did learn, however, that she and Bev weren't the only ones playing detective.

"And if half of what I heard today is true," she told herself as she turned up her acreage's driveway, "little Eagle River is a hotbed of scandal."

Murmurs about the possible sale of the auction barn had been circling for a week now. Over the weekend, those had apparently ignited into a firestorm of theories about not just the company's finances, but the personal reputations of the Wheelers and those in their inner circle.

From what Kate could gather, the bulk of the collection notices had arrived in people's mailboxes on Wednesday and Thursday. Their appearance, coupled with the chance to chew over the situation at weekend family dinners, social events, and church services, was likely to blame for the tidal wave of fresh gossip she'd heard on today's route. Every parcel drop had been an opportunity for someone to share their opinion on the situation.

As Kate unloaded her mail car, and tried to pet a happily

wriggling Hazel at the same time, she sifted through the tidbits she'd collected.

A number of the residents Kate had interacted with throughout the day, including a surprising majority of the women, had been quick to follow Jack's lead and point their fingers at the ladies in the business office. Some of that was probably due to the very thing the post-office guys had said that morning: administrative-support positions were most likely to be held by women. And that was especially true at a longstanding business like the auction barn.

Back in the day, it would have been unheard of for females to be working in the stockyards, or helping large, unpredictable livestock take a turn around the show ring. Their "place" was in the office, mostly away from the public, handling the countless marginalized-yet-important tasks that kept the company humming along season after season.

"But that's not all," Kate told Hazel as they came into the enclosed back porch. "Some of the women I talked to today had an edge of viciousness in their voices. Believe it or not, but I think they were jealous. Because from what I also heard, the Wheelers offer excellent pay and generous benefits compared to most of the office jobs around here. And those are few and far between, already."

Charlie ran into the kitchen, and Kate felt honored that he'd left his post by the living room's picture window long enough to greet her. A pair of robins was building a nest in one corner of the front porch's ceiling, and their spring construction project had kept Charlie entertained the past few days.

"Have you been nice to the Three Mouseketeers?" Charlie couldn't get outside to torment the robins, but he was an expert at throwing shade at Scout, Jerry, and Maggie through the windows when he felt like it. "I know they like to hang out on the porch. I hope you didn't give them a hard time today."

Charlie's "meow" was loud and clear, but Kate suspected

it had nothing to do with the outside cats. He wanted his long, luxurious coat brushed right this minute, and Kate decided to indulge his request rather than make him wait until after supper.

She was so tired; climbing the stairs to change her clothes felt like a bit too much to handle just now. A quick snooze on the couch would be needed before chores.

"There is something called schadenfreude," she explained to Charlie as he settled on her chest. "It's a German word. Basically, it means you find even a little satisfaction in someone else's misfortune. I think some of the ladies I talked to today are enjoying a big helping of that right now."

Charlie purred as his favorite brush smoothed the thick, furry ruff around his neck.

"I can't imagine that Betsy and Judy, and the rest of the office staff, have done anything to earn such harsh commentary other than holding what are apparently some of our community's most-coveted jobs."

But it wasn't just the administrative assistants who'd taken a turn under the microscope. Judgments had also been handed down regarding several of the men who'd worked at the business over the years. Members of that group ranged from past managers of the stock areas to auctioneers affiliated with the company, and of course members of the Wheeler family, as well.

Kate pondered the contrast between the positive opinions of the auction barn shared at Peabody's that morning, and the less-rosy views voiced along her rural route.

While many of Eagle River's residents and leaders appreciated the jobs and visitors the Wheelers' company brought to town, some of the country folks apparently saw the family in a much different light. How many of the stories were accurate, and how many were exaggerated due to anger over the collection notices that had arrived last week, Kate wasn't sure.

Either way, she'd found herself on the receiving end of several tales about decades of infighting within the Wheeler family. Rifts so deep that, more than once, they'd nearly caused the auction business to collapse.

More than a few people had grumbled about the company's history of excessively high sales commissions, a practice they claimed had continued even during the toughest economic times for the region's farmers. One elderly fellow had hijacked five minutes of Kate's afternoon to vent his still-simmering frustration over how one long-dead Wheeler had cheated his grandfather on a horse-trading deal some seventy years ago.

Even more surprising to Kate had been the whispers about the Wheelers' personal lives, including claims of infidelity, alcoholism, and gambling.

Beyond Dylan and his sister, Emma, Kate didn't know the family well enough to pass judgment on anyone's character. It was certainly possible that some of the scandalous rumors she'd heard were true. But Kate also wondered if some people were overly eager to blame the Wheelers themselves for the rash of accounting errors that had been discovered.

After all, if residents believed someone in the family was at fault, they wouldn't have to consider who else in their tight-knit community might be a first-class thief.

"Who knows what's real, and what isn't?" With Charlie's brushing complete, Kate leaned back into the throw pillow behind her head.

"Most likely, there's been a rotten apple or two in the family tree over the past century, while the rest of them have been decent-enough people. Jealousy is likely a factor there, as well. Too many family farms have disappeared over the decades, but the Wheelers' business continues to thrive."

When Chuck had sneered at Dylan for being a "rich boy," he probably wasn't too far off the mark.

Emma and Dylan had been on the same school bus route

as Kate and Bryan many times during their growing-up years. Kate recalled both the grand, porch-wrapped farmhouse that had been the Wheelers' home base for over a century; and the sprawling, vaulted-ceiling ranch Dylan's parents had built on an adjacent piece of land about twenty years ago.

For Kate, the most interesting thing wasn't what the rumors said about the Wheelers, especially when some of those were probably exaggerated, or outright false. It was the surprising number of people who, for whatever reason, resented the family.

A few people around Eagle River might even have a motive to undermine the auction business. Or just grab for themselves what they perceived as excess money the Wheelers would never miss.

Especially when Dylan's dad maybe wasn't paying enough attention to the company's finances.

Charlie was already asleep, settled in the crook of Kate's arm, and she yawned as she glanced at the clock.

"I guess it's better to be a Duncan than a Wheeler," she told Hazel, who had plopped down in front of the couch and now rested, jaw on paws, ready for her own catnap before chores. "We're the lucky ones. No one's raking us over the coals."

* * *

A light rain tapping at the farmhouse's windows woke Kate from her nap. It was five thirty, and nearly dark outside.

Charlie was no longer on the couch. Kate suspected he'd moved upstairs, to the window seat in the little office. But Hazel was still on the rug, and watching Kate with an expectant look.

"Should we go out and see the cats?"

Hazel gave a whimper of excitement.

"Yes, yes! It's chore time! Let me change out of these work clothes, first."

Kate soon pocketed her phone, pulled on her yellow galoshes, and topped off her ensemble with a waterproof jacket. Hazel didn't waste any time, pushing through her second doggie door to head out into the wet weather, but Kate lingered long enough to scoop kitty kibble from the vacuum-lidded canister in one corner of the back porch.

"I bet the raccoons and other critters aren't out here tonight," she muttered as she headed out into the rain, a covered food bucket in one gloved hand. "I'd be tucked in somewhere warm and dry, for sure."

The Three Mouseketeers had the same idea. None of the barn cats greeted Kate along her path to the machine shed, but she was met with meows of impatience when she let herself into the building.

"I know! It's nasty out there, right?" Kate flipped on the overhead lights, which chased the gloom into the far corners of the shed. She glanced around, then down at her feet.

"Hey, you guys ... where's Maggie?"

Apparently, Scout and Jerry had been the only sources of the meowing. The heat lamp still warmed the cubbyhole inside the cats' mesh-enclosed space, but the gray-tabby girl wasn't in there, either.

"I can't believe she's out in this rain." Kate set down the food bucket, and ignored the boys' comical attempts to open its lid with bared teeth and outstretched claws. "Where ..."

Then she heard it: growling that came from somewhere in the back of the shed. It was feline, and rather ladylike, but Kate was still cautious.

Maggie was in there, somewhere. She was probably crouched down in the jumble of leftover wood scraps, wire baskets, livestock halters, and discarded shovels and rakes that congregated in the back of the machine shed. But what sort of foe, exactly, was she facing right now?

Kate listened and tried to relax. There were no thrashing-about sounds, no other yowls that she could make out.

Jerry and Scout seemed completely unconcerned, and paraded around as if nothing was amiss. Hazel had followed Kate into the shed, and her demeanor was merely curious, not defensive.

But Kate couldn't be too careful. She shooed Hazel outside, reached for the flashlight kept on a nearby shelf, then tiptoed toward where Maggie was still on guard.

"There you are! What's going on, girl?" Kate sang in a gentle voice. "I can't imagine a mouse would bother you that much. You'd have pounced on it long before now."

Maggie was crouched on the floor along the outside wall, hiding behind a stack of wooden chicken crates, her ears flat with more annoyance than fear. The cat only blinked when Kate called her name and aimed the flashlight in that direction, but something else was suddenly on the move farther back in the shed.

Kate flicked her wrist just in time to catch a glimpse of another furry critter dashing from one hiding spot to the next. She gasped as a strikingly marked calico cat made a brief appearance, then wedged herself behind a pile of empty feed sacks.

And it had to be a "she." Genetically speaking, male calicos were incredibly rare. And this one, from what little Kate had seen, was either exceptionally well-fed, or ...

She groaned. "Oh, no! Don't tell me you're in the family way."

Kate looked down at Maggie, who hadn't moved from her post. "Count yourself lucky that Milton took care of that for you a long time ago. That poor girl!"

No wonder Jerry and Scout were unfazed by this visitor. It was just another cat, and one that was only interested in finding an easy meal and a warm, dry place to rest.

Kate was getting hungry, herself. Tonight's spread looked to be the last of Friday night's pizza and pumpkin pie, but she was eager to get inside and enjoy it. The sooner these cats had their dinner, she could, too.

Scout gave a yowl of triumph when she picked up the food bucket again, and let herself through the improvised screen door to the cats' area while her feline friends scooted in via their own opening. Even Maggie was more interested in dinner than guard duty.

The cats always had lots of dry food available, day and night, and Kate now recalled it had seemed to disappear a little faster in the last week or so.

"You might as well join them," Kate called softly to the calico, who had crept forward a few feet but was still half-hidden on the other side of the shed. "I brought plenty of kibble. I didn't know I was feeding four these days. And you're eating for a crowd, apparently."

The stray didn't move, but her stance relaxed a bit.

"Suit yourself." Kate picked up the water bowl, and started for the door. "I'm going to refresh this at the hydrant. Don't be scared when I come back in a few minutes." Then she had to laugh. "Who am I kidding? This kitty knows my routine. She's probably been watching me for several days, if not longer."

After finishing her chores, which included fluffing the straw in the cats' hideaway, Kate admonished Maggie to let the stranger share their meal, then headed for the house.

As she pulled her hood over her knit cap, Kate wondered what she'd do with another cat. Or more like, several more cats. If she was remembering it right, a cat's gestation cycle was roughly two months. Come late April, if not before, there would likely be a litter of kittens living in her shed.

Well, there were those spay-and-neuter clinics in Prosper when the time was right. Her friends Karen Porter and Melinda Foster, along with the post office crew, surely could help find homes for the kittens once they were old enough to be weaned.

It was raining harder now. Despite her surprise, Kate was

glad that stray girl had found shelter in the machine shed.

Or maybe the calico wasn't a stray, after all!

That possibility made Kate smile as she came into the back porch. It was more likely the cat had wandered over from a neighboring farm. She seemed healthy, and more cautious than feral. Someone was probably anxiously searching for their pet.

Hazel, wet and muddy and happy, was waiting for Kate on the rug outside the kitchen door.

"Let me get the towel." Kate peeled off her soaked layers and added them to the hooks on the wall. "And when we're done, I'm going to call Gwen. She's only a quarter mile up the road; maybe our new friend belongs there. If not, Gwen might know where 'home' is."

Gwen and her boys were still finishing their dinner, but she was glad to hear from Kate. As a divorced mom who worked full time, she didn't have many opportunities for socializing. Kate explained about the pretty cat while she popped her pizza into the microwave.

The Ashfords weren't missing any cats, much less a calico. Yet Gwen was somehow stunned by this news.

"Are you serious?" Gwen gasped. "It can't be! Does she have a black patch on her right ear? Is the last third of her tail completely orange?"

"Yep."

"You're sure?"

"One hundred percent. I didn't get a good look at the rest of her, though. She wouldn't come to me." Kate was so relieved. "But you know where she belongs, then? That's wonderful! I can just ..."

Kate heard Gwen's sons chattering in the background. Why did they suddenly sound so excited?

"Give us ten minutes," Gwen said. "We're on our way."

* * *

Kate was still in shock. Once Gwen had gotten a good look at the calico, who was still hiding in the back of the shed, she'd been confident she knew exactly where that cat belonged.

Here. At Kate's place.

"Or she used to." Gwen shook her head in awe as Kate stood next to her, speechless. "Oh, my goodness, she's come so far to get home!"

Minnie Trowbridge, the elderly woman who had lived at this acreage for decades with her family, had had only two outdoor cats by last summer. Both were rather tame, but not house cat material. Worried that the property's next owner may not care for cats, and wanting to ensure her furry friends had a stable home, Minnie had asked around for someone else in the country to take them once she moved to town.

"I have several already, as you know," Gwen said. "And Maisie likes them, but she's never been keen on feline visitors. Besides, being just up the road, I figured they wouldn't stay. Give them a chance to get their bearings, and they'd just head back here."

Minnie had finally found a friend's granddaughter who was willing to take in both cats. Her family had a snug barn and were animal lovers, had promised to supplement the cats' mousing chores with plenty of kibble ... and they lived twelve miles away.

As if she knew she was being discussed, the calico peeked out of her hiding place to watch Kate and Gwen with more curiosity than fear in her eyes. The rain had stopped, and Gwen's boys had been sent out into the yard with Hazel to give the cat some peace while the ladies tried to lure her out.

"I ... I didn't know," Kate sputtered. "When I toured the place, my realtor and I walked through all the buildings. Sure, there was stuff piled here and there, but I saw no signs of any cats. Or any other animals, for that matter."

"Minnie fed them up by the back porch steps. It was too

far for her to get out to the shed, at her age. And she often took the dishes inside when the cats were done, so the raccoons wouldn't be drawn up around the house." Gwen shrugged. "But she always kept water in that little tile dish in the flowerbed on the east side of the house."

Kate nodded as the pieces fell into place. "As you know, Minnie was gone by the time the house hit the market. So the cats were, too."

Her own barn cats were done with their supper, and Scout now wanted attention from Kate. Jerry was making the same request from around Gwen's ankles, but Maggie wasn't rolling out the welcome mat for anyone. She remained inside the cats' area, front paws tucked under her chest and her eyes narrowed with annoyance.

"This just raises so many questions." Kate crouched down and smiled at the new cat. She gave the concrete floor an encouraging pat, but the calico stayed where she was. "How did she find her way back here? When did she leave?"

"And was she on her way through the winter?" Gwen shook her head. "I can't believe she'd do that. If she left last fall, she must have holed up at another farm or two along the way."

Kate blinked back a few tears. "Can you imagine? One paw in front of the other, with miles and miles to go. It's more likely she didn't start out until that nice thaw we had a few weeks back."

"But it's stormed since then." Gwen shuddered. "Remember the gale that blew in with nine inches of snow? Where was she then? And you think she's pregnant?"

"I'm pretty sure of that. When I first saw her, when she went from one hiding spot to the next, that was the first thought I had."

They came up with a plan. Gwen thought she knew the name of the young couple who'd taken in Minnie's cats. If not, she would ask around to get it, and give them a call to let them know. The ladies hated to involve Minnie, at least for now, as Gwen said the older woman would surely get upset over her former pet's trials.

"It's nobody's fault," Gwen said. "If this girl was that determined to walk home, nothing short of being locked in a cage was going to stop her. Even though those two cats didn't live in the house, Minnie thought the world of them. Maybe we can get this kitty returned to her proper place without involving her."

"What if the cat won't stay? I mean, she's already made the trip once."

Gwen laughed. "Well, then I guess you have another cat, with more to come." She thought for a moment, then crouched down next to Kate.

"I'm not sure if this is right, but it might be. I'm going to give it a shot. Patches, will you come here? You're such a sweet kitty!"

The calico lifted her head, and her ears twitched.

"Here, Patches!" Kate joined in. "Here, kitty."

The cat took a tentative step forward, then a few more.

That one woman was a total stranger, but Patches had decided she seemed nice enough. She had been observing her long enough to know. The other one? Well, maybe Patches had seen a little of her over the years.

Minnie didn't seem to be around, but Patches knew she'd made the right choice. It felt so good to be back in her old shed, to be home, even though there were three new furry faces here.

The two boys were as harmless as they could be ... but that other girl cat? She'd better lay off the glares, and those flicks of the tail. And when it was mealtime, and the nice new lady left the shed, that girl had better make room at the food bowl without one yowl of complaint.

Because Patches was back, and *she* was the queen of this farm.

* 6 *

Kate tried to cut into her cinnamon roll with a fork, but quickly gave up and used the plastic knife, instead.

"It's no wonder this came with two utensils," she told Bev as she tucked into her treat in the auction barn's bleachers. "The counter clerk wasn't kidding when she said I'd need them."

Wheeler Auction Company was a bustling place on a Saturday morning, and the ladies had chosen seats high up in the arena to get a little extra elbow room. And so they could have relatively private conversations regarding who, and what, they were about to observe at this sale.

Because they were there for much more than the legendary food. While the auction barn held various livestock sales throughout the week, the last Saturday of every month was reserved for a higher-profile event that included a wide variety of animals and drew larger crowds from across the region.

Bev eyed Kate's plate-sized roll with admiration, but shook her head when Kate offered to slice off a section.

"Nope, I'm holding out for the pie." Bev took a sip of her coffee, then nodded her approval. It was hot and strong, nothing fancy. "I need to digest that breakfast sandwich first, then I'll head back down for a slice. I saw they had coconut cream today, which is my favorite."

"There you are!" Karen Porter, a veterinarian at the Prosper clinic, blew a stray wisp from her blond ponytail out of her eyes as she hiked the final stretch of concrete steps. She had a massive caramel-pecan roll in one hand, and coffee in the other.

"I'd need to run these stairs several times to work this off, but it would be worth it." She took her spot on the worn wooden bench. "It's a miracle that all three of us were off today so we could do this. Too bad Melinda had to work."

"Prosper Hardware is only closed on Sundays and major holidays," Bev reminded the younger women. "It's always been that way. This is their busiest day of the week, too." Then she grinned. "But at least we have a solid trio to investigate this situation."

The auction barn's cavernous space echoed with an unrelenting hum as the minutes ticked down toward the start of the sale. Crew members called to one another across the oval show ring as they made a final tour of the sawdust-padded concrete floor and double checked the various gates.

Two arched hallways on the north side of the selling ring led into the adjoining building, which was filled with rows of indoor stalls. Beyond those, on the far-east side, was the livestock loading and unloading area. A rounded hallway on the west and south sides of the pavilion provided several access points to the auditorium's bleachers, as well as the lunch stand and its small cafeteria, and the business offices.

A massive cupola encircled by two-dozen multi-paned windows rose high above the ring, and the sunlight beaming in this morning lit up the fine specks of dust that floated in the air.

The historical building's grand scale and ornate features reminded Kate of a church. And the more she thought about it, that was a fitting analogy for both this space and the people who had been visiting it for over a century.

If you wanted to buy or sell livestock, this was the only place in the entire region to do it. If you just wanted to soak up the atmosphere and enjoy the fellowship of like-minded people, you could find that here, too. All around her, people were laughing and chatting with relatives, old friends, and new acquaintances. This wasn't just a business. It was a gathering spot, just like Peabody's or the coffee shop.

Kate looked down at what was left of her cinnamon roll, and wondered how much longer this tradition would be able to continue.

But unlike in church, the most-eager attendees insisted on sitting up front. While several tiers of backless benches, their edges worn and their scratches and scrapes softened by time, encircled the show ring, five short rows of fold-down wooden chairs banked the auctioneer's stand.

This was where the day's biggest bidders tended to gather, as well as members of the company's various business partners, the auction barn's lead staffers, and the Wheelers themselves. It was the area that Kate, Bev, and Karen were most interested in today.

But Kate was also eager to take a walk through the holding pens in the back of the building, as well as a self-guided tour of the grounds. She had fond memories of this place from her childhood and teenage years, as she'd often accompanied her dad and Bryan regardless of whether they attended as buyers or sellers.

Grandpa James sometimes joined them, and the hustle and bustle of Wheeler Auction Company had often stirred his recollections of farm life when he was a boy. He'd shared tales of long ago that had captured Kate and Bryan's attention as much as the critters that circled the ring, and the breathless ramblings of the auctioneer.

So many years had passed, and the auction barn itself hadn't really changed. But the food ...

"Have these rolls gotten bigger?" Kate asked Bev. "I

remember them being amazingly good when I was little, but I think they've been super-sized."

"I can confirm that's true," Bev said as she gave into Karen's insistence that she try a bite of the pecan roll. "Portions are bigger, like what you find at restaurants." Then Bev glanced toward their nearest seatmates, who were about four feet away, and lowered her voice.

"A friend of mine works in the kitchen, has for years. She said they realized about a decade ago that people were happy to pay a lot more for a little more, if you know what I mean. That meant better profit margins for the lunch stand."

Kate chewed that over as she licked frosting from her fingers before wiping them on a paper napkin. She would never do that in a restaurant, but the auction barn's no-nonsense vibe meant it wasn't a big deal. "Interesting. How exactly is the lunch stand structured, business-wise? Do you know?"

Karen grinned. "Good observation. It's one more way money flows in and out of this place. Bev, what's the scoop on that?"

"I believe the Wheelers insist that it turns its own profit. It's just one part of the machine, if you will. From what I've heard, they have a separate budget. At least in theory."

Kate laughed. "I wonder if Jack knows that. He'd be all over it with his women-handling-the-money idea. But I can't imagine one of the pie ladies is skimming off the top somehow."

She dug another chunk out of her cinnamon roll, then leaned in. "Now, who are all those people milling around down there? Anyone know? It's been years since I've been at an auction. I think I only recognize Dylan and his dad."

Pete Wheeler, in a sharp-pressed Western shirt and dark blue jeans, lingered by the auctioneer's platform, deep in conversation with an elderly man sporting a worn baseball-style cap and clean overalls. Kate noticed that as soon as their chat ended, another man stepped into Pete's line of sight before he could move on.

But Pete didn't seem to mind the delay. Kate saw his wide grin for the second guy, and both of them were laughing broadly before Pete clapped the man on the shoulder.

Dylan was on the opposite side of the ring, his spotless checked shirt and still-shiny black boots very similar to those worn by his dad. But while Pete joked around with potential buyers, Dylan's forehead was creased with concentration as he moved from one sales-ring assistant to the next, making sure everyone had what they needed.

While Kate couldn't hear the conversations, she imagined Dylan reminding the workers about the order of the lots that would be auctioned, or how to guide a group of steers or a team of horses around the ring to ensure their best qualities were on display.

Kate nodded in recognition when she saw Dylan stop one young crew member and gesture for him to tuck in his polo shirt.

The Dylan she remembered was thoughtful and meticulous, but also incredibly smart. His math abilities were near-legendary with teachers at Eagle River High School, and he'd been valedictorian of his class. After four years away at college, it hadn't been a surprise when he'd come right back to Eagle River to officially join the family business.

Kate had done the opposite, while Bryan had followed a path more like Dylan's. As she reflected on how they'd all changed over the years, her attention was drawn back to Pete Wheeler.

How much older he looked these days! While he smiled and shook hands with those milling around him, his shoulders seemed slumped. The scandal regarding the auction barn's unbalanced books had to feel like a dagger in Pete Wheeler's back.

Bev must have noticed the same.

"I imagine he's taking this hard," she told Kate and Karen. "Clyde ran into him at the co-op a few days ago. He said Pete barely looked anyone in the eye, and hustled out of the shop as fast as he could. And I mean the Eagle River co-op," she added. "The Wheelers use it for the company's needs, as well as their own livestock. They don't do business in Prosper."

"I can imagine that drives Auggie nuts," Karen said. August Kleinsbach owned the Prosper co-op. "He has quite the kingdom built up. But the Wheelers are smart to get what they need at the co-op right here in town. There would be backlash if they didn't."

The Eagle River Farmers Cooperative had been in existence almost as long as Wheeler Auction Company, Bev said. The auction barn had a constant need for oats, hay, straw, and other such supplies, and continued to purchase those items from the cooperative under special agreements put in place generations ago.

The rise of corporate farming and expanded retail options meant the Wheelers could shave a bit off those expenses by going elsewhere, but the family refused to turn their backs on the local farmers who were some of their most-loyal auction customers. And a great number of those folks seemed to be at this sale.

"Just look at this crowd!" Bev gestured around the bleachers. "Not everybody's here to buy, of course; it's as much a social outing as anything else. And one of the lots up for sale today would be expected to bring in lots of gawkers."

Kate knew exactly what Bev was referring to; she'd considered it a lucky chance that she was off work today, and able to attend this particular sale. Because one of the most-prized teams of Percheron horses in the entire state, if not the Upper Midwest, was going to take a turn around the show ring.

"The Binghams are putting two of their show horses up for sale," she explained to Karen. "I'm sure many people are here to get a glimpse at them, and see what they sell for. My neighbor, Gwen, told me the horse market's been down lately. But this is still a big deal."

The Binghams' main farm was more like a ranch, as it encompassed more than nine-hundred acres about fifteen miles east of Eagle River. Kate wasn't familiar with the family, as they lived close enough to Charles City that their kids had attended that school system. But the Binghams were known for the champion horses they raised, along with the field crops they cultivated.

Pete Wheeler was now deep in conversation with a middle-aged man and woman in the front row of the audience, and Bev confirmed they were Elton and Andrea Bingham. The artfully applied highlights in Andrea's hair were noticeable from across the ring, along with the glint of her golden earrings.

"I wondered who that was." Karen leaned in for a closer look. "I know the name, but not the face. She seems overdressed. Do you think that's a cashmere wrap?"

Bev shrugged, adding that she'd never owned anything made from that luxury fabric in her life. But as Kate studied Mrs. Bingham's draped cardigan, she recalled the well-heeled ladies she used to see shopping along Chicago's Magnificent Mile. Andrea's saddle-brown boots also whispered of luxury.

"I hope she doesn't step in anything aromatic," Kate told her friends. "I'd hate to think of what it would take to get those boots clean again. They're fantastic. But not suited to an auction barn, in my opinion."

Bev seemed to consider something, then shook her head.

"What?" Karen wanted to know. "What were you going to say?"

"Well, word is Andrea and Elton are selling this pair of Percherons out of desperation. I've heard they do more than raise exceptional horses; they bet on them, too. Or, I should say, Elton does. If you get my meaning."

"Oh, I do." Kate considered this tidbit as Andrea turned to greet another woman and inadvertently gave the crowd a better look at her high-end designer purse. "So that's what everyone's here to see. Not just the team itself, but the Binghams' walk of shame."

Karen had heard the same about the Binghams. Apparently, the region's highest-profile horse breeders weren't strangers to the sort of scorching gossip currently swirling around the Wheelers.

"I shouldn't say where I got my info." Karen set aside the last third of her pecan roll. "But yes, it sounds like they need the cash. Doc and I don't treat their herd, of course; they are all-in with the vet clinic here in town."

"So are the Wheelers," Bev pointed out. "At their farm, and of course here at the auction barn. The Eagle River vets probably don't need to visit this place often, but still."

"Everyone's connected around here, one way or another." Kate sipped her coffee. "It's to be expected in a town this small. Even so, you can't help but wonder: How much of that is due to expectations created by tradition, rather than choice?"

Karen wrinkled her nose as she pointed toward the auctioneer's podium. "Exhibit A. *This* is the auctioneer today? I can't believe he's still working here."

"Is that the one?" Bev was curious. "The guy that handled the hay sale?"

Karen explained to Kate how she and Melinda had spent a few harrowing hours at the auction barn two years ago. The area had been suffering from a drought, and they'd been desperate to secure more hay for Melinda's sheep.

Dozens of anxious farmers had swarmed the auction barn's parking lot that morning, and the terrible heat had only compounded the worries and irritability of those in the crowd. When the auctioneer began to bounce from one load of hay to the other with no sign of reason, many suspected he was trying to send the smaller proprietors home early and push the big spenders into bidding wars on certain lots.

The disgruntled whispers had soon turned into angry shouts and direct challenges to the auctioneer. Someone in the office had called the police.

Karen recalled how the auctioneer had been pulled aside for a talk with law enforcement and management. He'd then offered a rather-dramatic series of apologies before starting the bidding back up again ... that time, moving down the row of hay racks as expected.

"I heard about that," Bev said. "One of our neighbors was here that day, too." She thought for a moment. "Hmm. I can't remember this auctioneer's name. Gary? Roger?" She shook her head. "He's not very local, it seems like."

Kate shook her head in disgust. "If he's so shady; sorry, allegedly shady; why would the Wheelers ever hire him again, much less keep him around this long? There aren't as many live auctions these days, for farm animals or anything else; so much of it is done online. You'd think they'd have their pick of people to call a sale."

"Seems odd, doesn't it?" Bev muttered as everyone in the crowd rose to their feet and turned their attention to the state and American flags on display behind the auctioneer's podium. "Maybe with the Wheelers, once you're in, you're in for life."

As the strains of the National Anthem drifted out of the speaker system, Kate placed one hand over her heart. She also took a few moments to carefully study the various employees and hangers-on who'd paused on the auction barn's floor.

If the Wheelers' inner circle was that small, this embezzlement case wasn't going to be only a matter of criminal activity. It was also likely to be scarred by deep, personal betrayal.

* * *

A cheer went up from the crowd once the anthem was over, and the ladies momentarily set aside their sleuthing as they enjoyed the variety of animals that streamed into the sale ring.

Several flocks of sheep were among the early lots for this Saturday sale, and some of the ewes already had young lambs at their sides.

"It's too early, in my opinion." Karen wrinkled her nose. "But the larger producers like to get a jump start on the season."

Bev nudged Kate. "Maybe you'd like a few, to keep that pasture in check. You could be just like Melinda."

"Yeah, and she also has a donkey. Nope, I'm going to pass today. Besides, my flock of *cats* will likely double in about a month."

"Your clowder." Karen raised her voice to be heard over the noise of the packed arena. "That's the official term. How's Patches getting along with Scout and his crew?"

"Scout and Jerry are just rolling with it. Maggie is taking her cues from them, most of the time. Patches has made it clear she expects to be in charge, and I think Maggie's decided it's not worth a fight."

"I can't believe she walked that far!" Bev said. "But then, I guess 'home' is wherever you really want to be."

Gwen had tracked down Patches' previous caretakers, but everyone had agreed to let the stubborn cat stay right where she was.

The young couple had last seen Patches in November and, after several weeks of searching, had given up all hope she was still alive. Minnie's other cat was especially bonded with two of the felines at his new place, which might explain why he remained behind when Patches decided to return home.

The Eagle River mail carriers were putting out feelers for anyone looking for kittens in the coming months. Indoor homes would be greatly preferred, of course; but sadly, there were always more than enough kittens to go around.

Kate had talked herself into settling for quality barn homes, if necessary.

A trio of ducks came next, and their waddling procession brought laughter and claps of appreciation from the crowd.

"Hey, Kate, there's another option." Karen pointed toward the ring, her voice teasing in its tone.

"You have that huge, fancy chicken house just sitting empty. Get these guys a wading pool, and they'd love to go home with you."

"We had some ducks once," Bev said.

"How did that go?" Kate wanted to know.

"Coyotes." Bev's shoulders sagged with defeat. "That's how it went. And that was that."

Kate shook her head. "No fowls for me, thanks. At least, not for a while yet."

She leaned forward to get a better look at the patrons in the rows closest to the auctioneer's podium. The crowd there had swelled to over two-dozen people since the start of the sale.

"Looks like we have some more high rollers in attendance. What time will the Percherons come through?"

Bev consulted the sale flier she'd picked up on their way into the arena. While everything was advertised online these days, the Wheelers still followed the tradition of having sell sheets for attendees. "Just after eleven, looks like. It says here that anyone seriously interested in the team needed to turn in financial information by noon yesterday."

"Smart." Karen nodded her approval. "As a seller, you'd want to be sure the cash flow is there. Especially if you desperately need the money."

Kate recalled how John Grant had walked out of the sale barn with almost two thousand dollars' worth of hogs after giving Pete Wheeler nothing more than a handshake and a promise to mail a check.

These Percherons were worth exponentially more than that, and Kate wondered if the barn's financial protocols varied based on the value of the animals changing hands.

Or were the rules sometimes bent based on who was doing the buying and the selling?

Kate was starting to see how money could disappear from this business, especially if it was being pilfered a little at a time. Despite its longevity, there didn't seem to be any clear set of professional standards at work at this company.

Several lots of beef cows, and then dairy herds, came through the ring. The bidding was spirited and quick, and Kate had to admire the auctioneer's skill even though Karen had understandably questioned his morals.

Maybe he was simply one of the best in the business, and the Wheelers were willing to watch him closely in exchange for his ability to encourage higher bids and keep a sale flowing smoothly.

After one lot of dairy cows, the auctioneer's chatter took a dramatic pause. Four of the floor assistants moved toward the ring's largest gated entrance as a ripple of anticipation rolled through the auction barn.

"Well, folks, this is the team you've been waiting for!" This proclamation was met with cheers. "They're on their way out, right now! We're all in for a treat today!"

A few moments later, a stunning pair of dark-gray draft horses stepped elegantly into the bright lights of the auction floor. Their glossy black manes and tails were woven through with navy ribbons, and the horses tossed their heads with pride when they were met by a round of applause.

With the ease of a pair accustomed to moving as one, they trotted into the ring pulling a vintage farm wagon decked out with red-metal trim and rows of brass-head fasteners. Their driver held the reins with ease in his left hand, and raised his cowboy hat to the crowd with his right.

It was a greeting, to be sure. But the casual gesture also

underscored the veteran team's reliability and confidence before a crowd.

"Oh, my!" Bev shook her head in admiration. "Aren't they beautiful?"

Kate couldn't speak for a moment. Her family had never raised horses, but even she could appreciate the strength and elegance of this team as they paraded around the ring.

"Folks, you've never seen anything like it!" the auctioneer exclaimed. "They are a one-in-a-million pair, for sure. Let's get this started!"

When he named the opening bid, gasps went up around the arena.

"Are they really worth that much, or more?" Kate asked. "They're fantastic, but in this market ..."

Bev was skeptical. "Hay and oats are still high; most people can't make a go of it. Show horses are a rich man's game, though. We'll see what happens."

Several of the pre-approved bidders were clustered at the ring-side rail, but Kate wondered how many more were a few rows back in the crowd, trying to keep a low profile. The auctioneer's assistants were apparently skilled at catching discreet bids, as the asking price for the team seemed to climb faster than the amount of motion visible in the front rows.

After the team finished their high-stepping trot around the ring, the wagon's driver eased them to a stop near the auctioneer's podium. With a quick word from their handler, both horses took a step back and bowed to the now-roaring crowd. The auctioneer gave a wide grin as the bids continued to pour in.

Karen clasped her hands in admiration. "I have never seen anything like it! Now they're getting apple slices as a treat. It looks like they are as calm and well-trained as they are strong."

"I suppose they'd have to be." Kate marveled at the size of the Percherons' hooves. "You'd need to be careful around horses that huge, feel confident they'd listen to you, and know they were gentle enough that you could handle them safely. Oh, look at the Binghams."

Both husband and wife smiled for the crowd, but the relief was clear on Elton's face. Andrea, meanwhile, wiped away a tear.

"Just how far in the hole is he?" Karen asked Bev.

"Don't know; but far enough to sell off their best driving team this morning." Bev nodded in understanding. "Our three are just pets, of course; they aren't worth a fraction of this incredible team. But I'd be crying, too, if I had to let them go. At any price."

When the bidding finally ground to a halt, it was as if the entire arena held its breath. Even the Percherons were perfectly still.

"Sold! Folks, we just set a new record here today at Wheeler Auction Company!"

The auctioneer pointed toward a casually dressed middle-aged man in the third row of the wooden seats. He smiled and raised a hand in acknowledgment as the crowd applauded his determination or recklessness, or maybe both.

Dylan's dad was already making his way through the throng of elite bidders, eager to shake the hand of the horses' new owner.

The crowd settled down as the prancing team left the ring, and a group of goats soon made their way into the arena. The murmurs that passed through the crowded bleachers noted the Percherons' new owner was a top-notch breeder from northern Wisconsin.

"Not everyone wears their money on their sleeve," Bev observed. "Some folks with deep pockets don't flash their cash. And he must have quite a bit of it, given what he just paid for that team."

"Pete Wheeler has to be pleased." Karen finished her coffee in one gulp. "I can about imagine the commission the auction barn is going to collect on that sale."

"If only it was enough to make their money problems go away." Kate's phone chirped news of a new text. "Hey, Bryan's here. He's in the back, looking over a lot of beef cattle."

Patrons were allowed to visit the barn's pens beginning one hour before the start of a sale, and could mill around throughout the event to get a closer look at the animals on deck.

Karen's eyes sparkled with mirth as she stood up. "Well, I think you need to weigh in on that decision. It's the perfect excuse to wander into the back of the barn, see what else we can dig up today."

The three ladies made their way out of the bleachers. Once they reached the main hallway, Bev pointed toward the lunch stand.

"I still want that piece of pie. I think I'll get it to go, and get another for Clyde. I'll meet you in the back in a few minutes."

While some of the animals in the holding pens called to each other, and the auctioneer's chatter wafted out of the speakers, the back portion of the auction barn was much quieter than the auditorium.

A sizable number of animals were still waiting for their turns in the ring, but others were now ready for rides to their new homes.

Bryan leaned on a steel gate, deep in conversation with someone Kate didn't recognize. "Thanks, Larry," Bryan told the other man before the guy moved on. "They're a fine group. I'll see how it goes."

"So, you're plotting to bring home more cows?" Kate raised an eyebrow at her brother. "What does Dad say about that?"

Bryan laughed and held up a hand in protest. "He's good, OK? But I haven't decided yet. Karen, you're the bovine expert here. Remind me why I don't need to add to our herd."

"Oh, no; I'm staying out of it. You have our number if you need it." A man across the aisle soon waved Karen down, and she wandered off.

"I bet she gets stuck giving out free medical advice at places like this," Bryan said as he studied the eight cows more closely.

One of the Duncans' neighbors soon appeared, and he and Bryan launched into a detailed debate over when spring planting should start.

Kate reached through the pen's gate, and offered a hand of greeting to the cows.

As she petted one just above its nose and admired its healthy coat, Kate wondered how the region's farmers would adapt if Wheeler Auction Company were to close.

How far would animals like these, and the people who owned them, have to travel to take part in a sale? Unless this situation was resolved, there would be repercussions far beyond the loss of one of the area's largest employers.

"Look out!" Karen hurried back across the aisle as a series of shouts echoed from a few rows over. "The Percherons are coming this way!"

Kate was confused for a second. The draft horses had been so calm in the show ring, despite the commotion and cheers of the crowd.

She couldn't imagine they'd do more than twitch their ears as they were guided toward the trailer that would take them to their new home.

Then she saw three stockyard workers running down the aisle, shouting at everyone in their path to get back.

And just beyond them, rounding the bend with their tails held high in fear, two gigantic horses bolted toward the daylight streaming through the open doorway at the far end of the barn.

"Runaways!" someone shouted.

"Joe, try to grab his halter!"

"Those gates won't hold them. Roll the door down!"

"There's no time!" another man yelled. "Shut the security panels! *Now*!"

On the far end, two men rushed to close a second set of gates just inside the barn's main entrance. While they were taller and thicker than the panels already locked across the aisle, Kate wondered if they would be any match for a team of spooked draft horses.

People up and down the aisle rushed to get out of the way. Their shouts, and the horses' agitated neighs, were soon joined by the frantic calls of dozens of other animals in the back of the auction barn. Sheep and goats bleated, and cows sent up cries of distress. A bull down the way let out an enraged grunt and shoved his forehead against the side of his metal pen, and one of the Percherons reared up in fright.

Bryan grabbed Kate's arm. "Someone's going to get hurt. Get over the fence!"

The once-docile cows on the other side were restless now, pushing and shoving each other, but Kate knew her brother was right. It had been years since she'd been in with a group of cows, much less ones as terrified as these, but it was a better risk than what was coming their way.

Karen quickly joined them. They clung to the other side of the gate, their feet planted on a lower rail. In the next pen, a man and his son did the same.

"Heads down, everybody!" Karen shouted a warning. "Don't look them in the eye!"

Kate felt a vibration echo through the hollow-bar steel gate as the horses' massive hooves thundered down the aisle. A rumble at the far end had to be the steel door rolling down.

Suddenly, a woman shouted over the din. Kate couldn't make it all out, but it must have included the horses' names.

She opened her eyes in time to see Andrea Bingham, her cashmere cardigan flying behind her like a cape, dash into the aisle and hold her hands up in a beseeching manner.

The man in the next pen wrapped his arm tighter around his crying son. "She's going to get herself killed! Has she lost her mind?"

"She may be the only person they'll listen to," Karen said.

Andrea called to her horses again. After a few more cries of distress, both Percherons slowed their speed. Andrea darted between them and the closed gates, and grabbed the left horse's halter.

"Andrea!" Elton climbed over the fence after his wife. "What in the hell did you do that for? They could have trampled you!"

A barn staffer grabbed the second horse's lead, and took the other reins from Andrea's hands. Their mad dash finally over, the Percherons breathed long and deep as a handful of grooms tried to soothe them.

"I don't care!" Andrea was in tears. "Someone had to do something! They love me the most, you know they do!"

And then, she slapped her husband across the face.

"This is all your fault! If anything had happened to me just now, or anyone else in here, or those two magnificent animals, you would've been the one with blood on your hands, not me!"

Elton stared at his wife in shock as she turned her back on him, then went to comfort her beloved horses.

The right one rested its chin on Andrea's shoulder as she cried tears of anger and despair. The Percherons' new owner, shadowed by Dylan Wheeler, carefully approached the group and put a gentle hand on Andrea's other arm.

"Are the horses crying, too?" the little boy asked his dad.

"Maybe. They might be sad. I bet that lady took good care of them."

The other animals took their cues from the Percherons, and started to settle in their pens. As the barn quieted down, Kate could once again hear the auctioneer's calls coming through the speakers.

While bedlam had broken out in the back, most people in the rest of the building likely had no idea what had just happened.

Dylan soon appeared next to Kate. "Well, the show goes on, no matter what." She caught the note of cynicism in her old schoolmate's voice, as well as the relief. "Everyone's OK, and that's all that matters. This could have turned into a nightmare."

Karen offered to give the horses a quick look once they were tethered to a nearby post. While Bryan went back to mulling over his potential purchase, Kate started toward the arena in a bid to catch up with Bev.

She found her, eyes wide with worry and clutching a takeout container, in the next aisle over.

"Oh, thank goodness!" Bev gasped. "Is Karen ..."

"She's fine; and helping out, of course. The horses don't seem to be injured, but she's checking to be sure."

"I can't believe this happened." Bev shook her head in disbelief as they stepped aside to let a few stable hands herd a pack of sheep toward the sale ring. "I know those horses are in a strange place, and it's been a lot of excitement for them. But they're used to the show circuit."

"You're right. It doesn't make any sense. None at all."

Across the way, Pete Wheeler and two other men were studying the Percherons' still-open pen.

"I heard those guys talking." Bev cut her eyes toward a group of barn assistants. "The horses weren't out in the aisle when all this started. They were in their pen, right where they were supposed to be. One of the guys swore he saw another of the handlers unlatch the horses' stall gate, then reach over and smack one of them on the rump."

It would take something significant to spook a team of experienced show horses that badly, but what Bev had just described would do the trick.

Even so, Kate could hardly believe it. Why would anyone

do something so dangerous? Especially when the back of the barn was teeming with dozens of visitors, like it was today?

Karen found her way over to where Kate and Bev stood against the wall.

"Well, that was a close call! But the horses are fine, and no one else was hurt." She noticed the container Bev had in her hands. "I'm glad you were able to get your pie, at least."

"It's the last two pieces of coconut cream. And they might have saved my life! At my age, I don't know if I could have scrambled over a fence fast enough to get out of the way."

* 7 *

Randy dropped the oversized envelope next to Kate's mail case. "Looks like you have a special delivery today."

Kate set aside her half-sorted pile, and gave the front of the new envelope a good look. "Hmm. A certified letter." She blinked when she saw the return address in the corner. "I can't believe it!"

Jack leaned over for a look, and let out a low whistle. "Duncan, you hit the jackpot! It's been a long time since one of those has come through here."

"April Fool's Day was yesterday," Marge said between bites of her energy bar. "But that looks like the real deal to me."

"The FBI?" Kate held up the packet for the rest of the carriers to see. "What in the world does the FBI want with this guy?"

"Can't they just storm his house?" Randy chuckled as he packed his mail case. "I'd think a certified letter might tip someone off that they're on the radar."

Roberta paused at the sorting table on her way to freshen the front counter. "It could be about any number of things." She gave all her crew members a warning glance, but saved the strength of her glare for Jack. "You know, things that aren't any of our business."

"Darn, I was going to steam it open before Kate headed out," Jack called sarcastically after the boss, then turned back to his co-workers. "Anyone have a glue stick I can use to seal it up again?"

Kate had delivered many certified letters and packages during her career, but she'd had only one or two while in Eagle River. And she couldn't recall ever handling one sent by the Federal Bureau of Investigation. The IRS generated a great deal of mail, of course, but those missives rarely required a signature.

The carriers soon turned back to their sorting, but the certified letter stayed at the forefront of their minds.

"It makes me wonder if the FBI, and other agencies, will ever fully switch to electronic communications," Jack mused. "I mean, email isn't tamper proof, but is it more secure than this?"

Randy rolled his eyes. "That's the feds for you: wedded to tradition, no matter how inefficient it may be these days."

Marge wasn't so sure. "I see why they still do it this way. The message goes from person to person, within the bounds of the government." She pointed proudly at herself, then her co-workers. "I'd say we're a safer bet than a series of internet servers where you can't verify if the right firewalls are in place."

"Either way, you probably won't be able to unload it," Randy told Kate as she prepared to head out. "It's a Tuesday. He's probably at work, not at home. That letter is likely to come right back here."

Randy was right, but Kate had to try. Postal carriers were required to make one attempt to deliver a certified package or letter. If they were unsuccessful, a note was left and the item was held at the post office for pickup.

While the mysterious letter had pulled Kate out of her exhausted fog faster than a cup of Jack's stout-brewed coffee, she still yawned as she headed south out of town. She'd been busy last night out in the machine shed, clearing a space for Patches' private maternity ward.

Kate had managed to get Patches into a carrier and to the Prosper vet clinic yesterday. The mother-to-be was in good health, according to Karen, which was a huge relief given what the cat had been through. The calico's delivery date was perhaps three weeks away. That meant Kate had a little time to prepare, but she was taking no chances.

Given the uneasy truce between Patches and the other feline residents of her farm, Kate wasn't sure this mama would want to deliver her kittens inside the Three Mouseketeers' enclosure.

Most of Kate's efforts had been focused on clearing a section of the shed of its leftover items. Then a new, deep-sided plastic tote had been filled with fresh straw, and an extra heat lamp installed above it.

Today's forecast called for rain by afternoon, which was when Kate would attempt delivery of the certified letter. She'd grabbed a gallon-sized storage bag from the break room before leaving the post office, determined to keep this unusual missive dry until she (hopefully) washed her hands of it after lunch.

As she piloted Bertha down the gravel roads, ever mindful of the deep ruts so common this time of year, Kate wondered about the story behind this letter.

"Donald Wellington. Hmm." She ruminated some more, but had to shake her head in defeat. "Nope, never heard of him. Or anyone named Wellington, for that matter. It's possible they're outside of the Eagle River school system."

Mapleville was as sleepy as ever this morning, except for the spring-season busyness at the co-op. Its manager, Gerard Abernathy, seemed to know everyone for miles around, and it was likely he was familiar with Donald Wellington.

As Kate reached for the small stack of letters destined for the shop, she wondered how she could possibly bring up

Donald's name. But there was no easy, safe way to do that without raising suspicion.

"Nope, I can't," Kate reminded herself as she pulled up her parka hood and got out of the car, the co-op's bundle tucked under her arm. "As soon as I mention the name, Gerard will want to know why I'm asking. It's too risky."

Not only because that delivery was supposed to be confidential, but because Kate still had no idea what the Federal Bureau of Investigation wanted with Mr. Wellington. As she worked her way around the township, Kate's mind bounced from scenario to scenario. All she could come up with was that Mr. Wellington was either a spy, a big-time criminal, or possibly both.

But the address started to sound familiar as Kate got closer to the letter's destination, and that eased her concerns.

"Isn't that the big Victorian farmhouse that's had all the renovations done? Just after I cross Badger Creek? It's a beautiful place; I find it hard to believe anyone living there is mixed up in something shady."

The two-story home had several porches, both open and enclosed, and its size hinted it had been built for a large family. New windows and fresh shingles indicated a great deal of work had been done to the house, and Kate had always wondered what updates had been made inside. Today would give her a chance to climb the front porch steps, and perhaps get a glimpse of what she imagined was a gracious front hall.

Because that was the most she'd be able to see. And maybe that was a good thing. Outward appearances were not always an accurate indicator of what was on the inside, a hard truth that applied to people as well as houses.

"I still need to be careful," she reminded herself as she pulled away from a neighbor's mailbox, and drove toward the next crossroads. "After all, I still have no idea who these people are." She cringed, just a bit. "Or what the FBI wants with Mr. Wellington."

Kate wondered if she should text someone, tell them where she was stopping next and what she was going to do. Roberta was probably busy at the counter, and Bev was off today. And then, Kate smiled. She needed to text Alex about their plans for tomorrow night; this was the perfect time to do both. Wasn't he always cautioning her about staying alert as she drove these back roads alone? Being aware of her surroundings, and all that?

"I guess Mr. Safety is my check-in pick this time." Kate guided Bertha to the shoulder and reached for her phone.

I'm glad you let someone know where you're headed, Alex texted back. *So they need to sign before you can hand over the letter?*

Yes. And it's from the FBI.

What?! Let me know when you leave the car, and the second you get back.

There was a pause before another text came through. *Who's it for?*

Kate smirked. Of course, Alex couldn't help himself.

That is confidential, she told him. *Post office regulations.*

"He's worse than a little old lady when it comes to gossip around here." Kate shook her head as she pulled back out on the road. "I guess running a bar will do that to you."

It was a waste of time to stop at the Wellingtons' mailbox with the rest of their items, since Kate had to go to the house. And at least two people lived here, according to the pile on Bertha's passenger seat.

"Vanessa and Donald," Kate muttered as she turned up the long driveway. "I wonder if they have kids? I finally remembered the house; surely I've stopped here before when Jared's been out. But I don't think I know a thing about them."

Even in this first week of April, there were many signs of spring in the yard: daffodils nodding along a well-maintained picket fence, a slightly green tint to the lawn, larger clumps of fresh vegetation hinting that several manicured perennial beds dotted the property.

Kate pulled up in front of the garage, which had likely once been an impressive carriage house, and parked next to a top-tier SUV. She texted Alex about her arrival, gave the yard a good look, then checked the corners of the barn across the way for any sign of movement. Nothing seemed amiss, and she took a deep breath.

"There's no sign of a dog." That alone gave Kate a measure of relief. "And someone is home, I think, between this vehicle and the lights that are on inside the house. Maybe this won't be so bad."

With her questions partially answered, and comforted by the knowledge that Alex was keeping tabs on her from town, Kate's mood switched from cautious to curious. This shouldn't take long, and she'd be on her way again.

A few raindrops had started to fall about two miles ago, and the skies opened just as Kate zipped up her parka and raised its hood. She'd been smart to grab that plastic bag for the certified letter.

She made a mad dash for the front porch, rang the bell, and waited. A minute or so ticked by. No one came to the door.

The window blinds along the front of the house were closed. Other than the glow of a few lights behind them, Kate couldn't see a thing. She pushed the button a second time, and heard the chimes' faint answer once again.

As she waited, Kate's gaze wandered across the porch. Its floor's dark-gray paint was relatively fresh but pockmarked with mud, like every other entrance this time of year. A "welcome spring" sign tethered to the vinyl siding was the porch's only decoration. But Kate could imagine a set of wicker chairs resting here in the summer, and baskets of flowers swaying on the small hooks tacked under the roof's edge.

She opened the screen door, and knocked on the heavy oak one behind it. "Hello?"

While it had to be a reproduction, the door's vintage style perfectly matched the house. There was an intricate stained-glass design near the top, just high enough that visitors couldn't peek inside. Expensive, just like everything else Kate had noticed at this place.

She tried again. "Post office! I have a certified letter for Donald Wellington. It needs his signature; I can't leave it in the mailbox."

Were those footsteps, at last?

Kate sighed with relief, then spotted the security camera tacked just below the porch's beadboard ceiling. It wasn't unusual to see one of those these days, even out in the country. But then she noticed how its wires hung down, useless and frayed on the ends. They weren't attached to anything.

Why would someone unhook their security system in that way? Or was it so new that it hadn't been installed yet? Or maybe ...

The shadows behind the stained glass moved, and the front door's knob soon did the same. Kate took a respectful step back and let the screen door close in front of her.

This woman was in her fifties, Kate guessed. She had the honey-blonde hair of a woman with a generous budget for beauty treatments. But she wore sweatpants and a faded cotton sweater, and there were shadows under her wary eyes and lines of exhaustion on her face.

She simply stared at Kate, and waited.

"Hello?" Kate squared her shoulders when she realized how timid she sounded. "Hello! I'm Kate Duncan, Eagle River post office." She put on a smile. "I'm guessing you are Vanessa Wellington?"

The woman took a small, nearly imperceptible step back, then raised her chin. Kate wasn't the only one ill at ease.

"Yes, that's me."

"As I said, I have a certified letter for Donald. For ... your husband?"

Vanessa waited for a second, then nodded.

Kate waited, too.

"Is he here?" she finally asked. Because Vanessa just stood there in the doorway, her eyes fixated on the lane. Kate checked over her shoulder, but saw no one.

Vanessa must have decided the same, because she finally turned her full attention to Kate.

"No, he's not."

More silence.

"Do you expect him back today?" Kate pressed on. "We're only required to make one attempt to deliver these," she added in an apologetic tone. "But Roberta, our postmaster, prides herself on excellent customer service. We might be able to try again tomorrow. After that, we'll need to keep it at the post office. He'd have to pick it up there."

Vanessa blinked back sudden tears that Kate couldn't explain. "What's it for?"

"I'm not sure. We're not allowed to open these. Or any mail, for that matter."

Vanessa seemed skeptical. "Well, who sent it, then?" She gestured at the still-bagged envelope as Kate handed over the rest of the mail. "There's a return on there, I'm sure, so you know ..."

"I'm sorry, I can't say." Kate instinctively clutched the plastic bag to her chest, and Vanessa frowned.

"Why not?" Vanessa's voice went up part of an octave. "I'm his wife, for God's sake! These things affect me as much as they do him! Maybe more!"

She glanced at Kate's left hand. "Oh, I see; you're not married, you wouldn't understand. 'For better or for worse,' they say. Well, I say, things aren't going so great at the moment." Then she started to cry.

Kate felt a chill that went far beyond the cold, damp wind blowing through the open porch. What was going on here?

She could tell Vanessa about her ex, offer a bit of solidarity, but this woman didn't want to hear about Kate's divorce. For the first time in a long time, Kate was thankful for the post office's strict regulations. There was no way she had clearance to tell this woman the FBI had business with her husband.

Kate thought of Alex; she wondered if he was staring at his phone, waiting for a text that all was well, that she was safe.

And then, it occurred to her that perhaps *Vanessa* didn't feel safe.

"Is there something ... do you need help?" Kate asked gently.

Vanessa burst out laughing. It was the sarcastic kind that cut through Kate's concern like a knife.

"Do I need help? Good God, honey, I don't even know how to answer that." Vanessa wiped her eyes with the back of her hand. Somewhere deep inside the house, a dog barked once, twice, then was silent. "I don't even know if ..."

She stopped, as if realizing she was about to confide in a stranger. And say something she wasn't supposed to share. Or was too afraid to share.

But Kate wasn't quite ready to let this conversation end. Something was off here, she could feel it. "I love your house, but it's rather isolated. Your nearest neighbors are, what, over half a mile away?"

Vanessa nodded.

"I live alone. My closest one is barely a quarter mile down the road, and even that is too far, sometimes."

"I don't know when he's coming back," Vanessa suddenly said. "It could be tomorrow, it could be days." She shook her head. "I don't know."

Her gaze zeroed in on the letter in Kate's hands, as if

she'd momentarily forgotten it was there, and Kate sensed her desperation.

Oh, no, Kate thought. *She's going to beg me to give it to her, or to tell her who it's from.*

"If Donald's not home, then I'll be on my way," she said briskly. "Like I said, we might try again tomorrow. Donald has fifteen days to sign for this letter, or we'll have to send it back."

Something about how Vanessa gripped the open doorway said she was perhaps a little sorry that Kate was leaving.

Kate looked down, then back at the woman's anxious face.

"If you ever feel unsafe, for any reason, you should tell someone. I can say for sure that Sheriff Preston is a good man; he's kind, a great listener. And they have a new deputy named Abby, she's wonderful. She would ..."

"I'm not calling the sheriff." But the way Vanessa said it made Kate wonder if she really, really wanted to. "That's not going to solve ... I can't ..."

Then she sighed. "Thank you for stopping by. And for ... asking, I guess. But I'm fine. Everything's fine."

All Kate could do was nod. "Have a good day" seemed like the cruelest thing to say to this woman. She nodded again, then turned away.

The front door closed swiftly behind her, and Kate heard the click of the lock before she'd even made it to the steps. She tucked the plastic bag containing the certified letter inside her parka, and pulled up her hood again. With her head low, she rushed out into the downpour and hurried back to her mail car.

As she rounded the porch's corner, Kate was so surprised that she nearly tripped over her own feet. She hadn't noticed it on her way to the house; but from this angle, it was clear that all four tires on the SUV had been slashed. And not in the past few minutes, as the bottoms of the hubcaps already squatted in the soft muck of the gravel.

Kate instinctively gazed up at the side of the house. Was someone there, inside that upstairs window? She couldn't be certain, not in this driving rain, but had the curtains just moved?

She hustled to the safety of Bertha's interior, and immediately locked the doors. As the heater cleared the windshield and thawed her chilled fingers and toes, she texted Alex back.

It's done. I'm fine.

Her phone dinged twice before she could even get down the driveway. She knew it was Alex, and that he was full of questions. But she didn't have any answers.

Or at least, anything she should share with him. Because Kate was now fairly certain the Wellingtons' security camera wasn't new, or had simply been turned off. Its frayed wires had been sliced by someone directly, or indirectly, responsible for the vandalism of the SUV now mudded down in front of the garage.

Was anything else at the Wellingtons' acreage damaged? Kate wasn't about to circle back to find out.

"It's probably not even worth Jared trying again tomorrow." She was relieved when she reached the road, and found it as empty as it had been before. "Donald is obviously not home, and it doesn't sound like he'll be back anytime soon."

Unless ... was Donald there, but he wouldn't come to the door?

"It could have been one of their kids at the upstairs window, if they have any. Or Vanessa, herself, making sure that I was leaving."

The woman's guarded behavior stayed on Kate's mind as she slowed for the next mailbox. "She's definitely afraid; I could feel it. If someone slashed those tires and cut off the security camera, she has good reason to be that way. But why won't she call the sheriff? And where is her husband?"

Kate didn't know, or how to find out. But as she wrapped up her route, she decided there was one thing she could do.

* * *

Kate leaned over Roberta's desk and dropped her voice to a whisper. "I need to talk to you. In private."

Jack and Randy were wrapping up their post-route tasks at the nearest sorting table, and deep in debate about the Chicago Cubs' chances for a winning season. But Kate knew the guys could catch every word uttered in this corner of the room if they wanted to. As far as Kate knew, everyone else had left already; she'd stuck around specifically for this errand.

Roberta nodded, but raised her eyebrows.

"It's not personal," Kate murmured. "But something happened today, and ..."

"Say no more." Roberta tipped her head toward the tiny hallway that held the restroom as well as the storage room. "I'll meet you in the bunker."

The Eagle River post office wasn't spacious, to say the least. There were no meeting rooms, no quiet areas to be found in the break room or anywhere else. The storage room was so packed, only one person could maneuver through it at a time.

But there was a unisex restroom with two stalls, and that space locked from the inside.

"What's going on?" Roberta peeked under the stalls before she slid the chain on the door. Kate had checked those herself, just seconds ago; they were alone.

"I tried to deliver that certified letter today, but was unsuccessful." Kate took a deep breath, and let it out. The more she thought about the situation at the Wellingtons', the more uneasy she felt. She couldn't keep it to herself.

"Donald Wellington wasn't home, but his wife was. And ... well, I noticed something really strange. A few things, in fact."

Roberta listened intently as Kate explained the situation. What Vanessa had said, how nervous she'd seemed. The slashed tires, the security camera's mangled wires, the movement at the upstairs window. About two-thirds of the way through, the postmaster put her hands over her face.

"I was right to bring it up, then," Kate said when she got to the end. "I'm not letting my imagination get the better of me."

"Always, always, trust your gut." Roberta's brown eyes glowed with conviction as she wrapped her arms around herself. "This is a perfect example of why I want my carriers to come to me with anything, and everything, that happens on a route."

Kate's damp clothes had finally dried, and the radiator in the small space clanged and popped as it filled the room with warmth. Even so, she once again felt cold.

"What is going on?" She studied her boss' face. "There must be something, and you know what it is! Can you tell me?"

Roberta shook her head at first, and Kate waited.

"Well, I don't know, exactly." Then Roberta gave Kate a level stare. "Have you ever heard of Donald Wellington? Do you know who he is?"

Kate shook her head. "No. I wondered, though. I mean, the FBI sent him a certified letter. And then his wife acts like that when I knock on their door?"

Roberta glanced at the restroom's entrance again, as if making sure the door was locked. She seemed to consider her next words carefully. Or weigh the implication of what she was about to say. Kate wasn't sure which.

"Donald Wellington is a CPA."

Kate nodded. "Sure, OK."

"I mean, he is the *Wheelers'* CPA. He's the accountant for the auction barn. Oversees their books, does their taxes."

Kate was stunned. "He works in the office?"

"No. He works for himself, has his own business. But he would be the person who signs off on whatever comes out of that office. Does the monthly tax filings for the company, fills out all the forms. The buck stops with him."

Roberta closed her eyes for a moment. "You're telling me that his wife doesn't know, or wouldn't say, when he's coming back? And that someone vandalized their property, and she hasn't called the sheriff?"

"That was the gist of it." Kate tried to piece together what she'd just learned. "So, let's say he's involved in ... whatever is going on. Why is the FBI in the middle of this?"

She reminded Roberta about what Chief Calcott had said last week at Peabody's. It had taken less than two days for his tone-deaf remarks to make their way around town, and it was still a topic of conversation among the locals.

Roberta shook her head. "Do you think this is what Calcott meant about bringing in outside experts? I assumed he was talking about other cities, and the state ..."

Her eyes widened. "Does this mean the embezzlement scheme goes beyond Iowa, crosses state lines? That's the only way the feds would even give it a look."

"Or is this about something entirely different?" Kate threw up her hands in frustration. "At first, I'd assumed this Donald guy was involved in something really shady; like he was a spy, or peddling drugs."

The two women stared at each other for a moment.

"His name looked familiar, when I saw the envelope," Roberta finally said. "But I wasn't going to say anything to the group this morning, add fuel to the gossip fire. Like I said, most embezzlement cases never reach a level where the FBI bothers to get involved. Actually, I was a bit surprised that none of the carriers, not even Randy or Marge, seemed to know who he was." Then she sighed.

"All I know is, he's an accountant. But that doesn't mean he isn't ..."

Someone pounded on the door.

"Open up, you two!" It was Jack. "I need to get in there."

Roberta's usual good humor quickly returned. "To hear our conversation, or for some other reason?"

"Number two."

Kate grinned. "Don't you have a bottle out in your truck for such emergencies?"

"That won't help, not this time around," Jack insisted. "No, I mean I need to ..."

"Got it." Roberta slid the chain off the door. Jack burst through, and hustled into the closest stall.

"I wonder if it's against federal regulations to have that door locked when staff are in the building," Jack called out as Roberta and Kate left the room.

Randy had left, which allowed the women to continue their conversation for a few more minutes.

"What do you think we should do?" Kate asked her boss. "Vanessa made it very clear she didn't want to call the authorities, but something's not right."

"As a wife, I understand why she thinks this is something for her family to handle. But as a public employee, I can't sit on this sort of information." Roberta considered her options.

"Sheriff Preston needs a heads-up about this. I can't blab to him about the letter; but it's not about that, anyway. You stopped at their house, and you saw what you saw. Thank goodness the Wellingtons live outside the city limits; I don't need to bother with Calcott." She pulled out her phone. "I'll be in my car for a few minutes."

Not long after Roberta went out the back door, Jack returned.

"What's the deal, Duncan? The bunker's reserved for serious conversations only."

"Exactly." Kate smiled as she picked up her purse and prepared to leave. "Have a good night!"

8

“Kate!” Stacy shouted over the folk music that drifted from the speakers surrounding the high school auditorium’s stage. “Show these ladies how the next steps and turns are done!” Kate’s cousin’s smile was wide and smug. “Please?”

“On my way.” Kate started down from where she’d been sort-of hiding several rows up in the seats.

“Perhaps wedding management would have been an easier gig,” she muttered to herself as eight teenagers, their tee shirts and leggings covered by the white-linen dresses that served as costumes for the town’s May Day festival, waited impatiently on the stage. A few of the girls rolled their eyes.

Maybe they already knew the traditional dances by heart, had learned them from older sisters and cousins. Or maybe, like Kate, they just wanted to go home.

Stacy had texted Kate a few nights ago, desperate for help. Her friend Lauren, another teacher who often helped Stacy with this sort of extra-curricular activity, had been tapped to direct the high school’s spring play while the drama coach was on maternity leave.

Kate had hesitated at first, but quickly changed her tune when her cousin mentioned she was still hip-deep in final preparations for her June wedding.

Last fall, in a rush of nostalgia-fueled goodwill, Kate had

promised to be one of Stacy's bridesmaids. But during Kate's years away, she'd forgotten how keyed-up Stacy became when a big project was in the works. Kate had sensed an either/or ultimatum was about to be offered, and she'd jumped at the chance to help with the May Day festival, instead.

How hard could it be to teach some teens to hop, turn, and twirl their way through a few dance numbers? Besides, this volunteer gig would vanish in less than a month. But tonight, Kate felt like the first of May couldn't come soon enough.

Her stressful visit to the Wellingtons' house that afternoon had drained her of focus as well as energy. She hoped the grande mocha she'd picked up at The Daily Grind would be enough to keep her energized for tonight's practice.

"Ladies, we have a real professional helping us out this year!" Stacy chirped as Kate mounted the handful of steps in front of the stage. "I'm so excited to introduce you to my dear cousin Kate, a former May Day festival queen!"

"Oh, no." Kate waved her hands in the air, eager to clarify the situation. "I was still a princess senior year. You know, just one of the court."

"Doesn't matter." Stacy shrugged. "You were divine that year, just like before." She turned back to the girls. "Kate was part of the troupe *all three years* she was eligible."

A few of the girls' smiles carried the smallest amount of interest in Kate's supposed triumph, but Kate suspected the others were simply amused.

Eagle River's May Day celebration dated back to the 1870s, but the honor of being tapped to participate in the dance had apparently waned over time.

Way back when, including Kate's high school years, so many girls were eager for a spot in the troupe that slots were filled by drawing names. The three lead dancers had then been chosen by a student-body vote, with the top girl being named queen of the festival.

These days, however, educators had to practically beg girls to participate. And a social-media scandal a few years ago had generated so much backstabbing and infighting that the two princesses and the queen were now chosen by the school's staff.

Many girls now seemed content to record such events from the sidelines with their phones, rather than be involved themselves. After all, when you were already the star of your personal digital platforms, who needed to dance around a maypole to get noticed?

Even so, Kate was sort-of glad she'd offered to assist her cousin this year. Since her return to Eagle River, she'd vowed to find ways to get more involved in the community. But it wasn't just that.

Bryan and Anna had welcomed their baby boy on Sunday and, while Kate was thrilled to be little Ethan's aunt, his arrival had stirred difficult memories of Kate and Ben's repeated attempts to start a family. And those thoughts sometimes caused Kate to reflect on Ben's cheating and their subsequent divorce. It was a challenge that wasn't helped by Stacy's breathless excitement about seating arrangements and table favors.

This volunteer gig just might be a blessing. Kate hoped this handful of Tuesday evenings at the high school, along with spending time with Alex, might keep her focused on the present, not the past.

She was suddenly determined to show those youngsters a thing or two. After all, if she had to help train this year's dancers, they were going to get it right.

"Here's the thing," she told the girls. "The steps are pretty simple for this one. It's sort of like square dancing, which I hear is still being taught in gym class these days. But it's better, because there are no boys around to step on your feet."

The dancers giggled. Kate was pleased she'd gained their attention, at least.

"You'll all be facing the same direction as you dance around the pole, so just keep an eye on the girl in front of you. Just *feel* the music." Kate swayed slightly from side to side, in time with the folk tune. "And always hold your ribbon in your right hand."

One of the girls frowned. "How is that going to braid the ribbons together? If we're all going the same way, won't they just get wrapped around the pole?"

"That will happen during the second dance," Stacy said. "That's when the weaving is done." She smiled, but gave Kate a cautious look. "We'll get to that next week; one thing at a time."

"I just need to know what my crown will look like." The queen-to-be ran one hand through the end of her ponytail. "I have to plan my hair, you know."

The first of May sometimes brought blue skies and warm breezes, but the costumes' charms had too often been buried under parkas, stocking hats, and snow boots. Before Kate could remind the troupe about the unpredictable weather, one of the princesses spoke up.

"I think I'm going to do braids. And your hair is longer than mine, so you could wind them around your head."

"What are those braid-buns called?" another girl asked. "You know, like the princess wore in that old spaceship movie."

The future queen shook her head. "Her buns weren't braided, they were plain. And I think they were fake. And they would look dumb with my crown, so ..."

"OK." Kate stepped forward and clapped her hands. "Let's not worry about our hair just yet. We have four weeks before that's a problem."

But Kate wasn't sure that would be enough time to get this queen, and her ladies in waiting, to fall in line. Or just dance in a circle, for that matter.

She walked over to the group, and clasped one girl's

shoulders with her hands. "Erica, you need to start from this position." Kate nudged the girl to the left, then sighed as she caught another dancer sneaking glances at her phone.

"No devices! When your great-great-grandmothers learned these steps, I bet they took it much more seriously."

"What else was there for them to do?" one girl sneered. "Eagle River's boring now, I can't imagine how dead it was during horse-and-buggy days."

"Didn't you live in Chicago?" the future queen asked Kate. "I bet that was cool."

Kate wasn't sure how to respond.

Cool, maybe; except for her cheating ex, being attacked while on the job, her divorce ...

"Ladies!" Stacy pulled out her best schoolmarm voice. "The sooner we knock out this first dance, the sooner we get to go home. Now, I texted all of you the link to that website; I hope you studied it before you got here." She gave the girl who'd been checking her phone a cutting glance.

"I'm going to start the music again. Let's run through the opening sequence twice this time." Stacy clapped her hands, as if trying to rally her team. "We are going to get this right! In just a few weeks, you ladies are going to be the best pole dancers this town has ever seen!"

The girls stared at Stacy in disbelief. Kate nearly choked on her last gulp of coffee, then searched her tired mind for something, anything to move the conversation along.

"Just focus on the music," she urged the girls as Stacy queued the tunes. "Try to get the basics down tonight, and we'll go from there next week."

With resigned postures that didn't reflect the dance's air of gentility, the girls started again. But this time, their promenade seemed a little better. Kate thought maybe this wasn't a lost cause after all, and told Stacy so.

"Don't jinx us," her cousin muttered behind her plastered-on smile. "Remember when this was a big deal, to be in the May Day dance? Now it's like twisting arms to get them to participate."

"Everyone's a celebrity these days, if they want to be."

Stacy gave Kate a good-natured elbow when she saw her peeking at her phone. "So, do you have plans for later? Perhaps with a handsome bartender?"

"Hardly." Kate laughed. "He's closing tonight. I'll be asleep long before he's off work."

"Well, I take full credit for whatever's going on." Stacy nodded her approval, which Kate didn't need. "After all, it was the Christmas Festival Spectacular that brought the two of you together."

Kate shrugged. She and Alex had known each other long before Stacy and Lauren had orchestrated a romantic duet in front of Eagle River's holiday bonfire.

"Perhaps," Kate said. "But there's maybe, what, twelve-hundred people in this town? And how many of them are single men roughly our age? And steadily employed? Maybe it was bound to happen."

"So, what is it?"

Kate tried not to smile like a fool. "You know, me and Alex."

"Right. I mean, *what exactly is it*?"

As Kate watched the dancers step mostly in time to the folk music, she wondered about that very thing. She'd wondered about it more and more lately. Then she laughed, but didn't say a word.

"Oh, I see." Stacy nodded knowingly. "Whatever it is, it's *good*."

"Yeah. That's the best way to characterize it." Kate saw another list of questions coming her way if she didn't change the subject, and fast. "So, what's the deal with the sponsorships this year? Are those all lined up?"

Stacy was game to take the bait. "I think so. It's the usual places in town. There are only so many, after all."

The pharmacy, which also housed a small floral shop, would provide the girls' hair wreaths and corsages, as well as flower petals to be tossed during the procession. Eagle River's historical society would host the German-themed community meal offered after the maypole dance. A handful of sponsors had picked up the tab for the food, most of which was cooked by the kitchen staff at Peabody's. The Eagle's Nest would contribute the soda and beer for the meal.

And, as part of the festival's longest-standing tradition, Wheeler Auction Company would pony up a vintage horse-drawn wagon to carry the May Day court from the auction barn to the festival site on the elementary school's lawn.

"Dylan promised me they would still do it." The note of doubt in Stacy's voice caught Kate's attention. "The Wheelers have always been a big part of the festival. But I can't help but wonder if it's the kind of publicity they'd rather not have just now."

"Well, there's always a fire truck." Kate tried to lighten the mood. "Those skirts are long enough to be decent from that high up. I think the girls could be persuaded to make their appearance that way."

"That would work, if the auction barn backs out on us. And I don't think the girls would care in the least. You should see what some of them are wearing to class these days. I don't care if they have bike shorts on underneath; it's tacky." Stacy sighed. "Or maybe I'm just getting old."

"You're only thirty," Kate reminded her. "Two years younger than me."

"Well, in Eagle River, I'm older than I'd like to be." Then Stacy smiled. "Of course, I'll be off the market soon; I already am. So, do you think we need to approach our volunteer fire chief, just in case? Or is that too awkward, given where he works?"

Stacy was right; they had to tread carefully. Ben Dvorak had said barely a word, at least publicly, about how the embezzlement scandal might affect his role as head of maintenance at the auction barn.

No one seemed to believe he'd had anything to do with the missing money. But Kate wasn't sure if his discretion wholly stemmed from being tactful and professional, or if he'd been told to keep quiet. By his employer, or Police Chief Calcott, or both.

"Maybe we should wait on that," Kate told her cousin. "For Ben's sake, as well as ours. The last thing we want to do is imply we lack confidence in the Wheelers because of what's going on."

"Appearances matter," Stacy agreed. "We'll keep that option in our back pocket, for now. Maybe that mess will sort itself out sooner rather than later."

* * *

Charlie jumped up on the worn pantry shelf and let out a pointed "meow!" Alex dipped his chin in deference to the regal, Himalayan-mix cat.

"Yes, King Charles, I know this is your castle. We'll consult you before every step of this renovation."

"Proposed renovation." Kate gestured at the tiny kitchen pantry's rows of wooden shelves. Their contact-paper coatings had peeled and faded over the decades, as had the tired scrap of linoleum floor that likely covered how-many layers of redecorating efforts. "I'm still not sure this is a good idea."

Alex put his arm around her. "Is it the reno you're worried about, or your new contractor?"

Kate laughed. "The first. Besides, the second one will officially be Richard Everton if you and I even get that far. I don't think my homeowner's insurance will cover any disasters if the two of us hack into this old house's plumbing system." She narrowed her eyes at him. "Are you licensed, sir?"

"Nope." Alex shrugged. "And I don't need to be. I hired out the heavy lifting for my own bathroom. Richard and his sons do excellent work."

Kate already knew that was true. The Evertons had done a wonderful job of making the most-needed updates to her lone current bathroom, which was upstairs. Unfortunately, Richard's crew was expensive, as well.

But Kate really wanted a powder room on the main floor of her farmhouse, and this walk-in pantry was the only place it could go. If she could get this space down to the bare walls, then teach herself to lay new flooring, patch plaster, and install subway tile, she could just afford to let the Evertons handle the difficult stuff. And since her house was a hundred years old, that was nearly everything else.

The upstairs bathroom was not above the pantry, but it was close; and the kitchen's pipes were nearby, as well. Even so, new water and sewer lines would have to be run into this space and down to the basement.

Several electrical updates were needed, too. The room's current light source was one bulb operated by a dingy length of string, and there were no outlets inside these walls. And while the pantry currently opened off the kitchen, Kate would prefer the powder room's entry be moved to the small hallway that ran past the staircase.

"It seems, I don't know ... unhygienic to have the bathroom practically inside the kitchen," Kate said as she gave Charlie a few reassuring pets. He was as curious as the next cat, but he loathed any sort of mess or disruption.

Kate felt the same, but there was only one way out of this: weeks of hard work.

"I agree." Alex reached for the measuring tape in his back pocket, and took two small steps to reach the pantry wall in question. "Yep. There's just enough space to move the door here. If you get a tiny sink, you can fit that and the toilet on the opposite wall."

Hazel, who had been getting a drink in the kitchen, nudged her way around Kate's legs. With two human adults and two animals now inside the pantry, there was hardly room to move.

"My only other option is to flip everything," Kate said, "and have the entrance in the dining room. But that would be nearly as bad as it coming off the kitchen." The fourth wall backed the front entryway's closet. "And I need to make sure everything is going to fit perfectly before we rip into this space."

Alex understood. "We're looking at significant wall repairs, no matter what. The old doorway not only has to be closed up, but we'd need to mud the drywall to match the plaster's texture. On both sides."

If they were careful when they removed the pantry's door, Alex said, both it and its frame could be reused. They could salvage the current baseboards, as well, to keep the house's character intact.

Of course, some of the old oak casings might not be in the best shape once they were pried from the walls. Which probably weren't straight, which would mean lots of cuts to get the old pieces of millwork to properly fit their new locations. Even if they could get the rehabbed pantry's outside walls to blend in with the rest of the house, it might be smart to use all-new trim in the bathroom ...

Kate closed her eyes for a moment. "This is a big job; it's like opening Pandora's box. Who knows what we are going to find?"

Alex grinned. "Well, you could always go really retro." He gestured around them. "Keep these nasty shelves for storage. A chamber pot should fit under them nicely; just pull it out when you need it. Or, a five-gallon bucket with a toilet seat on top. We could put an old wash basin in here on a stand, haul water from the kitchen. Hazel, what do you think?"

The spirited wag of the dog's tail said Hazel didn't care

what the future bathroom looked like, not one bit.

She just wanted to hang with Alex. Charlie and the Three Mouseketeers had also quickly warmed to this new visitor weeks ago.

Alex's eagerness to let Moose into his heart, as well as his home, left no doubt he loved animals. Even so, Kate had been pleasantly surprised at Patches' reaction the first time she saw Alex. The still-aloof cat had barreled around the corner of the house to circle his legs, then demanded he pick her up, pregnant belly and all.

Yes, everyone adored Alex; Kate had to admit she felt the same. It was a little scary, even, how much she liked this man. And, maybe "like" wasn't a strong enough word, but she wasn't quite ready to face that yet.

And seeing Alex surrounded by scuffed walls and warped shelves, grinning from ear to ear as he promised Kate that her sought-after powder room was within reach, was enough to make her want to kiss him, right now. So she did.

"Is that payment for this evening's consultation?" he murmured in her ear. "Or an advance on what's to come?"

"Hmm. Let me think about that."

The hand-cranked timer on the kitchen counter clanged with the news that their pizza was ready. Kate's stove was too old to have a digital clock.

"I think this project's on hold for now," she said, "and not only because it's time to eat. But because until Hazel clears out, I can't move even one inch."

Alex and Kate settled in at the dining room table, with Hazel at Kate's feet. Charlie posted himself on the empty chair closest to Alex, his regal nose on alert.

"He loves carbs," Kate explained, "and popcorn is his favorite. If you drop any crust, he'll pounce on it. He won't touch sausage; maybe he thinks it's too spicy. But he'll alert Hazel, and she'll clean it up."

"I really like this wallpaper." Alex eyed the subtle peel-

and-stick pattern Kate and Gwen had installed in the dining room before the post office's holiday party. "I can't believe I'm saying that. What I remember is what my grandma had in her house, and the floral border you have there in the kitchen."

"Things have changed." Kate considered her options as she looked around. "You know, maybe that's the way to make the powder room really come alive. A simple and modern design, of course. But wallpaper would certainly help hide the scars from moving the doorway. We'd only have to texture the kitchen side of the closed-in wall."

"That's a great idea." He smiled at her from across the table. "So, you really want to take this on?"

Kate nodded slowly as she chewed. "I can see it; all the possibilities."

That was true about more than the powder room. Alex himself offered many more, if Kate paused long enough to consider them.

She rarely had company at her house. She usually ate alone, except for the patiently observant Charlie and Hazel, and she realized how nice it felt to have someone across the table again. It was a small thing, really, but something Kate had nearly forgotten about since Ben had moved out and she'd filed for divorce.

This wasn't the first time she and Alex had shared a meal in this house, of course. But Kate realized she could get really used to this if she let herself.

It was a little ironic they were having pizza tonight, given her family's weekly tradition that she hadn't yet invited Alex to attend. Her mom had stopped asking, but maybe Kate should surprise her and bring Alex along sometime.

Of course, Fridays were one of the busiest nights at his bar. It would be hard for him to get away. This was a Wednesday, and while he hadn't had to open, he did have to help close. Once they finished dinner, there wouldn't be much time left before he needed to leave.

Kate decided she shouldn't get used to the idea of having Alex here in the evenings. How would they even line up their schedules enough to work on her powder room together?

While she wondered about the future, Alex apparently was thinking about past events ... of the unsolved sort.

"Any news on the embezzlement front?" He tore off a small corner of pizza crust and fed it to Charlie. Kate pretended not to notice. "I've been surprised to not hear much at the bar the past few days."

Alex knew all about Saturday's stampede at the auction barn. He'd heard the rumors that the champion Percherons were deliberately let out of their stall.

As for what Kate had observed at the Wellingtons' yesterday, she hadn't said anything to him about that. She still couldn't tell him who the registered letter was for, and there wasn't a way to share the rest of what had happened without him possibly figuring out the first part.

Kate had relayed the details to Bev, of course. As another post-office employee, Bev could have been tasked with delivering that certified letter herself.

Bev had agreed with Kate's decision to confide in their boss, but admitted she didn't know Donald Wellington. He probably ran his accounting business out of his home, Bev decided, as she wasn't aware of a storefront office around Eagle River.

That alone made it easy for him to keep a low profile with the public. Tax season was in full swing but, thanks to the internet, someone like Donald could work from anywhere.

Both ladies had kept their ears open today, but hadn't turned up any leads on Donald's whereabouts or his possible connection to the embezzlement scheme. Between the web of secrecy surrounding his letter from the FBI, and being discreet for Vanessa's sake, it was difficult to initiate conversations about Mr. Wellington.

Alex had only asked about the letter that one time,

yesterday when she'd texted him. But had he forgotten about it? Absolutely not; Kate was sure of that.

"I haven't heard anything new," she told him. And that was the truth. "I wonder if people are just waiting to see what happens next."

Alex also seemed to have hit a dead end. He frowned as he finished his slice of pizza. "I don't know what's going on. But it makes you wonder how many people are involved in this, and why."

Kate had pondered that very idea as she'd reflected on the vandalism, and also the fear, she observed at the Wellingtons' farm.

While it was possible the accountant was at least partially to blame for the stolen cash, it was just as likely he was an innocent bystander who'd had to blow the whistle on one of his largest clients. Who was behind those threats, and how far might they go to silence Donald Wellington?

"I've known the Wheelers for years," she told Alex. "Not really well, understand; but Dylan and his sister used to ride our school bus. And now, I'm starting to think I don't know any of them at all."

"Not everyone is who they seem to be." Alex's world-weary sigh made Kate wonder what he suspected. "I know that family does a lot for this town, and that's good; but you never know what's going on behind the scenes."

Kate had baked lemon cookies for dessert, and they were still in the kitchen.

"Families are complicated enough," she said when she returned, plate in hand. "And there are three generations of Wheelers involved in that business right now. It's hard to think one of them could be behind something like this, but it's possible that's true."

"You're right. It's all about access." Alex took a cookie with a smile of thanks. "My money's on someone on the inside, but they might not be a Wheeler. What I wonder is, do they have help on the outside? It's hard to make money, or just about anything else, disappear these days. Technology has forced people to get more sophisticated about that sort of thing. And sometimes, they can't cover their tracks by working alone."

It was an interesting theory. Kate was just starting to turn it over in her mind when a mournful howl echoed from the vicinity of the back porch steps.

"What is *that*?" Alex craned his neck toward the east-facing windows to get a better look into the twilight. Just in time, he remembered to snatch his cookie off his plate; Charlie was poised to steal it. "Do you have a lovesick raccoon, or something?"

Charlie and Hazel weren't the only ones who'd learned they could summon Kate with a bit of drama. "I almost wish I did." She pushed her chair back again. "That would be Patches. She wants her nightly tour of the enclosed porch."

Charlie had no interest in this ritual, which had occurred more nights than not in the past week, but Hazel was ready to go. While Patches sniffed the unheated room's corners, the dog stuck to her side in a show of solidarity that Kate found heartwarming but didn't quite understand.

"I guess she wants to check for mice," Kate told Alex as they lingered by the door leading outside, ready to let the calico escape once her investigation was complete. "Cats are creatures of habit. Minnie must have let her in here a lot for that reason."

"Maybe Minnie gave her treats from the kitchen too," Alex suggested. And then, he nodded sagely. "Oh, yeah, I think there's something else going on here."

"What?"

"Look at how she's mostly sniffing anything that's soft. Hazel's muddy towels in the corner, your sweatshirt there on the bench. Even that tote of stocking caps and gloves under the bench."

Kate cringed, just a bit. While her house was neat and tidy, the back porch was always a catch-all of tossed-around stuff.

"When is she due?" Alex asked. "Because I think Patches is looking to 'move on up' from the machine shed when the time is right. Or should I say, move on in."

Kate sighed. "I think you're right. My efforts in the machine shed may have been a waste of time. You've become rather smart about feline ways since Moose adopted you."

"Maybe," Alex conceded. "But it's natural for animals to seek out a safe space when they feel vulnerable. People do the same."

He seemed about to say something else, something personal; but his focus quickly returned to Patches' pregnancy.

"If her instincts are so keen that they brought her all the way home after all those months, they would definitely tell her to seek out the warmest, most-comfortable spot to give birth."

Hazel's pile of towels seemed to be the winner, and Kate decided to find a stack of clean ones as well as another tote to put them in. Even so, just a few minutes later, Patches went to the outside door and made it clear where she wanted to bed down until morning.

"Karen thought we had about three more weeks," Kate told Alex as they watched Patches waddle across the lawn under the faint glow of the yard light. "But I suppose I need to be ready sooner rather than later."

✻ 9 ✻

As Bertha slowed for the next rural crossroads, Kate pondered the directions she'd been given, and took a left.

"Auggie could barely contain his excitement on the phone. Whatever he's discovered, it must be really, really good."

She leaned forward to see down the unfamiliar road as far as possible. And also from anticipation. "Where is this place? I grew up about five miles from here, and I didn't even know it existed."

Luckily, she had the route west of town today, which meant she could burn her lunch break out here rather than head back to the post office. And that Auggie could sneak away from the Prosper co-op long enough to give her the scoop in person.

Why hadn't he just spilled the beans on the phone? Kate suspected that was partly because Auggie was as gleeful as a dog with a new bone when he came into possession of a hot bit of gossip. But she also wondered if this information was too powerful, maybe even too dangerous, for Auggie to share if he was anywhere someone might overhear. That would certainly explain his choice of a meet-up location.

A few tractors were visible in distant fields, but spring planting wouldn't really get rolling for a couple more weeks. April was hardly a week old, and the recent string of mild temperatures wasn't going to last. But the red-winged blackbird perched on a "curves ahead" road sign was singing its song, despite the stiff breeze that ruffled its mostly dark feathers.

Some might think a blackbird was a bad omen, but Kate knew better. These vocal fliers, with their trademark red and orange patches on their wings, were smart and quick. The sight of them reminded her she was in the country, and she was always thrilled when she found them gathered at the bird feeders in her own yard.

Patches liked them too, for a very different reason. Her feline instincts told her to observe, pounce on, and attempt to kill many of the feathered friends Scout and his crew mostly ignored. Full bowls of kibble in the machine shed were no match for the calico's hard-wired drive to survive. Even so, Kate was amused to notice how many times the chatty birds managed to outsmart the stalking cat.

Kate took two more turns, then found herself heading south on yet another gravel road that had one bend after another. She was more than three miles west of her parents' farm now, in an area serviced by the Prosper post office. The T intersection up ahead matched Auggie's directions, and Kate took a right and started up a rather-steep hill.

A small stand of trees arrived on the right, and Kate spotted Auggie's work truck backed into what looked like a field drive. As she neared the turnoff, she spotted an iron archway just past the edge of the ditch.

"I had no idea this little cemetery was here." Despite the strangeness of this errand, Kate felt the thrill of discovery. "I've never been on this road in my life, that I can recall. I guess I'll park on the shoulder of the gravel, which isn't much of one. There isn't anywhere else to go."

Auggie popped out of his truck and gave Kate a wave. She returned it as she picked her way across the soft, thawed earth behind his vehicle.

"Leave it to you to choose a place like this," she chided him when they met up in the lane. "I don't think we can get more remote."

"Well, they always say, 'dead men tell no tales.'" Auggie had apparently simmered down a bit since he'd called, but his brown eyes still twinkled with excitement.

"My oldest Benniger ancestors are buried here; I know this patch of hallowed ground well. Jane and I come out every Memorial Day to put out flowers. It's too bad more people don't bother to do the same."

A simple fence enclosed the tiny parcel, and a worn cattle panel bridged the deep ruts between the iron arch's posts. The makeshift gate's rusted padlock told Kate it had been some time since the cemetery had been officially open. The burial plot had only a handful of short rows, and most of its stones leaned with the weight of passing decades and rough weather.

But there were a few signs of life, too. A trio of overgrown evergreens kept watch over the northern boundary, and two majestic oak trees among the markers were setting tiny buds for new leaves. A squirrel in the closest oak trained its sharp eyes on Kate and Auggie, and chittered news of their arrival.

Auggie pointed toward a gap between the locked gate and the also-rusting metal fence, and they started in that direction.

"The grass gets really thick in here during the summer, since the township trustees only mow it twice a year. It's native prairie," he added proudly. "Best to leave it alone, I say. And no, we're not trespassing," he answered the question on Kate's face. "They just don't want vehicles driving in and out and disturbing the habitat, that's all."

They soon stopped beside an impressive monument with "Benniger" etched on its front. Kate admired the stone's carvings for a moment while Auggie brushed dead leaves away from its base.

"Well, are you going to keep me in suspense?" she finally asked. "What's the deal? Whatever it is, you pulled yourself away from planting-season craziness at the co-op to tell me what's what."

"Yep. And I need to get back to it, same as you." With one hand on his ancestor's stone for a little balance, Auggie got to his feet. "Good Lord, I should be doing more of those knee exercises. Anyway, last night I talked to a ... well, an associate of mine. And he told me something astounding."

Auggie crossed his arms and looked around for a second, as if anyone else could possibly overhear this conversation. If there were any birds perched in the oak trees' still-bare branches, they were silent. Only the squirrel appeared to be listening.

"So ... you know the Wheelers own the auction barn, right?"

Kate laughed in surprise. "Um, yeah. Everyone knows that."

"Well, it turns out they aren't the only ones."

She frowned. "What do you mean? Of course they do! Dylan's great-great-great-grandfather ..."

"Yeah, yeah, we've all been schooled in the illustrious history of one of Eagle River's most-beloved institutions." Auggie's voice took on a note of sarcasm. "Turns out, that's a fat lie. Or at least, it has been for the last forty years or so."

He leaned in, and Kate did the same.

"Silent partners!" Auggie whispered. "The Wheelers aren't the only ones keeping that ship afloat."

While many auction barns around the Midwest had consolidated, been sold to large agricultural corporations, or simply closed, the Wheelers' business continued to be lauded as a shining example of one family's ability to weather change and economic storms.

"But it's horseshit!" Auggie sputtered. "Every last bit of it!"

He turned sharply to his left. "Sorry, Nana," he called in the direction of another marker not far away, then gave Kate a sheepish grin. "She'd be reaching for a bar of soap right now, if she could."

"So you're telling me the Wheelers have backers? They aren't pulling off this stunning feat of financial success all on their own?"

"Yep, that's right."

The auction barn had faced hard times in its earlier decades, yet always found a way to survive. But the farm crisis of the 1980s had been more than the Wheelers could handle on their own, Auggie said.

In a desperate bid to keep the doors open, Dylan's grandfather had apparently reached out to some of his contacts and asked for handouts. Whether those had been intended as one-time loans that were to be paid back, or the start of ongoing partnerships, Auggie wasn't sure. But as those dark days dragged on, the financial alliances continued.

"And they do to this day. That's what my source is telling me." Auggie's agitation seemed to be as much about the underhandedness of the situation as who might be involved. After all, while he loved gossip, he prided himself on being a straight shooter as well.

"There are people around the region who are propping up that auction barn, in the same way those big beams are holding up the ceiling over the arena." He waved one hand over his head for emphasis.

"Is it a lot of money?" Kate was fascinated by this story. "I mean, small percentages here and there, or ..."

"Oh, no; I'm pretty sure of that. We're talking about *big* money. Like I said, to the point they are silent partners. They're taking a hefty slice of the pie, month in and month out. Part of it as shares of the proceeds, and the rest as a nice little incentive to keep their mouths shut, as they have for years."

This was an astounding bit of gossip, but that was what made Kate a little suspicious. "If everything is so much on the down low, why is this coming out now?"

She hated to say the next thing on her mind, as Auggie might take offense. She said it anyway.

"Are you absolutely sure what you're hearing is true?" Then she had to laugh. "You love a good story, and you love insider info even more. Is it even possible that ..."

"No way." Auggie was emphatic about that. "I got this from an excellent source, someone who would know." He nodded to reinforce the idea, almost more to himself than to Kate.

"It's the embezzlement scandal that's bringing all of this into the light. Before, it was merely interesting information; but now, this guy's getting worried. He's wondering if he should go to the authorities with it. What if it means something? Something that could solve this case?"

Kate understood. She'd felt the same weight of knowing after her unnerving stop at the Wellingtons' on Tuesday. In her situation, she'd done the right thing by telling Roberta as quickly as possible.

Auggie's source was right to be concerned. These long-standing silent partners were on the receiving end of countless transactions coming out of the Wheelers' accounts. There might be opportunities for more than that if someone had the knowledge to pull it off.

"So there are several new possibilities for who could be stealing money from the auction barn," Kate said. "This is making my head spin."

"This doesn't explain how they're doing it, of course," Auggie admitted. "But it certainly points to a number of potential suspects. And motive, too. I mean, what if the Wheelers have cut back on this profit sharing, or whatever you want to call it? Would someone think they had a right to grab more cash when no one was looking?"

Auggie was really on to something there. No wonder he'd begged Kate to meet him as quickly as possible. And in a cemetery, no less.

"So if one of the investors is behind this, they've been skimming for themselves for a while now." Kate brushed her hair out of her eyes. "It's not anything new. Wouldn't you think the Wheelers would have figured it out by now? Put a stop to it?"

As soon as she asked the question, Kate had an answer. More than a few people had accused Pete Wheeler of not paying enough attention to the auction barn's books.

Auggie likely thought the same, but he also had another idea.

"Unless they can't." He raised his eyebrows. "Unless they are so far into debt with these other folks that they can't say no."

Was that what had motivated the Wheelers to consider selling their business in the first place? The opportunity to wash their hands of these financial burdens, make a fresh start? But the more Kate thought about it, she wondered if the Wheelers had ever seriously considered putting their auction barn on the auction block.

No one seemed exactly sure what had prompted that rumor to circulate around Eagle River. The only concrete thing Kate had heard was that night at The Eagle's Nest, when Chuck and his friend had hinted at a secret meeting in the company's office with some guy in a pressed business-style shirt.

While that could have been a business consultant, or even a potential buyer, it was just as likely the visitor was someone else ... like Donald Wellington. If the Wheelers' longtime accountant had stumbled across something suspicious, Kate was sure he'd be as quick to call an emergency meeting as Auggie had today. Unless he was the one swiping the money.

Either way, someone had decided the Wellingtons needed

a little reminder about who held the upper hand. Kate could tell Auggie about the slashed tires without telling him about the certified letter. But this web of deceit was multiplying in size and complexity by the minute, and she decided she'd better keep that to herself.

"Here's what I'm most curious about, right now," she told Auggie. "Who are these so-called 'silent partners'? Do you know?"

"I was given a list. Maybe I shouldn't share that." He hesitated for a few moments. "But you've done a bang-up job of helping out around here since you got back. And I know you can keep a secret. Or five."

That statement made Kate feel rather guilty about hiding something from Auggie. And then, her mind quickly turned to how she should handle whatever he was about to tell her.

She and Bev were a team; they worked these cases together. But would this be something she shouldn't share with her friend? If total secrecy was a condition of Auggie's confidences, Kate would have to honor that.

Kate nodded her acceptance, even though she wasn't quite sure what she was agreeing to. "Who are they?"

"Well, I was told of three for sure. But there could be more. These people could be the key to unraveling this whole mess. Which we need to do, for everyone's sake. If Wheeler Auction Company goes down, it's going to deal a serious blow to our local economy."

First up was a major farm-implement dealer with a branch in Mason City. It was a franchise, to be sure, but the regional site was operated by another family owned business. Second was Eagle River's veterinary practice, a place that Kate was vaguely aware of but had never frequented. Her family had always relied on Doc Ogden in Prosper, and now Karen as well, as that office was closer to their farm and, quite honestly, more affordable.

And the third? Elton and Andrea Bingham, the former

owners of the majestic Percheron team that had set a new sales record at Wheeler Auction Company. Elton's family had been raising draft horses for over fifty years.

The more Kate considered each of the alleged silent partners, the more this all made sense. Which made her believe that what Auggie's source had told him was true.

She had to wonder, though, how much capital the Binghams really had at their disposal these days. "Elton and Andrea are up to their necks in debt, themselves, from what I've heard," she told Auggie. "I was at the auction barn on Saturday, when they sold that team."

"I've heard the same. And I missed all the excitement! I was too busy ramping up for spring planting at the shop."

His disconsolate tone almost made Kate smile. How Auggie loved to be in the loop! Between the buzz about the Percherons' sale and their unexpected, nearly disastrous bolt through the back of the auction barn, the event had been the talk of Eagle River for several days.

"Are there other silent partners, do you think?" Kate asked. "Anyone you suspect?"

"I've been trying to figure that out." Auggie sighed. "My money would be on something ag-related, of course. Like a meat locker, or a big-time seed-corn dealer with deep pockets. But I haven't heard even a hint about this, from anyone else."

"So, not the Prosper co-op, then?" Kate couldn't resist.

Auggie chuckled. "Nope! There's no criminal activity going on there, I assure you." He crossed his arms. "I think you'll find all the co-ops in the area are on the straight and narrow."

Mapleville's and Eagle River's sites were true cooperatives, Auggie explained. Their directors answered to boards made up of area farmers, shareholders who held voting rights on major decisions; the co-ops were officially nonprofit entities. Auggie's shop in Prosper was more like a traditional business, one that he owned outright. The Swanton co-op was the same.

It wasn't possible for the Eagle River or Mapleville co-ops to be silent partners in the auction barn, Auggie insisted, because the nonprofits' balance sheets were routinely reviewed by their governing boards.

Half of Hartland County would have gotten wind of any such arrangement years ago.

Kate agreed. But she suspected that someone connected to a local co-op was the source of the top-secret list Auggie had just shared with her.

She would never ask him to reveal his source; the information itself was enlightening enough. But given the sudden wariness in Auggie's eyes as they huddled in this cemetery, she wondered if he was bracing for that very question.

"I won't ask who told you. But thanks for letting me know what you know. Or, at least, what you suspect."

"Oh, it's golden, I'm sure of that. Now the question is ... what can you do with it?"

She shrugged. "What are *you* going to do?"

"Keep my eyes and ears open." He turned on his heel, and she followed him back toward the road. "Not much else I can do, at this point."

"You know," Kate said as they slid sideways through the gap by the gate, "I was half-expecting you to mention the Eagle River bank."

"I thought the same. But then, it doesn't quite fit, does it?"

The Baxters had operated Eagle River Savings Bank for about as long as the Wheelers had owned their auction service. It was almost a given the bank had loaned the Wheelers money over the years, Auggie said, but the Baxters always had the law, and emotional leverage, on their side.

Why risk trying to swipe cash on the back end when you

could take what you wanted through steep interest rates and fees?

"Leonard Baxter is one wily dude; so were his father and grandfather, and on back." Auggie opened his truck's door. "I'm sure the Wheelers let that wolf into the barn a long, long, time ago, and it comes and goes as it pleases."

Just before Kate reached Bertha, Auggie rolled down his window. "Hopefully there's something in there that you and Bev can work with!"

"Bev?" Kate tried to keep a straight face. It was hard, given the wave of relief she felt. "Why would ..."

Auggie laughed, and pointed to where his ancestors rested in the little pioneer cemetery. "I want to hear all about it. I'll be *dying* to know what you two dig up!"

10

Kate rolled over, and bumped against something small and furry. Still half asleep, she patted the cat's back.

"Charlie, you're hogging the bed," she murmured. "Why aren't you curled up by the pillow, like you ..."

Suddenly, Kate was wide awake.

What happened to Charlie's fur?

Charlie's thick coat was over two inches long. But all she could feel was a short, plush layer of feline hair. Her heart began to race as her eyes tried to adjust to the darkness of the bedroom.

"Oh, Moose; it's you!" Kate sighed with relief. "I thought I was having a terrible nightmare, that someone had given Charlie the biggest haircut of his life."

The brown tabby meowed in return, which further assured Kate this wasn't part of some awful dream. Moose's vocals leaned toward the raspy side, compared to her house cat's genteel greeting. Yes, this definitely wasn't Charlie.

"We're at your house, not mine," Kate said to Moose. "So, yeah, you can take the middle if you want."

She'd spent a few evenings at Alex's lately. But Kate still liked to head home and sleep in her own bed, when all was said and done.

And we've done plenty, she reminded herself, then almost

giggled. That was notable, in its own way. Because Kate liked to laugh, but she wasn't a woman prone to giggling about anything.

Where was Alex, anyway?

Her eyes had adjusted better to the dark, but it was still thick inside the bedroom. Since he mostly worked nights, Alex had total-blackout curtains on these windows. While there was no glow seeping in from the streetlights outside, the old panes weren't insulated. Somewhere far off, a dog barked. Then a car rolled past.

Alex's side of the bed was still warm; he hadn't been gone long.

Kate yawned, and wondered about the time. Her phone, resting on the floor by the bed, said it was nearly one in the morning. She could be dressed in five minutes, and turning up her own lane within fifteen, but that still felt like a monumental effort when it was the middle of the night.

"I'd better get home," she told Moose, who'd now settled himself squarely on top of Alex's pillow. "Charlie and Hazel will be waiting for me, and they're probably going to give me those guilt-inducing looks when I get there."

By contrast, Moose was the most laid-back cat Kate had ever met. Being brought in out of the cold meant he'd never have to struggle for food or shelter again, so he found it easy to take everything else in stride.

Kate rolled out of bed, and did the same with the top sheet. Tucking it around herself, she padded toward the bedroom door. It was closed, and the old iron knob made a clicking noise when it opened.

Just like her own house's doors. Most things at Alex's house were old, for better or worse. Either original to the structure, or so steeped in its history that they might as well be. It had that dated, worn-in, comfortable vibe that Kate loved.

No wonder I feel at home here, she thought as she started

down the short hallway and turned into the dining room, the back corner of the bed sheet following her like the train of a strapless dress. Of course, much of that had to do with the man who owned this house. The faint light radiating out of the kitchen told Kate that's where he was right now.

Moose had followed her, and he pounced on the end of the sheet as it moved along. When Kate stopped just outside the doorway into the kitchen, the cat rubbed against her bare ankles before settling at her feet.

Alex was murmuring something to himself. Kate couldn't make out the words, but she imagined he was prepping a bowl of cereal, or about to scramble an egg in the microwave while he made a piece of toast.

He loved breakfast food as much as she did, and his sometimes-odd work schedule meant he could eat it any time, day or night.

But Kate soon realized there were too many pauses in Alex's conversation for it to be one sided; he had to be on his phone.

The bar was still open. Steve, his assistant manager, had probably called, and Kate hoped there wasn't a problem at Paul's Place.

"No, that's all I know," Alex was saying. There was a long pause.

"I can't tell you exactly what's going on. I wish I could."

Kate heard a cabinet door open and close. She was probably correct that he was getting something to eat. But who was he talking to?

"We've been over this before." Alex's tone was more insistent than defensive. "There's only so much I can do. It's complicated, you know that."

And then ...

"Yeah, she's here right now." Another pause. "But that's not the problem, OK?"

Kate's toes turned to ice on the bare oak floors, even as

her face began to burn with ... what? Anger? Hurt? Jealousy? Or even a little bit of shame?

Because her boyfriend was having a secretive conversation with God-knows-who in the middle of the night while she lurked in his dining room wearing only a bed sheet.

Kate couldn't recall when she'd last felt this naked and vulnerable, if ever. She didn't know what Alex was going on about, or how it could possibly have anything to do with her. But maybe that was the problem.

He obviously wasn't talking to Steve. She couldn't imagine he would be on the phone with one of his parents at this hour, unless there was some sort of emergency. Alex sounded a bit frustrated, but not overly concerned. And this certainly wasn't the tone he'd take with his Aunt Helen, either, or any other family member.

Unless this was his cousin, Police Chief Ray Calcott, and they were having some sort of disagreement. But about what? Kate hadn't pegged them as close friends, but they certainly didn't seem to be adversaries, either.

Was it a friend? Kate's cheeks burned hotter as she realized she couldn't begin to guess who that might be. Shouldn't she at least have an idea? Had she been so pleasantly distracted by this ... relationship with Alex that she hadn't given too much thought to who he hung out with when he wasn't at home, at the bar, or with her?

Of course, there was another possibility. One that made Kate sick with regret.

The one thing, the only thing, she'd asked of Alex before they got this close was that she be the only one. And now, she wondered if he'd broken his promise. Or ever kept it in the first place.

Well, she was going to find out. Right now. Kate adjusted her cotton-percale wrap dress, raised her chin, and sailed into the kitchen.

Alex had pulled on his boxers when he'd gotten out of

bed. His muscled back was turned toward the doorway, and he indeed had his phone tucked under his left ear.

Kate couldn't have made more than a bit of noise. But Alex, as always, was very aware of his surroundings. He whirled around from the counter, a table knife loaded with peanut butter in one hand. He looked guilty; there was no other way to describe it.

Quite the opposite expression from the one that normally greeted Kate when she appeared in his kitchen in the middle of the night, looking just like this.

"Hey, I gotta go," he told the person on the other end. "I'll let you know how it goes, OK?"

They stood there for a moment, staring at each other in silence. Moose jumped up on the kitchen table and pranced across it, but Alex didn't even seem to notice the huge cat was in the room.

Kate was willing to give Alex a chance to explain. Because if there was someone else, she was going to be the better person about it. She wouldn't beg, she wouldn't ask why. She'd just give him a few seconds to make his lame excuses, then she'd pull on her clothes and be gone.

"What's going on?" Kate crossed her arms against whatever disappointment was about to come her way. "Look, I'd hoped you were better than that, but maybe I was wrong. I didn't ask you for a major commitment or anything, just to only be with me while we ..."

Alex barked out a laugh so loud, a startled Moose jumped off the table.

"Are you serious?" There was a hint of hurt in his voice, but Kate wasn't sure if it came from his heart, or just his ego. "You think I'm banging someone else?"

"Oh, that's what you call it?" Kate took a small step back. "Fine, fine; then I *really* need to get out of here."

Alex rubbed a hand over his face. "Sorry, I didn't mean ... it's late, and you startled me, and ..."

"Oh, please." Kate flicked her train in irritation and started to turn away. "You're a bartender. This isn't really the 'middle of the night' for you. But it is for me."

"Will you let me explain?" Alex set his phone on the counter and came around the table, but he knew better than to reach for her hand. "I'm not seeing anyone else, I swear."

"What's going on, then? Secret phone calls made under the cover of darkness?" Kate let out a bitter laugh. "That's pretty cloak-and-dagger, I'd say, unless you are cheating."

The sting of Ben's betrayal returned with a vengeance. Even though she was certain her expression hadn't changed, Alex picked up on that right away.

"I'm not your husband. Ex-husband, I should say." He crossed his arms. "As for what's going on ... maybe I should tell you. But if you don't want to hear it, it'd be a waste of time. Because if you don't trust me, it doesn't matter."

Despite her anger, Kate felt a cold stone settle in her heart. "Does any of it matter, anymore? What are you saying? Are you done, here? With me?"

Alex just shrugged. In the faint glow from the light above the kitchen sink, Kate saw signs of an emotional struggle on his face. And, she realized, she didn't want this to be over.

They'd been trying to keep it casual, other than keeping it exclusive; but the thought of losing him was suddenly devastating. How had she fallen so hard for him, and so fast? She'd promised herself that wasn't going to happen. It obviously had.

Which was why it was so important she got some sort of answer out of him. And he hadn't said another word.

If he wasn't cheating on her, then what was it? Was he involved in something shady, something criminal?

Running a bar, he came into contact with people from all walks of life. It was a good bet that some of them weren't on the straight and narrow. Kate's mind raced toward several possibilities, all of which made her wish this was as simple, and as obvious, as Alex seeing someone on the side.

Alex finally spoke. “I’m not done with you,” he said softly. He looked away for a second, then back at Kate with those soulful brown eyes that always seemed to look right through her. “At least, unless you want me to be.”

“If we ... go on like this.” Kate looked down at her bed sheet. “There can’t be any secrets between us. Nothing big, I mean. I’ve had enough of those, you know that.” She stared right back at him, not caring if he saw the tears in her eyes. “I need to know that I can trust you, that you’re not ...”

“How much do you want to know?” His question hung there in the gloom for a few moments. “Kate, *everyone* has secrets. I’m not the only one. So do you.”

He stared at the darkness on the other side of the kitchen window. “Everyone in this town has secrets. I don’t know them all, but I’ve heard enough to know some of the ‘good folks’ of Eagle River are hiding things that ... well, it’s not your business.”

“Fine. But I want to hear yours; I care about you.”

It was the truth; but there was a bit of fear mixed in, as well. Whatever Alex was keeping from her, she sensed it was something that could change the way she felt about him.

He blinked quickly and turned his head away. “I don’t know.” It came out as barely more than a whisper. “I don’t know if I should. I’m not sure you could handle it.”

“I’m tougher than I look, I promise.” Then her eyebrows rose. “Oh, I see. You think I can’t keep things to myself?”

But as soon as she said it, Kate understood. She’d spent a great deal of time snooping around since she’d moved back to Eagle River. Trying to figure out what was going on, collecting leads, chatting up residents on her routes. Passing pertinent information to Sheriff Preston, and anyone else she thought needed to know.

And dissecting cases in great detail with Bev. And Auggie. And Karen and Melinda. And Alex, himself.

"This is different," she said. "If there are things you want to tell me, I want to hear them. And I won't share them with anyone. I mean that."

Kate wasn't sure what she'd expected Alex's reaction to be, but she was caught off guard when he put his hands over his face.

"What if I don't want to talk about it?" His voice was raspy with anguish. "What if I can't?"

Kate's heart overflowed with compassion; but her head warned her to keep her distance, both emotionally and physically. This probably wasn't about another woman, at least, and that insight brought Kate some measure of relief. But Alex was indeed involved in *something*, and maybe he was right.

Maybe it was best she didn't know, and not because she'd betray his confidences. Whatever it was, there seemed to be some sort of danger involved. Something Alex was trying to protect her from. But how could she continue to have him in her life, especially in this way, if he wouldn't give her a clear picture of what was going on?

"If you have to walk away, I get it," he finally said. "It's happened before," he added, more to himself than to Kate. "It's a lot sometimes, even for me. If you think you need to be done, then ..."

"I wish I could do this." Kate meant it. "But you ... Alex, there's always this wall between us, no matter how close we get. I feel like I can't get over it, or through it, to really reach you."

"You're right about that," was all he said. No explanation, no begging her to stay, no promises to stop doing whatever he was doing.

Kate quickly realized that, at least for tonight, she didn't have one more thing to offer this situation. They were emotionally mature adults. There wasn't going to be any yelling and shouting, or drama. She just needed to gather up her things, and her disappointment, and leave. “I'd better get dressed.”

Alex nodded. “If you change your mind, you know where to find me.”

“Same here.” Kate couldn't help it; she reached for his hand, one last time. He squeezed it, and leaned toward her. But then he stopped.

“I wish I could explain. But maybe it's better if I don't.”

Better for you, or for me? Kate wondered, but she let it go. She was going to have to let a lot of things go; and the sooner she did, the better. And then, she saw movement on the counter behind Alex.

“Oh, no!” She couldn't help but smile as she shook her head. “Moose, what are you ...”

Alex whirled around, then tossed up his hands with a sigh. “Dude, you are the worst roommate I've ever had. That's my peanut butter sandwich! We don't steal food around here, remember? There's plenty for both of us.”

Moose's survival instincts had never left him. Even now, when he had a warm, safe home and a person who cared for him and catered to his every whim, the former stray apparently always stayed on his toes. Kate knew she needed to do the same.

And this was the perfect time for her to make her exit. She snatched up the bottom of the bed sheet, hurried down the hallway, and closed the bedroom door behind her.

* * *

Hazel and Charlie were indeed waiting for Kate when she got home, but their disdainful expressions quickly turned to offers of comfort when she wandered into the kitchen, bleary-eyed and exhausted.

“Yeah, I cried all the way home,” she told Charlie as he leaned in to rub his forehead against her arm. He'd jumped on the counter as soon as she'd set her things on it; Kate knew it was his way of getting close to her as quickly as possible.

With her arms now free, Kate put them around her cat. "You're the only guy in my life now." Charlie purred his sympathy. "Well, you and Scout and Jerry, too. It's for the best; it has to be."

Hazel whimpered at Kate's feet, her tail wagging only slightly.

"I know you liked Alex. So did I. But, well, to be honest, I have no idea what's going on. And I'm not sure when I'll find out, if ever. Or even if I should."

Kate sighed as the three of them started for the stairs. "Alex Walsh is one mystery I may never be able to solve."

Kate braced herself for a restless night, hours spent tossing and turning, but the opposite happened. Once she laid down, it was only a few minutes before she was ready to close her eyes.

My own pillow, she thought as her limbs grew heavy and her heartbeat slowed. *In my own house, that I don't have to share with anyone.*

Did that make her feel better, or worse? Kate didn't know. But morning was only a few hours away, and she couldn't think about Alex any more tonight.

11

Kate's foul mood the next morning was right in step with the dark clouds and relentless winds that had arrived while she slept.

But Charlie, Hazel, and the barn cats needed their breakfast; and as always, the mail must go through.

"Neither rain nor sleet, nor dark of night," Kate muttered as she trudged out to the garage, where Bertha waited to start another day on the road. "Nor bad boyfriends, or whatever else comes along."

It took all of what little energy Kate had to appear refreshed and calm as she entered the post office's back door. Maybe there had been too many evenings bouncing between her place and Alex's, trying to see each other as often as they could despite their polar-opposite work schedules. Or maybe, she was just sad and disappointed.

Bev, of course, saw right through the forced smiles.

"Honey, what happened?" Bev leaned over the table as they began their sorting for the day. Mae Fisher was off, so Kate had her northwest run; Bev was only in until one, and was organizing the parcels by route. "It's not Patches, is it? Or one of the other critters?"

"No, no," Kate assured her friend. "They're all fine. My family's fine, the furry members as well as the human ones."

She tried for a laugh, but Bev's concerned gaze still pinned Kate in place.

What could Kate say? Too many sets of ears were probably listening in. She had said very little about Alex at work, and she wasn't about to start now. Especially when, she realized with a pang in her chest, it didn't really matter anymore.

But she'd jump at the chance to confide in her friend. Bev was twenty years older, and her seasoned evaluations of situations always gave Kate a refreshing perspective. The post office, however, wasn't the place for such a heart-to-heart; it would have to wait.

And then, there was this: Kate could tell Bev that she and Alex had had a falling out, but it would be hard to say who dumped whom.

They both seemed to be done, whether they really wanted to be or not. As for why, Kate certainly wasn't ready to share the wide-ranging theories that swirled through her mind this morning.

Alex is too hot, and too bored in this little town, to keep his pants zipped. It's still possible he's "banging" some woman who hangs out at his bar.

Alex is dealing drugs out of his bar.

Alex is trafficking stolen goods, possibly firearms, out of his bar.

Alex is embroiled in some sort of underground conspiracy that causes him to make secretive phone calls in the middle of the night.

More than one of these may be true.

Bev stared at Kate with concern for another moment, then simply nodded. "You don't have to talk about it, whatever it is, if you don't want to."

She laid a hand on Kate's arm as she came around the

counter. "But I'm here, if you do."

"Thanks." It wasn't an adequate appreciation of Bev's friendship, but Kate was too tired to come up with anything more at this hour. "Maybe we can talk later."

Out on the gravel roads, Kate tried her best to keep Bertha on track under the threat of a strong northwest wind. Winter still had the upper hand, and Kate wondered if it was about to come roaring back with a vengeance. April snowstorms were rather common, and they were often vicious. She wondered about the farmers who'd tried to jumpstart the season, and started planting too early. How might they fare if another hard freeze, or worse, arrived?

And how many hopes had Kate nurtured about Alex that had turned out to be premature in their own way?

As she leaned out at mailbox after mailbox, the roaring gale threatening to rip the envelopes and circulars from her hands, Kate had to face what was left of that relationship.

"Not much." It was a relief to power up the window, and push her hands into the heat radiating from Bertha's vents. "I guess it's just as well I didn't introduce him to Mom and Dad yet. Much less bring him to pizza night, or any other family gatherings." Karen and Melinda knew about Alex, of course; but the three of them had never gotten around to organizing any couples' get-togethers.

This was hard, so hard. Yet maybe, if she gave herself a few days to process everything that had happened, it eventually might be as easy to cut Alex out of her life as it had been to let him in.

"It can be like none of this ever happened, if I let it," she told herself with grim determination. Even so, her heart was filled with disappointment and regret.

Despite the raw, blustery day, this endless grid of gravel roads gave Kate the solitude she needed to sift through last night's developments and search for some perspective.

Ultimately, she decided Alex probably wasn't cheating on

her. And not just because he'd denied it. Kate remembered all too well how it had felt to find out Ben was seeing one of his co-workers, and this just didn't feel the same.

That was a bit of a relief. But if not that, then ... what?

Along with all the other theories already spinning through Kate's mind, she considered the possibility Alex was somehow wrapped up in the auction barn scandal. But she couldn't come up with any solid reason why the embezzlement case was at the root of ... whatever he was up to.

It was highly unlikely that Paul's Place had ever been a silent partner in the auction company. Auggie was certain all the affiliated businesses were ag-related, and Kate agreed that made sense. And the bar was so small, and its crowd so low key, that Kate couldn't imagine sales at the pavilion ever brought even a few extra customers through the bar's doors.

Even so, there was still a chance that Alex, whether intentionally or unintentionally, was wrapped up in something criminal. What had he told her?

Everyone has secrets.

That was true, of course. But some secrets were worse, and far-more damaging, than others.

Kate had assumed she knew Alex well, or at least well enough, given the time they'd spent together. But maybe, how they'd been spending much of that time had clouded her judgment. Had she missed clues that she otherwise would have noticed?

* * *

Alex was still on Kate's mind as she washed the dishes and cleaned the kitchen after supper. It was raining now; a damp, bone-chilling night that made Kate grateful to be inside and warm.

Twice she went to the back porch to make sure Patches hadn't left the comforts of the machine shed, and both times she was relieved to find the stoop empty.

"It's a night not fit for man or beast," she told Hazel, who had followed her out into the enclosed porch on her second trip. Charlie had no interest in this errand, or anything else that would pull him away from his padded throne by the crackling fireplace.

It hopefully wouldn't be needed tonight, but Kate still checked the plastic tote packed with fluffy towels. "We have everything ready for Patches, if she decides to have her babies in here when it's time."

Kate's heart ached as she thought of how that stubborn kitty had wandered so far all alone, through barren fields and along windswept gravel roads.

Late last fall, before the snows arrived, Patches would have tried to find shelter inside weed-choked culverts, or the tight spaces under creek bridges. But both locations carried the risk of surprising wild animals doing the same thing. The calico must have found her way into at least one stranger's barn, or she never would have survived the winter. Even so, such a place would have been filled with unfamiliar felines, and possibly unwelcoming dogs.

The poor cat's ordeal made tears well up in Kate's eyes. Yes, that was the only reason she was crying again.

Kate knelt and wrapped her arms around Hazel. "I don't think you're going to see Alex anymore, unless you somehow happened to be at the post office when he stopped in. I'm so sorry."

The dog whimpered. Kate knew it was because Hazel was distressed by her tears, but she wondered what Hazel would think when Alex never showed up here again. Where was her friend? Why didn't he come back?

"That's over and done with, I guess." Kate brushed her hands over Hazel's ears and down her face. "And that's OK. We are going to be fine."

She didn't believe it, not yet. Maybe someday ...

Kate reached for the doorknob, which was cold to the

touch. Maybe this enclosed porch was better than the machine shed, but not by much. There was a lone electrical outlet in the wall that backed the kitchen, and Kate decided she could hang a heat lamp out here as easily as in the machine shed.

Once they were back in the kitchen, Kate refreshed Hazel's water bowl, adding a bit of hot water to warm her chilled pup. As she waited for the microwave to heat a mug for hot chocolate, her gaze landed on her toolbox parked just inside the open pantry door.

She was tired, of course; but it was still early. And there was a project that needed her attention. A project that could fill hours of her now-free time, give her something productive to do as she sorted out her feelings.

If she watched some online videos and asked Bryan and Dad for help, maybe Kate could handle much of the grunt work of the bathroom renovation on her own. Melinda had transformed her own old farmhouse, and Karen was certainly capable, too. Kate didn't have to do this alone.

As she sipped her drink and felt its warmth spread through her body, Kate studied the pantry with a fresh set of eyes. What was the bare minimum needed to make this powder room a reality? The fewer changes she made, the less money and time the project would take.

Moving the doorway and the trim boards was too much work, and not really necessary. Kate was usually the only person in this house, anyway; and her guests wouldn't mind too much if the space continued to open off the kitchen. She could remove all the shelves and their brackets easily enough. If she did it carefully, it wouldn't be that hard to patch the plaster walls herself.

The old flooring could stay for now, especially since much of it would be covered by a new set of bathroom rugs. Someday, if or when the kitchen got its own facelift, she could continue that new floor into here.

Once Richard Everton and his sons installed the toilet and sink, Kate could add the mirror and towel ring. She could easily paint the tiny space on her own. There was hardly room for two people to be inside at the same time, anyway.

"And there's always wallpaper." Kate tried to push her thoughts of Alex aside, and focus on the idea they'd shared. "Something modern, and simple, would really give this space some personality. Or, what about beadboard, just around the bottom? It would be right in style with this old farmhouse. I could paint the trim to match."

Everywhere Kate looked, she saw possibilities and potential. She didn't have a sledgehammer; and that was just as well, as she needed to proceed carefully.

But she did have a hammer, and plenty of frustration to burn.

She drained her mug, set it in the sink, and pulled on a pair of work gloves.

12

The glow of the heat lamps was welcome on this still-dark early Wednesday morning. Kate checked that all three were aimed at the makeshift pen Bev had constructed in one corner of the post office's break room, and cringed over how they also lit up the tired cream paint on the walls.

"This place could certainly use a refresh. But I doubt Roberta has the cash for that, or the time."

Kate was two nights in on her solo pantry renovation, so decorating was certainly on her mind. With every shelf she removed, every old screw or nail that was pulled from the pantry's walls and dumped into a bucket, she was erasing the past and making room for the future.

It was a far-more productive use of her time than thinking about Alex. He hadn't called or texted; Kate hadn't reached out to him, either. And other than chores, there wasn't much else to do around her little farm these days. It was too muddy to clear off the garden, and too early to pot flowers for the porch steps.

As for the embezzlement case, Kate felt like she and Bev had hit a brick wall.

Auggie's gossip about the possibility of silent investors in the auction barn was certainly fascinating, but the ladies had quickly realized it would be nearly impossible for the two of them to generate any new leads with that information.

Eagle River's veterinary clinic would never let people hang out in its lobby without good reason, and there would be the same challenges at the Mason City implement dealership. Kate wasn't in the market for a new tractor, and she wasn't about to entrust her animals' care to the Eagle River clinic when she had Doc and Karen. Kate couldn't even fathom how she and Bev might attempt to glean any useful details from the Binghams.

Any silent partners in the auction barn would be people who could keep a secret, and had done so for years already. None of them would be foolish enough to say, or do, anything in a public location that would put themselves under the microscope of public opinion.

So many things seemed to be out of Kate's control these days, but she did have the power to make one rather-important decision this morning: The postal carrier assigned to baby-chick duty got to choose the strength of the day's first batch of brew.

Kate yawned as she started the coffee maker, then checked the clock on the wall. It was just after five; her special delivery should be arriving any minute now.

This was only Kate's second predawn shift, as Randy and Mae were both especially eager to look after the little birds. Once Kate had the babies tucked into their makeshift nursery, there was cleaning to do.

The regional mail facility's crew had access to the post office, and came and went this early in the day with the understanding they'd stack their drop offs on and around the far sorting table, not make a mess, and lock up on their way out. While Roberta's first and third commands were always followed to the letter, the second was somewhat of a problem. Especially during this muddy time of year.

The regional staffers had been ignoring the postmaster's new sign in the vestibule, and not removing their shoes. Kate would tend to the floors before the other carriers arrived.

This morning's batch of birds was for Duane Albertson, who lived east of town. Roberta had said the Albertsons were chick-purchasing regulars, and Duane or Kathy would arrive by six to take the babies off the post office's hands.

Kate soon heard someone pounding on the back door. The older woman had a box of regular mail in her arms.

"I have your chicks out in the truck," she promised Kate. "I saw your car, but I wanted to be sure you were ready before I brought them in. They say it'll warm up this afternoon, but it's a cold morning, for sure."

"The heat lamps are on. How many sets of chicks do you have to deliver today?"

"Seven so far; that's what came in this morning. We might be making an extra run this afternoon with a few stragglers. Gotta get them transported and home before that deadline, you know."

The regional carrier soon returned with a cardboard box pockmarked with air holes. The tiny birds chirped incessantly as they were brought into the warm post office, but Kate didn't mind.

"I used to work in Chicago before I moved back home," she told the other woman, "and, well ... this wasn't something we handled."

The regional carrier laughed. "Oh, I bet! Well, I'll get the rest of your stuff."

Kate took the perforated box into the break room, set it in the pen, and carefully lifted the lid. The packing slip taped to the top noted there were six Rhode Island Reds and eight Plymouth Rocks, and Kate marveled at the differences in the baby birds' colorings. But all of them were fluffy and cute, and seemed to be healthy.

"Your new parents are on their way," she promised the chicks. "I think you'll be good without any snacks until they get here."

Duane knocked on the back door not twenty minutes later. Kate held the door while he carried the box, which he'd covered with a blanket, out to his truck. He settled the chicks on the passenger seat, then waved to Kate as he pulled out of the parking lot.

The chick-shift supervisor also tried to get a jump on sorting the day's packages, but Kate decided she had a few minutes to herself before starting that task. There weren't too many boxes that day; and a cat nap was unofficially part of the job, given the exceptionally early start.

"I wouldn't get away with this in Chicago," Kate muttered as she rolled her coat into a makeshift pillow, then hopped up on the other long table. The metal counter wasn't the most comfortable, but she set her phone's alarm for twenty minutes and closed her eyes.

Another cup of coffee and the breakfast she'd brought from home gave Kate the fuel she needed to get her workday in full swing. After mopping the back room's floor and organizing the parcels, she decided to tackle the front lobby.

She was rearranging the public notices on the bulletin board when a car pulled up out front.

Not just any car. A police car. Moments later, Chief Ray Calcott started for the post office's front door.

It was just before seven. Roberta would arrive soon, if she wasn't already making her way across the back parking lot, but it looked like Kate would have to greet the police chief on her own.

After she unlocked the door. The lobby didn't open until nine, as the sign out front clearly stated, but Calcott was just about to reach for the outside bar and push his way inside.

Kate plastered on a smile as she hurried to turn the deadbolt. What was he doing here at this hour?

Chief Calcott didn't have a parcel in his arms. Maybe he just needed some stamps, and didn't think he had time to stop in during the regular business day. Still, it was strange.

And rather egotistical of him to expect special treatment.

"Hello," Kate said as pleasantly as possible. It seemed rude to point out that the post office wasn't open yet.

"Well, hello again." The police chief returned Kate's smile, and it seemed somewhat genuine. "You're Wayne Burberry's granddaughter, Kate Duncan."

"That's me." Kate wasn't sure why the chief felt it necessary to reference Grandpa Wayne. Grandpa was well known in town, but still. She wondered if Calcott was trying to show how well-connected he was. It wasn't just that he remembered a name; he had context to go with it, too.

"I'm here to see Postmaster Schupp." The chief unzipped his work jacket and leaned against the counter. He was obviously prepared to wait.

"Oh." Kate glanced at the clock again. "She's on her way in, should be here any minute."

They had time to waste; Kate needed to keep the chit-chat going. It was tempting to ask him about the embezzlement case, of course, and a small part of her wanted to discreetly inquire about Alex, as well. But she wouldn't give the chief the satisfaction of bringing up either topic because, given the bemused look on his face, that might be exactly what he expected her to do.

"Do you need any stamps while you're here?" Kate went behind the counter and opened the cash register's drawer. Tallying its contents was next on her to-do list; she might as well keep working.

"No, no, I'm good. Thanks." The chief looked around the still-quiet lobby for a moment, then back at Kate.

"Actually, there is something. I still need to talk to Roberta, but maybe you can help me out." He leaned over the counter, and gave Kate a conspiratorial smile that she refused to return.

"You know all about the mess that's going on with the Wheelers and the auction barn. I really need to know if they've received any ... strange mail lately." This time, his smile came with an encouraging nod. "You know, something that seemed, oh, I don't know, out of place for them?"

Kate rolled the cash register's drawer closed, and let it latch with a bit more force than was necessary. Did Calcott think she was a stupid fool, or what?

"I can't talk about that. None of us here can."

She wanted to add: *I'm sure you know better*, but suspected that would just ruffle the chief's feathers. This rooster appeared docile enough, but Kate sensed he wouldn't hesitate to peck at her if he got riled up.

Chief Calcott frowned. Then he sighed and rolled his eyes.

"I understand there are ... protocols and such. But we're really in a bind here."

His voice took on a pleading tone. "There's too much paperwork, especially when it comes to the feds. It could take weeks to get that settled. You know how it is."

Kate did, but she wasn't about to take the bait. She just stood there, determined to make him wait for Roberta's arrival. If the police chief took her tired expression as a sign of disinterest or flat-out refusal, even better.

He finally tapped one index finger on the counter. "We gotta get to the bottom of whatever's going on! Being able to see the Wheelers' mail, as well as the business stuff that moves in and out of the auction barn, would be a big help. Those addresses might give us some leads."

Kate couldn't believe they were even having this conversation. And then, she remembered something.

Last year, when Milton Benniger went missing, the Eagle River post office had alerted Sheriff Preston when an envelope with an especially interesting return address had come through the shop. There had been spirited debate among the carriers about the ethics of such a move, but Roberta had endorsed it because an elderly person was unaccounted for and possibly in danger.

And there was another, very-important difference between that situation, and this one: The Eagle River post office had willingly volunteered that information.

Sheriff Preston had been grateful for the tip, of course. But through all his years in that job, he'd never assumed one of the county's post offices would hand over something like that without official permission ... nor had he ever demanded they do so.

As Calcott stood there, a confident smile still plastered on his face, Kate wondered if he'd gotten lucky with a similar request in the past, somewhere else where he'd worked in law enforcement. Perhaps he had; but it wasn't going to fly in Eagle River.

"You need to get a warrant," Kate said slowly as she looked him right in the eye. "I think you know that. And honestly, I'd have no idea off the top of my head what has come through here for the Wheelers, or anyone else."

There was, of course, Donald Wellington's certified letter from the FBI. It still waited in a locked drawer in Roberta's desk. Donald had yet to retrieve it, and he only had only one more week to show up before it was sent back.

"I don't need to *open* their mail." Calcott shook his head in bewilderment, as if he couldn't understand why Kate wouldn't comply with his request. "I just need to get an idea of what's been coming and going, that's all. You were there at breakfast, that morning at Peabody's. You heard us talking about how complicated this case is."

"Oh, yes; because nobody's died." Kate thought of Donald again. This time, she suppressed a shiver. *Where is that guy?* "Yeah, I remember."

Was that a bit of a blush creeping up from the chief's jacket collar? "Fair enough." He straightened up and took a small step back. "Even so, I'm sure you'll be interested in the latest developments."

Kate was now wiping the counter with a dust cloth, and

only made a small, noncommittal noise in response. If he wanted her to gossip with him, in the hope she'd let something useful slip, he was going to be disappointed again.

"Half an hour ago, I got a call from Dylan Wheeler," the chief said. "He'd gone into the auction barn really early, to get a jump on the paperwork for Saturday's big sale. Turns out, the place was vandalized overnight."

Kate's dust cloth stopped moving.

"The front windows, there along the parking lot? Four of them were busted clear out, like someone took a baseball bat to them. And in the back? Raw eggs all over two of the roll-down doors that open into the stall area."

Kate recalled the slashed tires at the Wellingtons' farmhouse. "Hmm. Sounds like someone might be trying to make a statement about something."

She wanted to ask about the auction barn's security system, where the outside cameras were located and if any of them had been damaged, but she wasn't about to give Chief Calcott the satisfaction of her taking the bait.

"Why would someone do this?" The chief seemed genuinely perplexed. "Embezzlement is a white-collar crime; or at least, it's usually not a blue one. Why trash a property if you've already found a way to get what you wanted, help yourself to the money?"

"Good morning, everyone!" Roberta sailed into the lobby, and Kate breathed a sigh of relief.

"Well, Chief Calcott! To what do we owe this early visit? Up with the chickens, I see." She turned to Kate. "Speaking of which, did our babies go home already? I didn't hear a peep out of the break room."

"Yep, Duane came right away to pick them up."

Kate wondered if she should leave, if Calcott wanted to talk to Roberta in private. And then, she was determined to stay. Because if the police chief tried to end-run any federal laws again, she could serve as a witness if Roberta decided to report the infraction to Mayor Benson, or anyone else.

"Ray?" Roberta chirped when Chief Calcott didn't speak. "Do you need something?"

Kate glared at him from across the counter. *Do it,* she thought. *Ask again, and see what happens.*

"Well, now, I could use some stamps." It took a few moments for the chief to reach for his wallet, as if he wasn't entirely keen on going through with a purchase he didn't need. "Emails are well and good, but a real letter? It just has an importance to it, you know?"

I'm sure the FBI would agree, Kate thought but didn't say.

"Certainly." Roberta opened the stamps drawer. "Would you like the flags? We do have some lovely floral stamps, as well."

The chief opted for one of each, and Kate moved to the end of the counter to let Roberta handle the sale. As she straightened the rack that contained the various postal forms residents might need, Kate saw Calcott look her way again. Before he left, he paused in front of her.

She braced herself for another wheedling request, but was very surprised by what he had to say.

"I heard about ..." Calcott looked away for a second. "Well, I'll just say this: My cousin's a good guy, one of the best."

Roberta, who was now organizing the pen caddy, pretended to not be listening.

"Perhaps," Kate said, too cautious to believe one word of it. There was a part of her that hoped it was true. But after what happened just minutes ago, she couldn't take seriously anything this guy said.

The chief gave her a slight nod, then walked out to his car.

Roberta turned to Kate, her eyes full of concern. "Oh, no! Did you and Alex ..."

"It looks like we're done." Kate glanced at the clock; it had already been a long day. "But maybe it's for the best."

She made sure Calcott had disappeared down Main Street before she told Roberta about the real errand that had brought the police chief in at such an early hour.

The postmaster sighed in frustration, then told Kate she'd been right to challenge Calcott's underhanded request. While Roberta grumbled about postal regulations as much as anyone else, this was another issue entirely.

"We could lose our jobs if we ever went along with such nonsense." Roberta squared her shoulders and crossed her arms. "He may be the police chief in this town, but *we* work for the feds. If he wants information, he needs to go through the proper channels."

Roberta stared at the door into the back of the shop, where the other carriers were starting to arrive. "It makes me wonder who else on my team he may have approached."

Kate raised her eyebrows. "Do you think anyone would help him, if they even had anything to share?"

"I don't know; I hope not. I'm not sure how well everyone knows Calcott. He can be rather persuasive, when he wants to be. The badge helps, of course."

Roberta smirked as she picked up the dust cloth Kate had abandoned, and attacked the counter with surprising vigor. "I get it; he's trying to close this case. But he'd better not interfere with my shop again."

Roberta told Kate she wanted to keep the chief's early-morning visit under wraps for the time being. But word of last night's vandalism at the auction barn had already made its way around town.

Jack shook his head in awe and disappointment as he dropped his things on the nearest sorting counter. "First, they swiped all that cash! And now, they trash the place! Who's behind all this? What's it going to take to get this resolved?"

"Why destroy stuff like that?" Aaron couldn't understand it, either. "Wouldn't you just take the money and run? Why draw attention to yourself?"

Marge had brought in cinnamon rolls, a treat that was always welcomed by the other carriers. "Maybe the vandalism isn't related to the embezzlement scandal."

Randy considered that idea. "You think someone else with a beef is taking an opportunity to raise hell?"

Aaron laughed. "Nice cow reference."

"Well, I could see that," Jack admitted. "With all the chaos going on within the company, and everyone trying to figure out who the guilty party is, other people might see their chance to destroy stuff and get away with it."

"Kick the Wheelers while they're down," Randy said sadly. "Man, I never thought I'd see the day when one of Eagle River's most-respected families would be facing this kind of trouble."

"It's not just the Wheelers who are suffering due to all of this," Mae offered from across the way. "Two of my nephews work at the auction barn. They're worried they're going to lose their jobs, one way or another."

Bev had arrived, and set up her sorting tray next to Kate's. The two of them stayed quiet while the rest of the crew continued to debate recent events.

"I heard something else yesterday." Jack now directed his words at Allison, who had just arrived. "Is it true that Judy Martin is retiring?"

Gasps went up around the room. "Why, she's been there for ..." Mae tried to think.

"Thirty-one years, and five months," Jack said. "That's what my wife said last night. The auction barn has always been considered a good place to work; and she's the office manager, no less. I can't believe that ..."

"She's sixty-three!" Allison leaned over the counter in Jack's direction. "Old enough to start taking Social Security, if she wants to."

Roberta had been at her desk, but took this opportunity to

wander by the counters on her way to the break room. "Judy's been considering this move for some time, I hear. Her daughter's family has moved back to the area, and she's looking forward to being a full-time grandma."

"Besides," Marge said, "if you'd been there that long, would you want to stay around under new owners, especially at her age? I mean, if the place is ever sold. Sounds like the perfect time to hang up your hat, if you ask me."

"Judy isn't retiring until the end of May," Allison said. "Betsy said she told all the office staff at the end of last week." She glared at Jack. "There's nothing shady going on there."

"A change in management isn't enough of a reason to quit." Jack wouldn't let it drop. "I mean, look at me, at this post office. I've been through how-many bosses."

"I'm not going anywhere!" Roberta yelled from the break room.

Randy clapped Jack on the shoulder and chuckled. "You're like those cockroaches in the storage room, my friend. I don't think we could get rid of you if we tried."

Everyone laughed, including Jack, and the conversation shifted to other topics. But Bev gave Kate a worried glance.

"I don't like this," Bev whispered. "It seems like the longer this situation drags on, the worse it gets. Do you think you'll be able to meet up with Dylan anytime soon?"

Stacy had called Kate yesterday, desperate for yet another favor. One that Kate had been eager to accept.

The president of Eagle River's historical society had informed Stacy that Wheeler Auction Company was about to drop its sponsorship of the May Day celebration. What had caused the Wheelers to change their tune in just the last week wasn't clear, Stacy had said, but Kate's off-the-cuff suggestion to have the dancers ride on a fire truck might need to be implemented.

Unless they could persuade Dylan to continue this decades-long tradition, even just one last time. Didn't Kate and Dylan ride the school bus together, back in the day? Maybe she could meet him for coffee, or lunch ...

"He never answered my text," Kate told Bev. "So I called last night, but all I got was his voicemail. I left a message."

"Whatever happens to the auction barn will have a major impact on this town," Bev said as she shook her head sadly. "But I can't help but worry about the Wheelers, themselves. This must be tearing their family apart."

* 13 *

Kate scanned the coffee shop, and didn't see who she was looking for. But she did spot an empty booth, and was quick to grab it before the Friday lunch rush started.

She still could hardly believe her luck. After nearly three days of nothing but silence from Dylan, he'd texted late yesterday afternoon to ask if she could join him for lunch today. This just happened to be Kate's weekday off, and she had errands to run in Swanton. Which also turned out to be where Dylan wanted to meet.

Kate wasn't surprised. Outside of Eagle River, the Wheelers' faces were less familiar. Here, there was a good chance she and Dylan could chat without being observed.

"He'll be here," she reminded herself as she shed her coat and knit cap. It was a blustery, cold day, and the warmth of the restaurant was welcome. "This was his idea, after all."

Finally, she spotted Dylan hesitating inside the doorway. He hadn't shaved that morning, and the rumpled shirt collar peeking out from the top of his jacket told Kate her meticulously neat school chum had to be struggling. He seemed tired and anxious, and Kate felt sorry for him.

This meeting was about the auction barn's sponsorship, but it was going to be nearly impossible to keep Dylan's personal challenges out of the conversation. She waved him over, and a wave of relief washed over his face.

"Thanks for meeting me all the way over here." Dylan surveyed the room one more time as he unzipped his parka. Given the way his shoulders relaxed, there apparently wasn't anyone here who he recognized.

"Oh, it's no problem." Unsure of what Dylan would be comfortable sharing with her, Kate was careful about what she said next. "Eagle River is quite the fishbowl. It always has been, but I really noticed it after I moved back."

Dylan's laugh carried an echo of bitterness. "I bet! And yeah, it's that, all right." He picked up the menu. "Especially with everything that's been going on. The water's been full of piranhas lately."

He'd already mentioned it; Kate decided being direct was best. "I didn't want to be the one to bring it up, but wasn't sure how to avoid it."

"It can't be helped." Dylan shrugged. "It follows me everywhere. The rest of us, too. Well, the turkey panini looks good. What do you want? I'll go up, and order for us."

"You don't have to pay," Kate protested. "I can ..."

"Nonsense." Dylan waved away her impending offer. "I'm not *that* broke, myself, despite what you might have heard."

He smiled and raised his eyebrows at Kate; she smiled back. It was encouraging to see Dylan trying to find a bit of humor in this dark situation.

"Besides," he went on, "you were always willing to share your leftover lunch snacks on the school bus, on the way home. I probably owe you, anyway."

"In that case, I'll have the club sandwich, with tomato soup. And iced tea."

"You got it."

Maybe this won't be so hard, Kate thought as he went to the counter. If Dylan was trying to keep some perspective through this scandal, surely he'd see the value of continuing the Wheelers' tradition of offering up a wagon and horses for a half-hour promenade through Eagle River.

Kate had her talking points ready to go: Someone else could drive the team, if none of the family felt up to it this year. They wouldn't have to help serve the community meal, or speak at the ceremony, or do anything else where they interacted with the crowd.

Pulling their sponsorship now, with less than three weeks until the festival, might be viewed by the community as a sign of defeat, or even guilt.

The Wheelers had always seemed to take pride in keeping up appearances. Perhaps that alone would be enough to convince the family to participate in the festival.

But even as Kate hoped her immediate task could be accomplished, she wondered about Dylan's sudden eagerness to meet up. Was he going to press her for whatever gossip she'd heard? He knew she was a mail carrier, and that she interacted with countless people around the region.

And there was always the possibility Dylan saw Kate's occupation as working in his favor. Would he take this opportunity to drop some positive talking points on Kate's plate in the hope she'd spread those around?

She thought it unlikely that Dylan was personally involved in the embezzlement at his family's business. But there was always the chance he knew, or at least suspected, that a relative was at fault. And even if Dylan didn't want to take part in a coverup for obvious ethical and legal reasons, she wondered if he was being pressured to do just that.

Kate decided she needed to tread carefully. When Dylan returned with their drinks, she cut to the chase. "We'd hate to lose your family's sponsorship for the festival. Is there anything the organizers can do to keep it going?"

"I'm not sure. I've talked to Dad and Uncle Bill, several times. I told them we can't stop now. It's tradition! They both try to cut me off when I bring it up; but from what I can gather, I think it's the procession that has them feeling uncomfortable. Not the two-hundred dollars we contribute toward the community meal."

Dylan leaned in with a wry smile. "You see, parading our troubles in public is something the Wheelers don't do."

"Never complain, never explain," Kate said with a grin. "Like the royal family, right?"

"Exactly."

Kate's instincts had been right about the situation, and that gave her a bit of confidence she could help Dylan convince his family to stay involved.

"Is there anyone else who'd be willing to drive the wagon? It wouldn't have to be your dad and uncle, this time. Maybe someone with experience managing horses at public events?"

The revelers along the parade route would know to stay on the sidewalks and out of the horses' way. But there would still be commotion and lots of noise. Kate's stomach dropped as she recalled the immense power of the runaway Percherons at the auction barn. The last thing anyone needed was a dangerous situation.

Dylan nodded. "I can think of a few people. You're right; that might be something Dad and Uncle Bill would agree to." But then he frowned. "Some of those folks, though ... I'm not sure this is the best time to ask for that kind of favor."

Kate was fairly certain Dylan was referring to the Binghams. A server dropped off their platters, and she turned her attention to her sandwich.

After a few bites of his panini, Dylan set it down. "You're probably wondering why I didn't get back to you sooner about meeting today. Or more accurately, why I kinda ghosted you, then suddenly wanted to meet."

"Well, a little. But I know things have been crazy lately. I understood."

"I appreciate you not pumping me for gossip about the ... issue with the business. But I have to admit, I'm wondering what you've been hearing."

Oh, here we go, Kate thought. But then, she realized, there wasn't much she could, or should, say.

Donald Wellington, and his letter from the FBI, were off limits. So was Chief Calcott's underhanded request the other morning at the post office. Dylan knew all about the vandalism at the auction barn, far more than Kate did.

He also knew that all the customers who'd received those delinquent-account letters had been absolved of wrongdoing. Even John Grant, who had managed to find his canceled check. And she wasn't about to ask Dylan about the possibility of silent partners in the business. But the pleading look in his eyes was hard to ignore.

"I haven't heard anything concrete," she hedged. "But as you know, the auction barn is one of Eagle River's largest employers. I think everyone is eager for this to be resolved. People are concerned, of course. For the business, but also your family."

That last part was true. And it did seem to bring Dylan a measure of comfort.

"It's just that ... this is such a mess." He ran one hand through his hair. "And the authorities are having a terrible time getting very far. They've looked at some obvious people, as I'm sure you can imagine. And several other theories have been offered, but none of them seem to be panning out. I feel like we're hitting dead ends, left and right."

"Whoever is doing this somehow created a system that's flown under the radar for years," Kate gently reminded him. "That's no small feat; it has to be incredibly complex. I could see how it's going to take some time to figure it out."

Kate wondered how much Pete Wheeler's alleged lack of concern for business matters was slowing things down. If the company's financial systems were outdated, it would make it that much harder for authorities to track down the thief.

"The investigators keep telling us to be patient. But I don't know how much more time we have to give." Dylan picked at his sandwich, as if he'd suddenly lost his appetite.

"It's my dad," he whispered. "He's taking this hard. Of course, you'd expect him to, but ... it's more than that."

When he was satisfied none of the other diners appeared to be listening in, he leaned over the table.

"He's despondent, Kate. I'm afraid that he'll ..." Dylan blinked rapidly. "All he talks about anymore is that this is all his fault, that he should have figured this out long ago. We're a six-generation business, counting myself and Nate, and Dad really feels the weight of that. He has it in his head that he's a failure, that it'll be all his fault if this ship goes down."

"And likely hurts our hometown in the process," Kate finished Dylan's thought. This situation was far worse than what she'd even expected. "Can he get help? Talk to someone? There are resources available, even in an area this rural."

"He won't go. I've tried; and my mom and sister have begged him, several times." Dylan lowered his head in defeat. "But it's not just the stiff-upper-lip thing that's stopping him. I keep telling him that mental-health professionals know their conversations are confidential, but he's paranoid that someone could use something he says against us."

Dylan might truly be in the dark about a family member's possible role in the embezzlement, Kate decided. But she wondered if Pete Wheeler was hiding something from his son.

"I'm scared." Dylan put his face in his hands for a second. "It's terrible about the money, I get that. But that doesn't mean a damn thing in the end. All that we've built, our family? It's nothing to me if I lose my dad over this."

He placed his palms on the table, as if needing its support.

"I've asked Dvorak to make sure all the halters and ropes, which are stored in the back of the barn, are locked away when he closes up at night. I told him it's because we don't want anything stolen, especially after the vandalism, but it's really because of Dad. He has the keys to everything, of course. But if he has to take those extra steps ... maybe it'll keep him from doing something he shouldn't."

Kate struggled with how to respond. "I'm sorry" wasn't going to cut it; not this time. She wondered if Pete Wheeler had access to any guns, and hoped he didn't.

No wonder Dylan was so anxious for this case to get resolved. Although she still wondered about the whereabouts of Donald Wellington, Kate hadn't assumed anyone's life had been put in danger by this whole ordeal. But now ...

"Don't worry about the May Day festival," she finally said. "You have far-more important things to deal with. We'll figure something out. There's always a fire truck; or a few tractors, even ATVs. The girls could hoof it if they had to, but they won't want to ruin their cute shoes."

Her effort to lighten the mood, just a little, seemed to work. Dylan laughed.

"That would shake up things for sure, get everyone's attention. In a good way," he added. "Maybe even keep people from focusing too much on why we're not involved this year."

He finally picked up his sandwich again. "Dad's always enjoyed being part of the May Day procession. Truthfully, I think it might raise his spirits to participate. So, don't count us out just yet. I'm going to keep trying, see if I can get him and Uncle Bill to come around."

"We have a little time yet." Kate returned to her own lunch. "Stacy and I will firm up a Plan B, but maybe we won't even need it. I wish I had something more to offer, something that would help."

"You already have; just listening has been a great help to me. So, how is it being an aunt? I heard Bryan and Anna had a little boy."

They spent the next half hour talking about everything else. Kate caught a glimpse of the carefree boy she remembered from those school bus rides so many years ago. While both of them had adult responsibilities now, the burden Dylan carried was certainly more than he should have to bear.

As Kate ran her errands that afternoon, she considered her options. And not only regarding who might step up for the May Day procession if the Wheelers bowed out.

The authorities weren't the only ones losing traction with this case; she and Bev seemed to be doing the same. But given the heartbreaking update she'd just received from Dylan, this wasn't the time for them to take their foot off the gas.

Nothing Kate had uncovered in the past week went beyond the community's ongoing concerns. Maybe it was time to take a different approach. She wrestled with sharing Dylan's worries with Bev, but knew her friend could be trusted to keep them to herself.

She always did, always had. And now, there was so much more at stake.

"Oh, poor Dylan!" Bev said when Kate called her that night. "I can't imagine what he's going through, what all of them are going through. You're right. We need to step up our efforts, somehow. And quick."

"I don't know where to go next." Kate stared out the dining room window that overlooked the backyard. There was no sign of Patches tonight, but her due date was likely to arrive within the week. "We need fresh sources, I feel like. New perspectives to get new information. But where can we find those?"

Bev didn't answer at first, and Kate could almost hear the gears grinding inside her friend's mind.

"What are you doing after work on Monday?" Bev asked. "I have some shopping to do, and I think you should come along."

The Stewarts were running low on dog food, as well as some things for their horses. And they couldn't stock up tomorrow, because they had an Easter-weekend celebration to attend out of town.

"It's fun to enjoy a cup of coffee with a different crew, for once," Bev said with a hint of mischief in her voice. "How about we sneak around behind Auggie's back and visit his competition?"

* * *

Kate and Bev drove separately to the Eagle River co-op on Monday afternoon, and not just to simplify their departure. Bev had driven her old farm truck to work that morning, and intended to have its loaded down before she headed home.

As for Kate, she didn't expect to come away from this visit with much of anything. There was always the chance that one of the guys hanging around in the co-op's shop, drinking coffee and swapping stories, would drop some crumbs that would add to the case. But that wasn't likely to happen, because this entire situation hinged on the invisibility of the missing money.

There simply wasn't anything for members of the public to see. And if they didn't witness anything of interest, they didn't have a story to share with their friends.

The Eagle River co-op was on the south edge of town. As Kate turned out of the post office's lot and drove down Main Street, she reminded herself that whoever was behind the theft likely hadn't executed even one illegal keystroke while sitting in the auction barn's office.

"Stealing passwords, cracking encryptions, disabling multi-factor IDs ... you could do all of that from anywhere. You could steal thousands of dollars in a matter of seconds while couch-surfing at home."

And it was the same for those on the right side of the law. Kate had never expected to see dozens of vehicles from various levels of government lining Main Street, day after day. But the lack of out-of-town visitors was, well, very visible. There was no hustle and bustle at city hall, and few unfamiliar faces had been spotted around the tables at The

Daily Grind or Peabody's.

Kate imagined the financial crimes investigators were holed up in some government building far from Eagle River, tapping away on their own keyboards for hours on end. Some of them might even be stationed out of state.

"Maybe I should buy something while I'm here," Kate decided as she pulled in next to Bev's truck. "I doubt they carry the wide selection of doggie treats that Auggie keeps in stock, but it would be rude to leave empty handed."

Compared to the beige siding that wrapped Auggie's main office in Prosper, the Eagle River co-op's shop looked like something that should be on the national historic register. The farmers' nonprofit had been in existence since the late 1800s, and in the 1940s it had purchased a former automotive shop adjacent to its initial property.

The red brick, single-story structure had multi-paned windows and crisp white trim under a ridged metal roof. Its two arched garage-door entrances now provided parking for staff. Kate couldn't remember the last time she'd been inside. Maybe in high school?

"It hasn't changed since then," Bev promised as they started toward the front door. "It still has the dark wood floors, not to mention those candy machines with the glass globes, and the same faded tan paint on the walls. This place is like a time machine."

"But they have a coffee maker, right?"

"Oh, yes! On a little table in one corner, where the old coal stove sat long ago. Clyde's been known to dawdle here longer than he needs to; I hope some of his buddies are sitting around today. It would give us an easy opener."

The ladies blew into the shop with a gust of wind, and it took Kate's eyes a moment to adjust after the bright sunshine outside. The place was immaculately clean, yet spartan in its offerings. There were just three short rows of products, a far cry from the retail extravaganza offered at Auggie's shop. But this was a true co-op, she reminded herself, whereas the Prosper location had morphed long ago into a private retail business that also aimed to offer farmers a fair price for their crops.

Kate couldn't be sure, but it seemed like Bryan and their dad had said Auggie's payouts were a bit better than those offered here. His expanded for-profit inventory, and higher capacity for grain storage, likely gave him more flexibility in his business model.

And the Eagle River co-op had a board of farmers who had to be consulted before any major decisions were made. That meant the man behind this counter wasn't as influential as Auggie, but he was just as friendly.

"Well hello, Bev!" Vernon Millard kept his white hair cropped close to mitigate signs of his receding hairline, and his wiry frame told of years of hard work in all kinds of weather. "No Clyde today?"

"Nope, I have a different partner in crime." Bev grinned; she hadn't been able to resist. "This is Kate Duncan, our newest mail carrier."

"Nice to meet you." Vernon's handshake was firm and hearty. "Curtis and Charlotte's daughter, right?" Kate nodded. "How are James and Lillian doing over in Fort Dodge these days?"

"Oh, they're liking it fine. They were back for a visit a few weeks ago. And Bryan and Dad are itching to get in the field. They hope to get started next week."

Kate had verified her family's planting plans last night, as it was exactly what Vernon, and the gaggle of guys gathered around the coffee pot, would be eager to hear about.

"They're out west of town, right?" one of the men called over to Kate. She nodded and smiled. Norm offered his hand in greeting, and Kate was quick to take the empty chair next to him. Bev gave Vernon her order for dog food, as well as oats and a few salt blocks for her horses, then settled in the last spot next to the coffee maker as more introductions were made.

"Mercy, it's chilly today." Bev rubbed her hands together as Kevin, the youngest man in the circle, fulfilled her request for a cup. "Black with a little sugar, thanks."

"There might be a storm brewing later this week," warned Jacob, who looked to be in his seventies. "I'm retired, of course, so I'll just kick my feet up and watch the flakes fly."

"That would put a real wrench in everyone's efforts to get in the fields," Norm said, "but we're due for another bout of bad weather before spring decides to stick around."

If the guys were surprised to have two women in their circle, they were kind enough not to show it. But the ladies knew they couldn't linger too long. Because even during this busy season, Eagle River's co-op was known for its efficient load-out service.

Despite the number of called-in orders, along with those made in person, Bev's number would be up in thirty minutes, if not before. The weather was a good opener, but the ladies needed to move on.

"That was quite the big cattle sale Saturday, over at the auction barn," Kate said. "Dad doesn't need any more cows, so he didn't even get a number. But he loves to go, anyway."

"Clyde and I love it, too," Bev said wistfully as she sipped her coffee. "Why, that place brings people together in such a special way. It'd be a real shame if its doors ever closed."

Norm shook his head sadly. "It doesn't look good. Enjoy those big cinnamon rolls while you still can."

"I hope that doesn't happen," Kevin said. "That stolen cash had to leave some sort of a paper trail, even with everything done electronically these days. Someone has to get to the bottom of this, and quickly."

Jacob leaned in. "They have a whole team of accountants on it, I hear. Not sure who they all are, but I've been told the authorities are bringing in outside advisors."

Bev raised an eyebrow. "Exactly how much money's missing? What have you heard?"

"I was told twenty thousand, at least," Jacob said.

"Oh, it's worse than that," Norm said. "Two people have told me it's well north of fifty grand."

Kevin let out a low whistle. "What a haul! But it'd never be enough if you got caught."

Jacob shook his head in disgust. "What I want to know is, who's paying for all those consultants? It'd better not be the taxpayers."

Today was April 15; no wonder the conversation was veering in that direction. People were concerned about the case's impact on the local economy, of course, but how it could hurt their personal pocketbooks was also a concern.

Kate saw a chance to share a few facts with this group. They'd be likely to spread them around, along with their gossip, and it might do some good.

"I was reading about this online. The company that was stolen from is on the hook for the consultants' fees, but these cases are still a lot of work for law enforcement. All the more reason I hope they find out who's behind this, and soon."

Would her last comments drive the men's chatter toward possible suspects? Kate caught Bev's barely perceptible nod from the other side of the coffee pot, and they waited.

As the ladies had expected, awkward silence was something these men hated more than having to foot the bill for the investigation.

"It's gotta be one of the Wheelers, themselves," Jacob finally said. "I don't think anyone else in the front office would do such a thing."

"My wife knows Judy," Norm piped up. "She'd never steal from anyone, not one cent. She's devoted her career to working for the Wheelers. Judy knows it looks bad that she's retiring now, but word is she's so disgusted with the whole mess, she wants nothing to do with them anymore."

"I heard the place was vandalized last week," Kate put in.

"Oh, that's a whole other thing, entirely," Kevin promised as he got up from his chair. Vernon had just waved him toward the counter to finish up his order. "I bet that's just some kids acting out. They saw an excuse to cause trouble, and they took it."

After Kevin left, the other two guys hitched their chairs closer together. Bev and Kate did the same.

"I know Pete doesn't pay much attention to the books," Jacob said, "but I don't think he is the culprit. He's a straight arrow, like his dad; and Marvin is too old to be messed up in this sort of thing, anyway. Why, he's eighty-two."

Norm rubbed the gray stubble on his weathered face. "Dylan's a good kid. So is Nate. That leaves Bill."

Only Wheeler men currently held official roles within the company, but their wives and daughters were still involved.

Kate recalled that Pete's sister, Betty, had worked in the office all through high school, and long after she'd married Bill Kirkland. Betty had only stepped aside after Nate and his sister were born.

Kate found it interesting that while these guys were so sure a Wheeler relative was at fault, there wasn't a woman's name in the bunch. Jack, she decided, might have a hard time believing that.

Norm suddenly turned in his chair. "Hey, Vernon," he called across the room. "What do you think? Is Bill Kirkland the mastermind behind this heist?"

Vernon was in the closest of the three aisles, a cardboard box tucked inside one elbow as he restocked the co-op's meager selection of vitamin supplements. "Oh, come on now, I'm trying to stay out of it," he said with a sheepish smile.

Norm and Jacob stared at Vernon with such hopeful expressions that Kate had to work to keep from laughing.

At that moment, no one else was in the shop. Finally, Vernon set his box of merchandise aside.

"I don't know anything about the money." He waved that all away with his hands. "But I did hear something interesting about the Wheelers last week. A few times over, in fact. Let's just say that Bill and Betty are ... having problems. I guess that's the nicest way to put it."

Bev widened her eyes at Kate from across the way. *What*?

"You know, it seems like Bill's always had a chip on his shoulder," Vernon mused. "Maybe he kinda feels second best to Pete. Pete is Marvin's son, and he's only the son in law."

Vernon shook his head, then went back to stocking shelves. "I always say, it's best to be careful around folks like that. If they have an axe to grind, you never know when, or how, they'll decide to sharpen it."

"I don't know if I should say anything," Norm said in a tone that told Kate he secretly wanted to.

"But I've heard something similar. Bill's seeing some woman from over by Charles City. My wife said she ... oh, I can't remember the name! But she's some big deal, I guess, she and her husband. They raise horses."

Bev nearly choked on her coffee.

Kate was too shocked to stay silent. "Do you mean Andrea Bingham?"

"Yep, that would be her." Jacob shook his head in disgust. Since the fire was already burning, he couldn't help but throw a little gasoline on it. "I heard those two have been fooling around for some time now."

Kate thought this line of conversation was more likely to be found among ladies chatting at a beauty salon, but Norm and Jacob wouldn't let it drop.

"Betty won't give Bill a divorce," Norm insisted. "She still loves him, first of all; and second, she'd be so humiliated to have her dirty laundry dragged up and down Main Street."

It already is, Kate thought with a pang of sympathy.

"Bill's my bet for the sneak," Jacob proclaimed. "If they'd divorce, the rest of the family would have to pay him to go away. While Pete's usually the one out in front, Bill's helped keep that company going, too. My money's on him getting his revenge by helping himself to the cash."

Norm chuckled. "He's sneaking around, then, twice over."

"Hey, Bev!" Vernon called over his shoulder as he rushed to answer another phone call at the counter. "Your feed is just about ready. Might as well pull up around back."

The ladies offered the men quick goodbyes and hurried out the door. Kate was glad to go.

"I feel like I need a shower." She grimaced as she walked Bev to her truck. "That was the last thing I expected to hear today. And from some men, too."

"They gossip as much as the ladies do, once the conversation gets rolling." Bev reached for her keys. "But if all of that is indeed going on, I can see why people might think Bill would be motivated to steal from the company."

Kate wished the phone at the Eagle River co-op didn't ring so often this time of year. Vernon might have added more insight to the conversation if he'd been allowed to linger in the aisle.

Or maybe not. And maybe, Kate had learned enough too-personal information to last her for a while. Especially after the heartbreaking details Dylan had shared with her on Friday.

"Well, I guess we got what we came for," she told Bev. "I'm not sure if it's of any use. Or if I'd even want to go down that path, anyway."

"I agree. I wouldn't feel right spreading that around, even if it helped the case." Bev sighed. "Poor Betty. Just goes to show, you never know what people are dealing with behind the scenes. And hiding from the rest of us."

14

Roberta joined Kate at the counter on Thursday afternoon. "You'd better head straight home after we close. I just got a weather alert; we could have six inches of snow by morning."

"Six?" The view out the lobby's large windows showed a bank of dark clouds closing in from the west. "Last I'd heard this morning, we were going to get a dusting, at most. I guess it's better than an ice storm."

"You're right; it could be so much worse." Roberta waved goodbye to the last customer. "We're prone to those this time of year. That, and thunderstorms. April is always a toss-up around here; we never know what to expect. A few degrees this way or that, and things can change in a hurry."

Kate mentally inventoried what supplies she had at home. She'd planned to stop at the Evertons' pharmacy/grocery store for a few things on her way out of town, but decided it could wait a day. One good thing about April snowstorms was that they usually didn't last long.

She was about to share how one of the guys at the co-op Monday afternoon had predicted this storm, but stopped herself. It would cause Roberta to wonder why Kate had been at the Eagle River shop, since she got all her pet supplies from Auggie, and Kate just wanted to forget everything she'd heard about Bill Kirkland.

Besides, there was something else Kate wanted to talk to the boss about before she left. "I haven't worked the counter for a few days. Did Donald Wellington ever show up?"

"Nope. I sent that letter back yesterday. I get that it's tradition and whatnot, but you'd think the FBI would have other ways of getting ahold of people nowadays. After all, they're the FBI."

"True. But maybe they already have. Maybe that letter, whatever it was about, was just a formality. Or when they didn't get a quick notification that Donald had signed for it, they started working other channels."

"Well, they have plenty. I'm sure they got in touch with him days ago, and everything's fine." Roberta seemed eager to reassure herself, as well as Kate.

"You know, when I called Sheriff Preston about what you noticed at the Wellingtons' place, I couldn't get a read on him at all. I mean, if it was news to him, or if he'd already gotten wind of it, somehow."

Kate began to tally the cash in the register's drawer. "I guess having a good poker face is part of the job; or, in that case, a good poker voice."

Roberta shrugged and stared out at the darkening skies. "Who knows what's going on around here?" She glanced at the lobby's clock. "The others should be trickling in soon. I'll tell them the same thing: get home as soon as you can."

Kate hadn't been outside since just after one, when she'd finished up a shorter-than-expected route south of town. A vicious gust of wind slapped her face as she exited the post office, and she was glad to get inside her car and crank the heat.

"You never give me any trouble." She patted Bertha's dash. "We got through our first winter together just fine. And the mud hasn't stopped us yet."

A few stray raindrops soon pelted the windshield, and the skies opened up with a bone-chilling rain just as they left town. Kate shivered as she rolled the window down at her own mailbox, and she was soaked after her mad dash from the garage to the enclosed back porch.

Hazel met her in the kitchen, her dark eyes dancing with welcome.

"I hope you blew off some steam in the yard this afternoon," Kate told the dog as she pulled off her damp coat. Charlie was already nestled in his bolstered bed by the hearth. "I'll light a fire for us as soon as everybody gets fed."

Kate's chore coat and boots were dusted with the first flakes of snow by the time she made it to the machine shed.

"No, I didn't forget about you guys," she said in answer to the Three Mouseketeers' demands for lots of pets and more food, in that order. Water and dry kibble were always available under the heat lamps, but they loved to pretend they had suffered greatly all day whenever Kate arrived with their dinner.

While Patches now allowed Kate to touch her, she refused to beg for attention and never wanted to be held. More than once, Kate had caught a fleeting expression of confusion on the calico's face, as if Patches half-expected someone very different to enter this shed.

"Do you miss Minnie?" Kate asked Patches while she refreshed the water bowl. "What a shock it must have been for you to walk all the way home, then find a different lady in charge around here." She gently stroked the cat's wide flanks. "Sweetie, you're as big as a house! Or more like, a machine shed."

Kate briefly considered staging some sort of "catnapping," but ultimately decided against it. Patches was too wily to be easily tricked into a carrier. Such an attempt was likely to be met with wailing and thrashing, and Kate didn't want the mama-to-be to harm herself or her kittens in the process.

And even if Kate could get lucky enough to force Patches into confinement, the cat would dart out the porch door the second an opportunity presented itself.

A gust of wind-driven snow sighed around the northwest corner of the building, and Kate shook her head.

"I wish you'd come to the house right now, just in case. With this weather ..."

But Patches turned her back on Kate, and focused on her supper.

* * *

Charlie had his coat brushed to his liking, then returned to his hearthside bed for the rest of the evening. Hazel had taken over the big chair, and watched the merry flames with half-closed eyes.

Kate lounged on the couch, but she couldn't seem to relax. While she streamed one of her favorite shows, she scrolled social media and kept an eye on the time. The snow was falling fast and thick now, and wet flakes splattered against the farmhouse's windows.

"I know I was out there twenty minutes ago, but I'm going to check again," she announced just before eight. "I have a feeling tonight's the night."

The back porch's floorboards were ice cold under Kate's thick socks. She peered out into the faint gloom provided by the yard light, and scanned the steps for any sign of Patches. None. She even opened the storm door and looked toward the garage and the machine shed. This time, she left the porch light on before going back into the kitchen.

There was no cat at eight-thirty; but fifteen minutes later, Kate heard Patches' demanding yowl as soon as she stepped out of the kitchen.

"Get in here!" Kate didn't have to say it twice. Patches slipped into the back porch, her coat flecked with snow, and waddled toward the tote banked with soft towels.

"I have everything ready," Kate promised as the cat sniffed every corner of the box and its contents. "See the heat lamp? It's really cold tonight, though. How about I warm some of those towels in the dryer and rebuild that nest?"

Patches answered Kate in her own way ... by going to the kitchen door and letting out another demanding yowl.

"Are you serious?" Kate was suspicious. "You don't even like to be held! Do you really want to go *all the way inside*? Your friend Hazel is in there, but you haven't met Charlie. And I don't think he'd like you moving in, not one bit."

What if Patches became frantic, bolted around the house, and hid under the furniture? Charlie would be furious. Hazel would think it was all a game, and start dashing around herself, barking and carrying on. This was a catastrophe in the making.

But Patches was right. Even with a heat lamp, this back porch was too damp and chilly on such a snowy night. The cat looked up at Kate again. This time, there was a pleading note in her guttural meows.

Could Kate herd her into the basement? The cellar door was only a few steps from the kitchen's entrance. If Patches was out of sight, Charlie wouldn't mind so much. And it would be warm down in the furnace room, far better than it was out here.

"OK," Kate finally said. "I don't know if this is a good idea, but we're going to try. Give me a few minutes."

Patches' growing discomfort meant she was less agile than usual, and Kate managed to slip around her to get inside. She readied a space next to the furnace, then dragged most of the dining-room chairs into the kitchen and draped them with a sheet to create a chute of sorts from the back door to the basement. Hazel watched these preparations with great interest.

"I hope Patches knows what she's doing," Kate told the dog as she checked that things were relatively secure. "Maybe Minnie let her in sometimes? I guess we are about to find out."

Patches darted through as soon as the kitchen door creaked open and, after a split-second pause of confusion when faced with a wall of fabric, quickly aimed for the only exit available. Kate made sure the calico was on her way down the steps, then shut the door.

"That was easy. Maybe too easy." But Kate already felt better.

Karen had said it was unlikely Patches would need assistance once she went into labor. But Kate knew she'd be checking on the calico several times throughout the night.

She brought the makeshift bed and heat lamp in from the back porch, and took them down to where Patches was hiding behind the furnace ducts.

"You have a warm spot there, huh?" By the way the cat moved, and the look in her eyes, Kate sensed Patches was already in the early stages of labor. "I'll warm these towels in the dryer while I work up a litter box. I'll bring down some food and water, too."

Charlie met her on the other side of the basement door, his thick coat standing on end. "Calm down, it'll be OK." Kate tried to soothe her boy with some pets, but he caught Patches' scent on her hands and gave a polite growl. "How about you go back in by the fire and forget she's in your house?"

Hazel's reaction was the opposite. She whimpered at the basement door while Kate worked, eager to get down to where all the action would take place. "No, you need to stay up here. I know you two are friends, but Patches needs her space right now."

Kate programmed a set of alarms on her phone at bedtime, then stumbled downstairs several times overnight to see how the delivery was progressing. During her three-thirty trek to the basement, she found an exhausted-but-proud Patches nestled in her tote with four tiny, wriggling newborns. Kate was mostly relieved, but a little excited, too.

Now the question was: how long would Patches want to

stay in the basement? It would be weeks before the kittens would be old enough, and the weather warm enough, for them to move out to the machine shed. And until then, Hazel would want to be on one side of the basement door, downstairs watching the babies; and Charlie would guard the other side, grumbling his disapproval of this uninvited guest.

Kate suddenly felt really, really tired.

"Let's just go back to bed," she told Charlie and Hazel when she returned to the kitchen. "We all need to get some rest. It's going to be very interesting around here for some time to come."

* * *

Morning brought weak rays of sunshine that promised to melt all the snow within a day or two. It was hard to tell, thanks to last night's wind, but Kate suspected the total at her farm was closer to four inches. As she cleared the sidewalk and scooped the drifts away from the garage door, she hoped this would be the last time she'd need this kind of shovel until at least November.

The other mail carriers felt the same.

"I'm so tired of winter," Marge grumbled as she unloaded a container of oatmeal-raisin cookies on one of the back room's counters. "It put me in a baking mood last night, sure; but I can do that on my own when I really feel like it."

Jack reached for a cookie and nodded his thanks. "These are perfect. They'll hit the spot on a day like today."

"We need to be careful," Jared reminded the group as he helped himself to a treat. "That was a heavy, wet snow; and it's supposed to hit fifty tomorrow afternoon. The roads are going to be a mess until things dry out."

Everyone groaned. "I'll need another of these to face that," Jack said as he picked up a second cookie. "Jared's right, though. We're in for several tough rounds of big thaws during the day, then refreezes at night."

"Can't we just fast forward to May?" Allison wanted to know. "I mean, that's only ten days away now. We'll be good by then."

"Oh, I don't know." Randy had his doubts. "About a decade ago, we had that one snowstorm that ..."

"Shhh!" Marge waved her hands in a beseeching manner. "Let's not jinx ourselves, OK?"

It wasn't just the mail carriers that had spring fever. The arrival of Patches' kittens had made it clear to Kate that Hazel needed to get out of the house, if only for a few days.

A quick chat with Roberta garnered Kate permission to have a doggie co-pilot starting Monday. Kate had Randy's town route tomorrow, so she'd need to hoof that one on her own.

"Hazel's coming in? That's wonderful news!" Allison said after Kate made her announcement. "You're right; she can sense that those sweet kittens are in the basement. Poor Patches won't get a moment's peace if Hazel keeps begging at the door, wanting to go down there and sniff them."

"Charlie doesn't seem to have any interest in the maternity ward," Kate told her co-workers. "I think he'll try to ignore our guests and stick to his routine. But it's just as well that Hazel has to tough it out today and tomorrow, as well as Sunday. I'm hoping the novelty will wear off, and she'll decide it's more fun to go out into the yard and get dirty."

"Thanks for taking my shift," Randy said. "We're going out of town on Sunday, so I'd like to get some things done around the house tomorrow." He gazed out the nearest window. "Of course, all this snow means I can't work outside like I'd planned."

Allison nodded in sympathy. "We're at the mercy of Mother Nature this time of year. All year, actually." Then she grinned at Kate. "But I can't wait to see Hazel again! It's been too long."

15

Hazel whimpered with excitement on Monday morning as Kate packed her travel harness, snacks, and a few doggie toys in a canvas tote bag.

"Yeah, you get to ride along today! Tomorrow, too; and maybe one or two more days after that."

Kate already had Bertha's back seat covered with an old blanket, and Hazel didn't need any encouragement to jump into the mail car. As they passed Gwen's place, Hazel pushed her nose against the closed window to get a better view of her friend Maisie, Gwen's black-and-white Collie.

Maisie was romping in the Ashfords' yard this morning, which was dotted with puddles and dirty tufts of leftover snow. Hazel's eager whimper told Kate it was time to set up a play date sometime soon.

"Maisie's going to get terribly muddy," Kate reminded Hazel, even though she knew that was exactly what her dog wanted to do, too. "She'll be a mess by the time she goes inside. I'm hoping you won't end up the same way today, but I have plenty of old towels, just in case."

Hazel's arrival was greeted with cheers from the post-office crew. She lapped up all the attention while Kate sorted parcels and letters for her route, then was eager for a potty break out back before they started their rounds.

As Kate and Hazel made their way north and west out of town, it was clear that the signs and sounds of spring had returned: Birds perched on fence posts trilled their melodies, residents raked the last of the dead leaves from their lawns, and farm cats of all colors and sizes absorbed the sun's strengthening rays from sidewalks and patios.

The felines lolling about made Kate ponder Patches' future. There was no doubt the calico would stay on after her kittens had left for their permanent homes, but would Patches ever drop the queen act and fit in with the rest of Kate's furry tribe?

And what about Moose? Would a case of spring fever cause Alex's big brown tabby to strike out on his own again?

Alex had made sure Moose was neutered and had received all his vaccinations. Moose seemed devoted to his new cat dad, and grateful for all the comforts of an indoor life. But Kate knew Moose was driven by his instincts, just like Patches. If they told him to pack up and move out, would he leave, or would he stay?

While Kate wondered about Moose, she wasn't going to reach out to find out what was going on. Not about the cat, or anything else about Alex, for that matter. She still missed him, but the pain had eased as the days rolled on.

"It's a new season," Kate reminded herself as much as Hazel. "Time for a fresh start, right? If it wasn't meant to be, then ... well, I guess it's better I found that out early on."

Kate was about to add, *before my heart got too involved*, but it was no use. That had happened months ago; and it was something she hadn't been able to fully see, to really face, until things were already over.

Like most people, Kate could offer a little falsehood from time to time when it seemed necessary. But she'd never lie to her dog.

They dropped another package and completed a few more miles of mailbox stops, then Kate turned down a rather-familiar road. She smiled and blinked back sudden tears when she saw the "for sale" sign posted at the end of one acreage's driveway.

"Oh, Milton, it's really happening! It's still a sellers' market, so I bet your home won't be available for too long before it's snapped up."

Hazel was watching Kate closely from the back seat. Suddenly, Kate had to laugh.

"See that barn?" she pointed up the lane as they rolled past. "This was Milton Benniger's place, where the Three Mouseketeers used to live. Scout used to hang out down here by the mailbox from time to time."

They dropped two parcels at another farm, then more mail at the end of several driveways, and soon started down a slight slope toward one of the countless creek culverts that crisscrossed Rockwell Township.

The roads were slowly improving, and the sunshine of the past few days had certainly helped. The higher areas dried out first, of course, but the dips were still pockmarked with ruts. Kate edged Bertha to the right as she followed the soft tracks in the gravel, then braked carefully as they glided over the bridge.

"The next stop is the MacGregors' place," Kate told Hazel. "Their chocolate Lab is named Brownie. Actually, I think Mae said they have another dog, too. Maybe a Golden Retriever?" Kate shrugged. "He's probably a mix, though; not a purebred. Just like you, most farm dogs ..."

Bertha wasn't going very fast; but Kate soon realized that might be a problem. There was a slight rise in the road up ahead, an incline so subtle that most people probably didn't notice it. Kate stepped on the gas, but it was too late.

The front tires pulled to the right and, in a sudden spray of mud and gravel, Bertha jerked to a stop.

"Oh, no. This is not good." Kate closed her eyes for a second as Hazel began to bark in the back seat. "It's OK," Kate chirped as she put the car into reverse. "I'll just back up a little, and we'll steer out of it."

Bertha moved, but only by a few inches. She was now more crooked in the road than she'd been before. Kate tried again, cranked the wheel this way and that, but it was no use.

"Yep, we're stuck! Hold tight, I'll be right back."

As soon as she opened her door, Kate knew it was bad. Bertha was mired down something terrible. Kate could now see that an especially large vehicle, probably some sort of field machinery, had recently chewed this stretch of gravel in a bid to get out of the tough spot Kate currently found herself in.

"I think they made it out on their own." She studied the way the tracks moved forward, then finally met up with the middle of the road. "But they dug it up in the process. And I'm too close to the ditch to try the same."

She got her rubber boots out of the trunk. But she couldn't steer Bertha out of the muck and push from the back at the same time.

Kate almost had to laugh at the hopeless possibility of Hazel somehow being able to give the car a little gas while Kate leaned against the trunk. Her dog was smart, but ...

Hazel was restless in the back seat, and kept looking out the windows. *Why aren't we moving? What's going on?*

"I'd better call Roberta." Kate reached for her phone. "We're going to need some help."

Eagle River's only auto body shop offered towing services, thank goodness. But they had only one truck, so it might be a while since the gravel roads were such a mess.

The MacGregors were still a ways off, as there were no farmsteads between here and the next crossroads. But Bertha had just stopped at the Bischoffs' place, and Kate had spotted a car in that yard. She wondered if she and Hazel would be better to stay with Bertha, or if she should leash up Hazel and start out for their last stop. Did the Bischoffs have a dog? Kate hadn't seen one today, but wasn't sure.

Roberta advised Kate to stay where she was, at least for now.

"I'll call it in. Maybe it won't take the garage very long to come out and give you a pull." Then Roberta laughed. "I bet Hazel wants out of that car! She'd have a blast in all that mud."

"Well, I'm already a mess," Kate said wryly. "She might as well be, too. And Bertha's sprayed with slop from bumper to bumper."

Kate got Hazel into her travel harness, and they decamped to the side of the road. Despite the pinch they were in, it was a beautiful day.

Kate pulled out some treats for Hazel, then two of Marge's cookies for herself. The leftovers had spent the weekend in the post office's fridge, so they were still fresh. Jack had been right; they would go perfectly with a cup of coffee.

But as Kate eyed the tangle of rotten, dead weeds in both roadside ditches, she set her insulated mug aside. She couldn't risk needing a bathroom break until they made it back to town.

Roberta called with the news that a tow truck would soon be on the way. That made Kate feel better.

"I'm lucky this hasn't happened already this spring," she told Hazel, who didn't even look up from where she was sniffing the road's soft shoulder. "Last year, it was May by the time I started, and the roads had all dried out by then."

Kate shook her head as she finished her first cookie. "In a few weeks, I'll have my one-year anniversary with this post office. Where has the time gone?"

A blue pickup truck appeared over the crest of the next hill, and Kate tightened her grip on Hazel's leash. She waved, and got a wave in return. And then, the truck stopped and a middle-aged man got out. He shook his head in sympathy as he stared at Bertha.

"Man, that's a tough break. She's wedged in there tight,

for sure. I told my wife, the county needs to fix this spot right away! I called it in last night, but who knows when they'll get a grader out here? By the way, I'm Clark Dittmar."

Kate introduced herself, and Hazel, too.

"My, that's a fine-looking dog you have there. German Shepherd?"

"Mostly." Kate couldn't help but smile. "At least, she claims to be."

Clark adjusted his worn baseball cap and laughed. "Ours are mutts, too. No telling, really, what they are. I say, those DNA tests are a waste of money. A good dog is a good dog. A piece of paper can't tell you that."

He walked over to Bertha's front bumper, then came back.

"Tell you what. I know you said there's a tow on the way, but it might be awhile. I'm less than a mile from here. I need to get these groceries home, but I'll come back with the tractor."

Kate raised her eyebrows in surprise and relief. "Are you sure? You think you can get us out?"

"Sure do." He grinned. "My brother George used to deliver the mail, way back when. I know you folks are on a tight schedule. It's too wet to get in the fields right now, anyway. Might as well have a little fun. Hold tight."

"Did you hear that?" Kate asked Hazel as Clark drove away. "We've found ourselves a Good Samaritan. Well, he's probably a *bored* one, too. But it doesn't matter."

Not long after Kate gave Roberta an update, a massive green tractor appeared over the hill. Clark was back, and he'd brought two of the thickest log chains Kate had ever seen. Hazel began to bark, sensing that something exciting was about to happen.

"I'm going to winch it up from the front," Clark called over the rumble of the tractor. "You girls hop back in. Once I'm in the cab, I'll signal when it's time to give it some gas."

There were a few hair-raising moments, as Clark hollered instructions to Kate while Hazel offered her two cents' worth from the back seat. But after a few forceful jerks, Bertha was finally back in the center of the road.

Clark waved away Kate's offer of payment, even after she reminded him that Roberta would expense it to the federal government. He did, however, allow her to give him two free packs of stamps.

"Those are worth their weight in gold these days," he said, and Kate had to admit that was just about right.

* * *

"Hazel's getting quite the job-shadowing experience these days," Jack said as the carriers gathered for their Wednesday-afternoon staff meeting. "Today was, what? Three in a row? A few more rounds out on the road, and she could just about be our newest sub."

"Well, she has the people skills for the job," Kate said as Hazel soaked up attention from the other carriers.

There wasn't time to run the dog home before the meeting, so Hazel was going to lounge in her favorite back corner while the rest of the staff gathered around the break room's table. "But I think the driver's license thing might trip her up."

Kate had granted Hazel several short, supervised visits with Patches and the kittens, and the dog finally seemed less interested in keeping her nose to the kitchen side of the basement door. The novelty of those new, if temporary, roommates had apparently worn off, and just in time.

While Bertha didn't seem too worse for wear after being winched out of the muck, Roberta still insisted Eugene's Garage give the mail car a once-over. That meant counter duty for Kate tomorrow, and a full day at home for Hazel.

"I just hope Bertha sails through her checkup," Kate told Jack as they took their seats. "We don't exactly have a whole fleet of mail trucks at our disposal if she needs to sit out for more than a day."

"Oh, Roberta will work some of her magic if that happens," Jack promised. "We'll figure something out."

Bev soon came in, and took a seat next to Kate.

"Any news?" Kate asked. Bev shook her head, and Kate could tell it wasn't just because Jack would get an earful of anything she said. Since the salacious gossip they'd collected at the Eagle River co-op early last week, neither of the ladies had unearthed any new details about the auction barn.

"But I am wondering about that fancy black SUV in the parking lot," Bev said. "It's not one of our cars, I'm sure of it."

"SUV?" Jack frowned. "I didn't notice anything when I came in. But then, that was twenty minutes ago."

Roberta soon breezed into the break room with a big smile on her face. "Hello, everyone!" She glanced around the table and nodded with satisfaction. "Good, all of you are here. Randy, I really appreciate you coming in on your day off for this meeting."

"What's the deal?" Jared wanted to know. "Do you have big news for us?"

Allison leaned forward. "New uniforms, maybe?"

"I doubt it." Randy shook his head. "I bet we're getting triple pay for overtime."

That brought laughter around the table. Roberta rolled her eyes. "Hell has yet to freeze over, I'm sad to report. No, it's neither of those. Actually, we have a very special guest today." She checked the clock.

"Two, really. One's running late. But the other is here."

The carriers exchanged curious looks. These meetings rarely lasted more than fifteen minutes, and were mostly held to satisfy management requirements. With such a small staff, it was rather easy for Roberta to keep everyone up to speed throughout the week.

"Greta," Roberta called into the short hallway, "we're in

here. Ignore that sign, don't worry about your shoes. Just come on back!"

A woman in a very expensive navy pantsuit strolled into the break room, and deposited a gleaming briefcase on the worn table. Her shoulder-length dark hair included a few elegant streaks of gray. A warm smile spread across her face as she shook Roberta's hand. "Thanks for having me stop by today."

"I'm so glad you could join us. I think it's going to be a big help to my team." Roberta turned back to the carriers. "Everyone, I'd like you to meet Greta Carlisle. She's an investigator from the FBI field office in Waterloo."

Even Jack was speechless.

Bev was the first to recover her composure. "Nice to meet you, Greta. Um, Agent Carlisle, or ..."

"Greta is just fine, thank you." The federal agent was certainly friendly, but there was also a hint of amusement in her brown eyes as she glanced around the table.

And then, there was a knock on the post office's back door.

"Oh, I'll get that," Roberta offered. She and Greta exchanged a glance that Kate couldn't quite read. "That must be our other special guest."

The carriers stared at each other, and the federal agent, as they waited for Roberta to return. While they were surprised and confused, Greta Carlisle was the opposite. She calmly opened her briefcase and rifled through its contents.

"We'll get started shortly. I'm sure all of you are eager to finish your tasks and head home on this lovely spring afternoon."

Roberta soon returned, with Ray Calcott trailing a few steps behind.

"Chief Calcott!" Greta exclaimed as if she'd just bumped into her best friend. "I'm so glad you could get away long enough to join us today."

Ray Calcott nodded solemnly at Greta as he took the last empty chair. "Yes, thank you. Ma'am."

It was difficult, but Kate managed to keep herself from snorting or laughing. There was an obvious pecking order at this meeting. Outranked by two federal employees, Eagle River's police chief clearly understood he was last on the list.

Calcott glanced nervously around the room as he removed his jacket. Kate couldn't be sure, but had she just felt a glare aimed in her direction? Bev elbowed her, and Kate decided she'd been right.

As soon as she'd acknowledged the police chief, Greta had turned back to Roberta.

"Postmaster Schupp, I was thrilled to hear from you last week. Due to the situation here in Eagle River, I agree this is the perfect time for a little refresher course on what information postal carriers can, and can't, share with others."

Bev elbowed Kate again as Chief Calcott stared at the floor.

"And we do have one other item to discuss today, albeit briefly," Agent Carlisle said. "I can confirm that federal investigators are assisting with an embezzlement case connected to a local business. Financial transactions in this digital age are nearly always handled electronically, which increases the probability that some of the unaccounted-for funds may have crossed state lines."

All the carriers leaned forward, eager to hear more. A few staff members raised their eyebrows in surprise.

This possibility wasn't news to Kate and Bev. Or to Roberta. It was the same for Chief Calcott. But his glum expression made it clear his role in this high-profile case had been shoved to a back burner.

"Is that something we are allowed to tell people?" Randy was almost bouncing in his chair. "But if it's classified ..."

"Oh, no, you're fine," Greta promised him.

"One of the bureau's most-important tasks is to help

coordinate the investigation of multi-state cases."

The degree to which the FBI was involved in such situations varied widely, Agent Carlisle said, as it depended on the severity of the case. She wasn't at liberty to discuss the bureau's specific role in this embezzlement investigation, or provide any further details.

Kate knew that no press conferences had been held regarding the investigation, and not a word had appeared in the local or regional media. That was common in embezzlement cases, according to what Kate had read online. Most of the time, nothing official was shared with the public until charges had already been filed.

"But there is one other thing I want to tell you today," Greta said. "This complicated situation is in excellent hands. Countless experts from the local, regional, and state levels are working together, and with us, to seek justice in this case."

As she continued to speak, Agent Carlisle made eye contact with each of the carriers in turn. "In fact, I encourage you to share that as you see fit. Many people are concerned about this situation, for many reasons. We want them to know it is being taken seriously."

"We'll help out in any way we can," Roberta promised.

Greta gave the postmaster a big smile. "Wonderful! We federal employees are all on the same team. Roberta claims she has the best crew west of the Mississippi in her office," Greta told the carriers. "And I like to say the same about our people. So, there you go."

Kate had wondered exactly how many strings Roberta had pulled to get a federal agent to attend this weekly huddle. But now, it was clear why Greta Carlisle had been eager to meet with them this afternoon. The FBI had a message they wanted to share with the Eagle River community. What better way to spread the word than to involve their counterparts at the post office?

Greta now pulled a sleek laptop from her briefcase. Next

came a hefty stack of paper that was soon revealed to be copies of a memo for everyone in the room, including the police chief.

"We're a little old school at the bureau," Greta said with a self-deprecating laugh as the paperwork was passed around. "Email has its place, of course; but I wanted to make sure everyone had a hard copy for their files."

"Thirty pages?" Bev whispered to Kate. "I hope there's not going to be a quiz."

Agent Carlisle spent the next half hour leading an in-depth, tedious review of the single-spaced document. It all boiled down to this: While there were a few exceptions, federal privacy laws generally prohibited members of the postal service from opening mail, or sharing information visible on the outside of packages and letters.

Common sense, obviously. But Agent Carlisle and Postmaster Schupp still seemed determined to drill that concept into the minds of everyone in the room, including (or perhaps, especially) Chief Calcott.

Kate noticed more than a few yawns hidden behind hands around the table. Her own attention kept wandering ahead to what sort of dinner she could make out of what was in her fridge, and when Patches and her babies might need a larger tote with taller sides. The kittens would be one week old tomorrow, and Kate hadn't decided on names yet ...

"That is something very important for all of us to remember," Agent Carlisle was saying. "Even members of law enforcement are subject to these rules. They must file a warrant to obtain access to information that passes through the postal system, and that request has to be approved by a judge."

Roberta jumped in. "And that is something I must oversee. Proper protocol needs to be followed. As you know, the post office has its own team of inspectors, as well." She smiled at each of her carriers in turn, but ignored the police chief. "If you ever have any questions, come to me. I'll sort it out."

Chief Calcott seemed to be staring at the floor. Or was he? Kate couldn't see his hands from across the table, and suspected he was checking his phone.

"Before I go," Greta said, "I'll remind all of you that these federal guidelines only apply to information that passes directly through the postal service. I urge you to keep your eyes and ears open for any leads that don't originate from the packages and letters you handle as carriers."

The federal agent reached back into her briefcase, then handed around her business cards.

"If you come across anything that might be helpful to the case, no matter how small it may seem, please let me know. And encourage everyone else to do the same."

As the meeting came to a close, Chief Calcott shook hands with Roberta and Greta, then quickly made his exit.

Only after he was gone did Kate realize Agent Carlisle had not specifically mentioned alerting *local* law enforcement about any leads. One could always do that, of course. Was it so obvious that Greta hadn't felt the need to mention it? Or was there some slight included in her message?

Either way, Bev was delighted as she pocketed the federal agent's card.

"Clyde's always telling me I should mind my own business," she told Kate. "'Leave it to the authorities,' he says. Well! Wait until I tell him I'm collecting evidence under a special order of the FBI. That'll take him down a notch or two."

16

Eugene nodded at Kate, then pointed at the door that opened into the auto shop's garage bays. "You can head on back. I think she's just about ready to go."

"Great, thanks." Kate smiled, but she wasn't exactly thrilled. Bertha might be "just about ready to go," but Kate's mail car had needed a front-line adjustment after their adventure on the muddy country roads.

Kate reminded herself that it could have been worse. And Bertha had now received her seasonal checkup, oil change, and brake inspection, too. She shouldn't have to bring Bertha back for several months ... if they managed to stay out of trouble.

Kate's mood brightened a bit when she stepped into the garage part of the shop. Because a somewhat-familiar face had just grinned at her from under Bertha's propped-open hood.

"Hey, Brody! I didn't know you were working here again."

"I sure am." Brody Donegan straightened up in a smooth move that easily cleared Bertha's hood. "I'm full time now," he said proudly. "Have been since December."

"I'm glad to hear that. Between this, and farming with your dad ..."

"Yep, things are looking up. An apartment's next on the

list. The parents are fine and all, but I'm determined to get my own place again."

The Donegans lived a few miles east of Kate, but Brody was the sole owner of a parcel just south of her farm that had been in his family for generations. While the house was long gone, the old barn had remained standing.

Until last fall, when an arsonist set it ablaze.

But the destruction of his family's old barn was only the start of Brody's troubles. Before the flames had even been smothered, gossip in and around Eagle River pointed the finger right at Brody himself. Insurance money had been the alleged motive, even though the long-vacant barn had been in such terrible shape that it carried hardly any value at all.

Even so, the scrutiny had been difficult for a young man who hadn't had many opportunities in life, and was trying so hard to make the best of the few available to him.

"I like her name," Brody said now as he gave Bertha a friendly pat on the left headlight. "It suits her just fine."

Kate shrugged. "The name came with the car. But thanks! She's normally very reliable, but we got into a tight spot on Monday, as you know."

"Oh, you're far from the first one we've had this spring. The gravel's been a mess for weeks."

"I'm eager for real spring to get here, and stay. Not the mud season."

Brody nodded. "Me, too. Of course, it won't last long. Before we know it, it'll be hot and humid, and we'll complain about that, too. Anyway, let me show you what to look and listen for, just in case you get stuck again."

Kate leaned on Bertha's front frame with Brody as he pointed out various things under the hood.

"Sounds good," she told him. "I'll keep an eye on her. I feel so much better knowing everything's fixed, and fixed right."

"I wish we could say the same about the auction barn

mess." Brody frowned. "My uncle used to work there, long ago. He's never had a bad word to say about the Wheelers. It's a shame. And one of my buddies works there now; he's worried he might lose his job before this is all over."

"Can he work on cars? If he's half as competent as you, then ..."

Brody's grin was back, but it vanished quickly. "Thanks; I wish it were that easy. But Eugene's full-up on staff. Unless someone quits, I don't think we'll have any openings for a long time." He raised his chin. "I'm definitely not going anywhere."

"Hopefully something will shake loose soon with the embezzlement case," Kate told Brody as she recalled Dylan's desperation to help his dad. Money was important, but some things were priceless. "I've heard there are several people working on it, on many levels. Maybe someone will come forward with the information the experts need to solve those crimes."

Brody looked down at his dusty work boots, then turned away to check Bertha's windshield washer fluid reservoir. It was an odd thing to do, Kate thought, as the semi-transparent tank showed he'd already filled it to the top line.

Was he stalling for some reason? From the look of concentration on his face, Kate suspected Brody was carefully weighing something that was on his mind. She decided to wait quietly, and see if he would speak.

"So ..." he finally said. "What if somebody knows something, and ..." Then he shook his head. "Scratch that. They don't *know*, but something doesn't seem right. And they aren't sure what to do about it?"

Two other mechanics were at work in the bays, and country music was blasting from the sound system in the corner. Eugene came out of the front office with an elderly woman in tow, and Kate waited until they'd walked past and reached the end car before she spoke.

"What exactly do you mean?" she asked Brody in a low voice. Kate was grateful for Bertha's propped-open hood, which gave her and Brody some privacy. Because her younger neighbor was certainly struggling with something.

Brody glanced around the garage, then leaned in. "Well, I was at a party Saturday night. You know, the rural kind. Out in a pasture in the middle of nowhere, some pickup trucks, a couple coolers full of beer, some girls."

"Like a bro-country song?" Kate couldn't resist as she gestured toward the closest speaker.

"Yeah, exactly. But everyone was legal." Then he backtracked. "Well, I think they were all old enough to drink. Whatever, I didn't plan it. It's not that, though. There was something like thirty people there already, quite a crowd, and then these three guys showed up that I didn't know. But Jaimie knew them, I guess. That's my buddy at the auction barn."

"So, what happened?" Kate expected to hear about some sort of argument. Maybe over a girl, or who'd brought the nasty, cheap beer.

"Well, everyone was getting really lit. And these guys? They were cool, I guess. But then they were whispering about something amongst themselves, you know? And then they started laughing, and getting loud." Brody wiped his hands on his work pants.

"The one dude said to his friends, 'make hay while the sun shines,' and they laughed harder and toasted each other like it was the smartest thing any of them had ever said."

Kate frowned even as she chuckled. "That's strange. People say the stupidest stuff when they're drunk."

"Tell me about it. This went on for a few minutes. They were repeating it back and forth like it was something really important, like it had real meaning for them, you know? It was so strange." Brody rolled his eyes. "Maybe it's nothing. It's just an old saying; my grandpa was fond of it."

Kate had heard it, too, if not often. But it wasn't the sort of thing she'd expect some young guys to say to each other while drinking beer in a field.

But slang had evolved over the years, like everything else. If Kate had attended that very-same party, she probably wouldn't have understood half of what people ten years her junior were chattering about.

"'Make hay while the sun shines,' huh?" Kate turned the phrase over in her mind, several times. "Well, I guess it means, 'get it while you can.'"

And then, she realized it could be the sort of vulgar comment drunk young guys would make at such a party. "I can't believe I'm asking this, but ... how many girls were there?"

"You know, I thought that myself, for about a second. But it wasn't about *that*, I'm sure of it. It was more like ... some sort of secret code to them."

"Like a password?" Kate was intrigued. "And you think one of them works at the auction barn?"

"I'm sure of it. Mitch, Mike ..." Brody shook his head. "I can't remember; we were barely introduced. All I know is that one of them works with Jaimie."

"What did they look like?"

"Like normal dudes, I guess. I've never seen any of them before in my life. And they were all wearing ball caps and hooded sweatshirts, since it was kinda cold. Everyone else was, too. We had a few battery lanterns, but otherwise it was pitch dark out there. You know, so we wouldn't get caught."

Other than one of the guys working for the Wheelers, Kate couldn't see how the situations could possibly be connected.

But she could see why Brody was still pondering it, days later.

He was right; there was something odd about their behavior. How they kept repeating that one phrase amongst themselves, and toasting each other as if they had something to celebrate.

Or ... were they commiserating about something good, *really good*, that maybe was about to come to an end?

"I couldn't pick those dudes out of a lineup, but I know what I heard." Brody was certain on that point. "That was exactly what they were saying. I'd had a few, myself, but I hold my booze pretty well."

He crossed his arms. "Then my girlfriend started picking this silly fight with me, and that ruined the fun, you know? She got mad and said she wanted to leave, go to her house where it was warm. We took off soon after that."

Kate was glad to see none of the other mechanics were paying attention to this conversation. She and Brody were still discussing car stuff, as far as anyone else in the shop knew.

"Maybe you should tell someone. It's a small thing, and you aren't sure if it means anything. But what if it does? If you ..."

"No way." Brody stared at the concrete floor. "Nope. I can't. Not after last time."

Then he looked at Kate with resentment in his eyes. "You know how that went down. I was guilty, everyone said so. Judged and shamed even though I was actually a victim."

Kate wasn't surprised Brody felt that way. Even so, she tried again.

"It could be an anonymous tip. You overheard something at a party; it has nothing to do with you. Like you said, dozens of people were there. Chief Calcott ..."

Brody gave a rueful snort. "Calcott pulled me over for going thirty-eight in a thirty-five last year. He laughed as he worked up my ticket. I'm not talking to him."

Kate thought of Agent Carlisle, but knew Brody was too distrustful to reach out to federal investigators, either. She had only one card left to play.

"Well, Sheriff Preston is a good guy."

Brody seemed to consider that option, but finally discarded it as well. And then, his face lit up with an idea. "Maybe there's another way to go about it. I mean, if you'd ..."

"Me? I wasn't there. I didn't hear it."

"That doesn't matter. You said yourself, it would be an anonymous tip." The sudden hope in Brody's voice made Kate's stomach sink. "Just say you heard it while on a route. Or, I don't know, anywhere but here."

In other words, *anything that leaves me out of it.*

"You know," Brody said, "I've always meant to thank you for speaking up like you did, in the fall. You noticed something then, and you told the authorities." He swallowed hard. "It meant everything to me, to have my name cleared in the end. I just ... thanks for doing that."

"You're most welcome." Kate smiled at her neighbor, and wished she knew him and his family better. "I did what I felt was right, I guess."

Eugene wandered past, and gave Brody a questioning look. Brody was a talented mechanic; Kate didn't want his boss to think he was dawdling, dragging his feet about getting back to work. She needed to leave.

"Just think about it," she told Brody as he dropped Bertha's hood.

He shrugged. "You do the same, OK?"

Kate accepted her keys when Brody held them out, but didn't make any promises about anything else. "Thanks again for fixing up Bertha. And tell your parents I said hello."

* * *

Kate barely saw Main Street slide past as she headed through town. At the lone stoplight she turned east toward home, her mind still focused on the twists and turns of her conversation with Brody.

He was right, and Kate knew it.

"Make hay while the sun shines" was indeed some sort of code, a shorthand ... but for what, exactly?

At least one of those guys worked at the auction barn, maybe more than one. Maybe they weren't involved in anything directly. Maybe they'd just overheard a few things.

"But they were celebrating, gloating about something." Kate gripped Bertha's steering wheel tighter as she turned off on her gravel road. She slowed at the end of Gwen's lane to wave to her neighbor, who was grubbing last summer's dead plants out of her front flowerbeds.

Of course, there was always the possibility Brody wasn't telling Kate everything he knew, or suspected. How drunk had he been that night, really? Was it possible he'd actually recognized Jaimie's coworker, even the other guys, but refused to admit it?

After all, Brody was trying his hardest to stay out of it. Even so, what he'd told Kate felt like it was the truth. And that was something she couldn't ignore.

"Make hay while the sun shines," she recited as she eased Bertha over the creek bridge.

"Get it while you can. Make hay ..."

Scout was at the end of Kate's driveway, waiting for her to come home. She stopped in the lane to check the mailbox and, while she tussled with Bertha's door latch and the stack of mail in her arms, the big tuxedo cat slipped inside the car.

"Too lazy to walk up to the house, huh?" Kate set the pile next to Scout on the passenger seat. "You're in charge of the mail, then. I see Jerry and Maggie up by the garage, waiting for me like civilized cats."

Hazel soon bounded around the back corner of the machine shed, her flanks splashed with muck. Kate sighed as she started for the house. "I'll get the towels. Meet me inside the back porch in five, Miss Hazel."

As she wiped the dog down for the umpteenth time that week, Kate continued to ponder what Brody had told her. All through chores, and dinner and dishes, she tried again and again to piece together what it all meant, if anything.

If she was even going to consider speaking up, Kate wanted to have some sort of idea where that might lead.

"But I shouldn't worry about that," she reminded herself while she cleaned Patches' basement litter box and fussed over the kittens. They now responded to the sound of Kate's voice, as well as their mother's.

"What did I tell Brody? It's really important to pass it on, let the authorities take it from there."

So, then, which authority might she tell?

Kate shared Brody's reticence to talk to Chief Calcott, if for very-different reasons. Agent Carlisle would take this seriously, of course. Even so, Sheriff Preston would likely be the one to get Kate's call.

But it was already after seven. Charlie needed his hair brushed, and Kate yawned as she reached for the novel resting on the coffee table and opened its pages.

"This can wait until tomorrow." She yawned a second time, and wondered if she'd even get through a few chapters before she called it a night. "It's been a long day, and this is a lot to process. 'Make hay while the sun shines' ... that could mean so many different things."

Kate was thinking about it again as she waited to fall asleep. She told Hazel and Charlie goodnight, then silently sent the same message to Patches and her babies in the basement, and the Three Mouseketeers out in the machine shed.

A faint rumble of thunder echoed over the fields as Kate mentally walked her farmhouse one more time. All the curtains were closed, the outside porch lights were on, and both the front and back doors were locked.

Her safety check made her think of Alex, and she sighed over how often her mind still turned toward him. Day and night, if the truth be told. At work, at home. It was odd, really, that they hadn't run into each other somewhere in the past few weeks. Eagle River wasn't exactly a metropolis.

She wondered how he was, what he was doing. There always seemed to be something she'd like to share with him, but couldn't.

Or wouldn't, she reminded herself.

I'm the one who put my foot down and called it quits. Or more like, when he did, I didn't try to convince him otherwise.

"Make hay while the sun shines," she whispered as Charlie settled in next to her pillow, and Hazel snuffled at the foot of the bed.

A few raindrops threw themselves against the bedroom's windowpanes, then the tap-tap-tap picked up in tempo as Kate closed her eyes and tumbled down into a deep sleep.

* * *

Her eyes flew open. The bedroom was nearly invisible in the thick darkness. It was raining harder now, and lightning flashed across the rumbling skies as Kate's heart hammered in her chest.

"Oh, my God!" She wrapped her arms around herself. "Oh no, oh no! What if it's true? What if that's it?"

Somehow in the night, Kate's mind had reached deep; and then it had grasped something that, earlier, it hadn't been able to find.

She reached for her phone. It was much later than she thought, only a few minutes before six in the morning. With a thunderstorm raging outside, there would be no gentle, lovely spring sunrise today.

Kate stared at the wall above the dresser as the pieces fell into place. This theory made sense ... in an amazing, twisted sort of way.

No, it wasn't a theory. Kate couldn't explain it, but she *knew*. Knew she was on to something.

Make hay while the sun shines. Get it while you can ...

Somebody was. Or several somebodies, if Kate's hunch was correct. And she was going to stop them, if she could.

There was only one person that could help her unravel the rest of it, confirm or deny the scenario that played out in her mind. And that hunch was crystal clear now, despite the dreary rain and fog outside.

"He gets up early, I know he does," Kate told Charlie as the cat glared at her with a quizzical expression. She scrolled through her phone's contacts.

I need to talk to you, she texted Auggie. *Today. I think I'm on to something.*

Not even a minute went by before she got an answer.

What's up? You got a lead?

Kate needed to get to the post office; Auggie would soon be on his way to work, too, if he wasn't already there. There wasn't time to talk just now. And then, the weight of what Kate would say, of what she suspected, made her breath catch in her throat.

We need to meet up, was all she told him. *But I shouldn't come to the co-op. Too many ears.*

Is it OK if my family listens in? The ones no longer on Earth, but in it?

Kate's shoulders sagged with relief. Only Auggie would crack a joke like that, and at such an early hour. Yes, it was the right place to go.

Perfect. Anytime midday works for me. Let me know when you're free, and I'll make it work.

* 17 *

This time, Kate beat Auggie to the cemetery. She sat behind Bertha's wheel for a moment and tried to gather her swirling thoughts, but then decided to get out and walk among the graveyard's stones.

The weather this morning matched her mood. The rain had stopped, at least momentarily, but sullen clouds still lowered overhead and a stiff wind roared across the fields.

She'd only told Roberta that she had a "sudden appointment" and needed to take an early lunch.

The postmaster had simply shrugged and nodded, and Kate was relieved when her well-meaning boss didn't inquire about Kate's health or how her family was faring. Because she was too worked up to come up with an innocuous lie.

If Kate was right, this was *big*.

So big, that she'd only given Bev a quick smile this morning and moved on, afraid her face or voice would betray the secret hunch she shouldered alone.

But only for a few more minutes. Auggie would be the first, and maybe the only, person to hear this theory. His reaction, and what else they were able to sort out about the situation, would help Kate decide what to do next.

She stopped pacing long enough to duck under the largest oak tree. Pausing beneath its unfurling leaves allowed her to momentarily escape the worst of the wind.

"He's here." She let out a deep breath when Auggie's work truck crested the hill. "Good. Let's get this over with."

Auggie met her at the gate, and grinned as he edged through the opening between the cattle panel and the fence.

"Goodness gracious, I need to lay off those doughnuts! A few more, and I'll be too fat to slide my way in here. I'll need to get the gate's key from the county. Jerry brought treats for coffee hour this morning, for no real reason. He drove all the way over to Swanton to pick them up, so I couldn't say no. There were some chocolate ones with sprinkles, and that's good enough for me."

Auggie blinked twice when he finally noticed Kate's pained expression.

"What the hell is going on?" he gasped. "I thought you had a good tip. Did something else happen this morning?"

There was no easy way into this conversation. Especially since Kate now suspected one of Auggie's closest business contacts, a man who was likely also his friend, was at the center of all this deception and theft.

"Vernon Millard," Kate shouted over the roar of the wind. "It has to be Vernon!"

A weight lifted off her shoulders as soon as she said it. She knew she was right. But the magnitude of what she'd just said stopped Auggie in his tracks.

He stared at her in disbelief for a few moments. Another gust howled over the ridge, and he clutched his faded cap. "That wind is terrible today," he muttered. "I should have left this thing in the truck."

And then, he shook his head.

"Look, I know you're getting good at this," he said gently. "*Really* good at this. But Vernon's a straight arrow, as straight as they come." Auggie's brows knitted together over his dark-rimmed glasses. "I've known him for, oh, almost forty years. Why, he's a Prosper kid! He was in the same grade as my oldest brother, in school. Vernon and Martha go to our church, he ..."

"Is he the one that told you about the silent partners?"

Auggie didn't answer, even as his eyes widened in surprise.

"He did, didn't he?" Kate gave a rueful laugh. "Yeah, I figured as much. I thought that before, that it had to be one of the co-op guys from around here. And then..."

The questioning look on Auggie's face quickly hardened into anger.

"What have you heard?" He spoke slowly, and bit off the end of every word. "Tell me everything you know."

She explained about the party in the field, about the trio of young guys who showed up, their behavior and what they said. She didn't reveal her source, and Auggie was too focused on the details to care. Maybe later he'd ask for a name, but Kate would never let on that it was Brody. Auggie wasn't the only one who could keep a secret.

"'Make hay while the sun shines,'" she told him as they stood there in the cemetery, their hoods up and their shoulders hunched as they tried to stay warm.

"They kept saying it to each other, over and over, like it was shorthand for something. I couldn't figure it out, at first. And then I realized: Who around here has a personal, vested interest in keeping the auction barn afloat?"

"There's no way the Eagle River co-op could be a silent partner," Auggie reminded her, "it's a nonprofit."

"Of course it is; *officially*," Kate said sarcastically. "But it provides all the feed and bedding for the auction barn, right? On sale days, and if farmers need to bring their animals in the night before. The Wheelers have to stay stocked with feed pellets and oats, and straw, and ..."

"Hay." Auggie placed his hands over his face for a moment. Kate just waited.

"Yes, they do," Auggie said as he stuffed his hands into

his coat pockets. "And yes, the Wheelers pass those charges on to the livestock owners with a reasonable markup for their time and effort." His eyes narrowed. "Maybe the markup isn't as 'reasonable' as what I've been led to believe."

"And Vernon does the books at the co-op, right? He handles everything himself? Money in, money out ..."

Auggie shrugged. "But he answers to the board."

"Do they review the accounts carefully, or not? Do you know?"

"I'm not sure, exactly," Auggie admitted. "But, yeah, Vernon runs the whole show; he has for years. Decades, even."

"They trust him, then, the board. All they see is what Vernon puts in front of them. They probably don't ask any questions."

Kate crossed her arms against the damp air, as well as the fury she saw on Auggie's lined face. "Are you sure Vernon's not hooked in with the Wheelers, somehow? It wouldn't have to be through the co-op; maybe he personally has some sort of long-running deal with the family."

Auggie shook his head. "All he told me was the names I told you."

"A lie of omission, perhaps. Or maybe he told you the truth."

Kate was restless with emotion, a mix of anger and frustration that seemed to match Auggie's mood. She couldn't just stand there any longer. As she turned to walk down the nearest row of headstones, Auggie was eager to match her step for step. If they could cover some ground, maybe they could figure this out.

"It's like what you said about the bank, how they have leverage through their fees," she reminded him as they aimed for the ancient pine trees that marked the graveyard's back boundary. "Vernon doesn't need to steal anything directly. Through the supply chain, he has a money pipeline that's been in place for decades. He skims off the top as he pleases."

"They'd have to be small amounts, if he's running it through the co-op. That would be the way to do it. Over time, little by little." Auggie stopped short. "But what about the auction barn's delinquent account notices?"

Doubt had crept back into Auggie's voice, and Kate wasn't surprised. She felt the same way. "That's a whole other game from the one Vernon could be playing with the co-op's invoices," Auggie said. "The auction customers' accounts are the entire focus of the investigation, from what I've heard."

Kate was stumped by that, too. And it made her worry this theory was as leaky as a rusted-out feed bucket.

Because if Vernon was behind all the missing money, someone else still had to be involved. Someone who was taking kickbacks on the inside to look the other way. Fixing the books to make it look like everything added up, or that some customers hadn't paid their bills.

Auggie threw up his hands. "And who in the hell is *that*?"

"I have absolutely no idea. That's what I can't figure out."

"Is it one of those young guys, do you think?"

Kate shrugged as she stared out over the weathered headstones. But this desolate place offered her no answers.

"Maybe, somehow. Maybe not ... But those men know *something*. My source was sure of it, by what they said and how they behaved. They were drunk, of course, but ..."

Auggie sighed. "And more often than not, that's when the truth comes out."

"Here's the other piece I'm missing, and it's a big one," Kate admitted. "Why would Vernon do this? What's his motive? Greed, obviously, but there has to be more to it than that. These are serious crimes. White-collar ones, of course, but ..."

"Oh, no."

"What?"

Vernon grew up dirt poor, Auggie told Kate, but he was

intelligent. He wanted to get away from here, go to college, be something other than a farmer like his dad and grandpa.

While there was no money for tuition, Vernon had a shot at some scholarships that would have helped pay his way. But his parents pressured him into staying on as a hired hand at the Eagle River co-op, a part-time job he'd taken as soon as he was old enough, to help support their large family.

Vernon gave in; his family meant everything to him. And after he and Martha married young and started their own family, those other opportunities were gone. Instead, he stayed with the co-op and quickly moved his way up until he was named its manager in his late twenties.

"He was rather young to take on so much responsibility," Auggie recalled, "but Vernon was known for both his book smarts and his winning ways with people. The board didn't hesitate to make him their top employee when old Fred Bennet retired. That was over thirty years ago, and Vernon's been in that job ever since."

Kate thought back to the day she and Bev had stopped at the Eagle River co-op, and the salacious gossip they'd heard about Dylan's uncle and Andrea Bingham. She shared it with Auggie now, and he raised his eyebrows in surprise.

"And here's the thing," Kate told him. "Vernon just happened to be stocking supplies in the closest aisle. He put that whole conversation in motion, cast doubt on Bill Kirkland without saying anything specific. When the other guys jumped in with all the sordid details, Vernon just stood back and let them roll."

Kate shook her head. "The more I think about it, the stranger that seems. The Wheelers have been a cash cow for that co-op for decades, probably since it was founded. You'd think Vernon would've taken the high road from the start."

"Unless he's trying to divert attention away from himself, no matter the cost." Auggie's face turned red, and not from the wind. "He did the same damn thing with me! Told me something I'd be eager to hear, tossed me a bone in the hopes I'd spread it around. Maybe it's not even true!"

"And maybe it is, but that's not the point."

Auggie turned down the next row of graves, and Kate followed. "So, Vernon is spreading disinformation," he said through gritted teeth, "trying to control the narrative. If he's really the one behind all this, he's more than a liar and a thief; he's a master manipulator. And he has a great deal to lose if he's found out."

"He's dangerous, then." Kate tried to push down the fear that rose in her chest. This wasn't the time to walk away from this case; too much was at stake.

She thought of Donald Wellington, and the vandalism at his home as well as the auction barn. Of Dylan's desperation, and the possibility that his father might try to take his own life. Of how one of the guys at the co-op had claimed the stash of stolen cash was upwards of fifty-thousand dollars. A number that was nowhere near what Vernon may have pocketed through a couple decades' worth of inflated co-op invoices. The stakes were so very high here. She couldn't afford to be wrong.

Auggie came to a halt in front of one of his ancestors' stones, and Kate was relieved. He was so upset; this couldn't be good for his heart.

When he lowered his head, Kate worried it was a gesture of defeat. But Auggie was looking at something.

He nudged the steel toe of one of his work boots into the native vegetation starting to emerge in this pioneer cemetery. "Vernon's like a snake in the grass," he muttered. "Cunning, deceptive, watchful. And not afraid to strike back."

And then, Auggie stared at Kate.

"This source of yours. What do they plan to do with this information?"

"Nothing." Kate shook her head. "They're afraid to come forward, in any way. I was trying to figure out what to do, myself. I think I need to reach out to the authorities; I was trying to decide who."

"Who else knows? Did you tell Bev about this?"

"No, not yet."

"Thank God. Please don't."

Kate wasn't so sure. "We're always honest with each other, no matter what we find. It doesn't feel right to ..."

"Listen to me." Auggie leaned in and put one hand on the arm of Kate's jacket. "You know how I like to ramble on, and throw my opinions all over creation. But if you only ever take one bit of advice from me, it should be this: Tell *no one* what you heard. Understand? It's too dangerous, for you and for them."

Kate had never seen fear in Auggie's eyes, for any reason. But she caught a glimpse of it now.

"OK, I won't. But what if this is the lead the investigators are looking for?"

Auggie rubbed his chin, deep in thought. "You need to be very careful with this. *We* need to be very careful."

And then, his face hardened in anger. "All these years, Vernon's been playing too many of us for a fool." He pulled his phone out of his pocket.

Kate stared at him. "Who are you calling?"

"Sheriff Preston." Auggie turned his back to the wind, and yanked off his gloves.

"I'll do it," she said. "You don't have ..."

"Nonsense. Vernon thinks he threw me off the trail with that crap about the silent partners. Even if he ever figures out there was a tip from the public, he won't look my way." Auggie shrugged. "Besides, I'm too well-known around here. He wouldn't dare mess with me."

And then, Auggie gave a short, sharp laugh that sounded like retribution and righteousness all rolled into one.

"I can do it. No, I *want* to do it." He grinned as he put his phone up to his ear. "I'll turn him in, myself."

18

Kate wasn't sure what she'd expected to happen once Auggie shared their suspicions about Vernon with Sheriff Preston. But after four days without any news, and not one new lead in the case, she was more than tired; she was exhausted.

And the dreary weather didn't help, not one bit. Friday's early-morning thunderstorms had ushered in a stretch of rainy, cool days that required constant vigilance as Kate piloted a restored Bertha down the mushy gravel roads. The rest of Kate's working hours were spent dodging downpours as she reached out the car's window to drop mail, or hustled to people's porches and back. Even at night, once she was home and out of her soggy work gear, Kate still felt cold and damp.

So the idea of driving over to Swanton, with its myriad of shopping choices, was more than she was willing to consider on this Monday afternoon. The handful of aisles at Eagle River's pharmacy lacked fresh produce, but the Evertons' store had a cooler stocked with milk and frozen foods.

Kate stifled a yawn as she reached for two rolls of paper towels, and reminded herself for the umpteenth time that she'd done the right thing by passing on what she'd heard from Brody. And now, she needed to step aside and let the real detectives do their work.

This was a complicated situation. Even if her hunch about Vernon was correct, it could take weeks for law enforcement to get the computer access, and then the proof, they would need to take action.

But that wasn't all that was bothering Kate these days. She hated keeping secrets from people she cared about, and Bev was one of those people.

It was a lonely thing, to carry the weight of what she suspected about Vernon Millard and not be able to talk it over with someone. She and Auggie had agreed not to speak of it again; even to each other, and certainly not to anyone else. The best thing was to try to forget about it, Auggie had said, because it would make it that much easier to act surprised whenever the truth came out. Kate knew he was right.

She paused at the end of the aisle, and tried to recall everything she needed. She'd forgotten her grocery list at home, of course. It wasn't long, but she still struggled to remember what was on it.

"Cereal? Some soup? What else? I can't wander around in here for hours. I need to get home, then get back to town in time for tonight's dress rehearsal."

The May Day dancers' efforts were paying off; and, even better, Dylan had called Friday night with a promise that the auction barn would continue its tradition of providing a wagon and horses for the procession.

Kate wasn't sure how Dylan had managed to maintain his family's role in the festival, and she had yet to hear who would be driving the team. But it didn't really matter. She and Stacy hadn't had to find alternate transportation for the girls, so that was one less thing. The weather forecast promised sunny skies and warm breezes for Wednesday's celebration, but Kate wondered if it was all too good to be true.

She wasn't going to get her hopes up. Not about the festival, or the possibility that she'd helped solve the embezzlement case, or anything else. Kate was burned out;

she needed a break from all the drama. So why did she find herself wanting to reach out to Alex?

She missed him, far more than she'd ever expected she would. And it wasn't just their physical connection that made her want to pick up her phone.

In fact, that was only a small part of it, Kate had realized over the past few weeks. She missed their long conversations about anything and everything. His quick wit, his intelligence, the way he could size up a person or a situation within a few moments.

Alex's razor-sharp intuition had been a little off-putting to Kate at first, possibly because hers was the same. But once she'd let her guard down, just a little, the keen sense of perception they shared had simply become one more way they connected.

It was probably just as well they weren't in touch, given the potentially explosive secret she now carried, Kate decided as she wandered down the next aisle. And while part of her longed to see him, she hadn't forgotten that strange phone call in the middle of the night, or Alex's defensive behavior.

She could never trust Alex with what she suspected about Vernon Millard. And she certainly couldn't trust him with her heart.

I need to forget about Alex, too, she reminded herself as turned toward the refrigerator case. All she needed was that half gallon of milk, and she'd be out of here.

I'm fine on my own. Everyone in my life needs to be reliable, open, honest. I don't have the time, or the patience, for anything else.

"Kate?"

Her shopping basket almost fell to the floor; she caught it just in time. Alex was right in front of her, a frozen pizza in one hand and a bag of hash browns in the other.

"I was just thinking about you," Kate blurted out before she could stop herself.

"Same." Alex frowned, but then he smiled.

Oh, Kate had missed that knowing smile.

They stared at each other for a few long seconds. And then, Kate noticed Chris Everton watching them from behind the pharmacy counter in the back of the store.

A woman pushing one of the store's three full-size shopping carts needed to wheel past. Kate and Alex stepped into the nearby aisle to get out of her way, a move that brought them closer together.

Kate took a breath before she spoke. "How are you?"

"I'm good. It's been busy at the bar, and Moose ..."

"How is he?" She was glad for an easy topic of conversation.

"Lazy and fat." Alex laughed. "Other than that, he's wonderful."

Kate quickly explained about Patches. The mama cat now demanded outdoor access a few times a day, but always came back to her babies. Doc and Karen had donated a playpen, which would go a long way toward keeping the kittens corralled as they grew.

"That's great news! It sounds like she's made up her mind to stay, then. Congratulations, Kate Duncan; the cat distribution system has chosen you." Alex shook his head in awe. "Several times over."

Kate didn't know whether to laugh or cry. She remembered that night at Alex's, not so long ago, when she first met Moose.

By the suddenly wistful expression on Alex's face, he hadn't forgotten, either.

"Well, I don't know if that's technically accurate," Kate said to fill the silence between them. "It's more like: Patches missed her old digs, decided to walk home, and found a strange woman handing out snacks in the machine shed. My place belongs to her, I think, as much or more so than she belongs to me."

"It's amazing what animals can do. There's so much more going on in their minds than what anyone gives them credit for."

"It's the same for people, sometimes." Kate couldn't resist.

Alex nodded slowly. "Have you come across anything good?" He didn't need to explain.

"Nope," she lied. "Nothing new. Dead ends everywhere I look."

"Uh-huh. Same here." He glanced around, then shook his head. "I remember the first time I ran into you here. I'd taken the last shopping cart ..."

Kate finished his sentence. "And you let me put my stuff in it."

She hadn't forgotten that day; and now, to hear he hadn't, either? That put a lump in her throat. And he was as handsome as ever. But Kate's heart was determined not to get ensnared. Last time, she'd been able to pull herself free. If she got too close again ...

"I miss you," Alex whispered. The hurt in his brown eyes was real; Kate could feel it. And then, she felt a few tears welling up in her own.

"I don't know." She blinked and looked away. "That last night ..."

"I can explain." He seemed to think for a moment. Then he nodded with conviction, as if he'd just talked himself into something that, before now, he hadn't been willing to consider. "If that's what it takes to get you back in my life? I'll do it."

Kate was surprised, momentarily touched ... and then, suddenly wary. Alex didn't say more; he just stood there with an anxious look on his face.

"How bad is it?" She took a few steps back, clutching her hand basket close. "I mean, do I even want to know?"

"I guess that depends." He looked away, then back again.

And then a smile appeared, a genuine one that seemed to cost him a great deal of effort. "Will you think about it, at least?"

Kate found herself nodding before she even had a second to do just that.

"OK, then. You know where to find me."

Alex moved on, and Kate made herself stay right where she was. Part of her wanted to hurry down the medical-care aisle, and wrap her arms around him before he made it as far as the sparse selection of grabber sticks and walkers.

But this wasn't the right time, and it certainly was the wrong place. Besides, she needed to give his request some careful consideration, first.

Kate kept one eye on Alex as she slowly selected her skim milk, and tossed a frozen pizza into her basket to waste a few more minutes. Because Alex was at the front counter, where Janet Everton was ringing up his purchases, and she didn't want to talk to him again. Not yet.

After he left, Kate carried her now-crowded basket to the front of the store.

"Hey, Kate," Janet said. "You certainly have your hands full."

Something in Janet's tone made Kate wonder if she was talking about more than Kate's purchases. Janet gave her husband a look, and Chris ambled up from the back.

"Lots of messes at home these days, I bet," Chris said as he sacked the paper towels. "How are the kittens?" And then, before Kate could give him an update, he spoke again. "I saw you talking to Alex."

Janet gave an exasperated sigh as she scanned the milk. "Honey, you're not exactly subtle, are you?"

Kate had to smile, just a bit. "Yeah. I haven't seen him in a while."

Janet leaned over the counter. "But are you going to see him again? I mean, will you ..."

"Now who's being nosy?" Chris asked his wife.

"I'll just say this." Janet reached for the cereal. "Alex Walsh is a bit ... complicated, I'll give you that. But he's a genuine soul, deep down, and all the way through."

Kate just nodded. She wondered if Janet, like many of the ladies in Eagle River, was too distracted by Alex's good looks to really see him clearly.

"Besides," Janet added with a shrug, "there aren't that many single guys around here, especially those worth wasting your time on. And even then, most of them have packed on the pounds and lost most of their hair."

Both statements also happened to apply to her husband. Chris stared at his wife as Kate burst out laughing.

"Well, you can forget about that lovely bouquet I was planning to get you for your birthday next week," he huffed.

"We get the flowers wholesale, and our discount is decent," Janet reminded him.

"Besides, if you really want to do something nice for me, you can clean out the gutters this weekend. And I love you," Janet added while she rang up the last of Kate's items. "Even if you don't look like Alex Walsh."

"Fine. But I used to," Chris told Kate. "Look like him. Well, almost." He playfully elbowed his wife. "I was quite the catch, back in the day. Janet was lucky to land me."

"I was," she admitted with a big grin. "That's for sure."

Chris and Janet's joking raised Kate's spirits, but it also made her a bit sad. They weren't just husband and wife, and business partners; they were best friends. Two people who'd shared over two decades of their lives together, and were going to do just that for many years to come.

Kate had plenty to be grateful for, but she didn't have *that*. Maybe she never would.

"I'll help you out with these," Chris promised Kate as he picked up one of the bags, "if you can manage the rest."

Kate didn't have that many groceries. It was obvious Chris had more he wanted to say. And she was willing to listen.

“All joking aside,” Chris said as Kate popped the trunk. “Maybe you should give him another chance.”

Kate sighed. “Oh, I don’t know.” As soon as Alex had left, her doubts had been quick to creep back in. “Maybe it’s just best to let it be.”

“Whatever went wrong between the two of you ...” Chris held up his hands defensively. “I don’t know anything about it, honestly; Alex never gave me the details. But it’s hurting him, not having you in his life.”

Kate wasn’t sure what to think. “Did he put you up to this?”

“Absolutely not. My meddling is all my own.” Chris looked up and down Main Street for a moment, as if making sure no one else was within earshot. Kate waited, intrigued.

“Alex Walsh is a good man. One of the best I’ve ever known. He’s just ... there’s baggage, that’s all.”

Kate raised her eyebrows.

“But that’s a story I’m not authorized to share.” Chris pulled his plaid shirt’s collar up against the breeze. “You’ll have to get it straight from the source, if you want it.”

Did she? She’d stopped at Eagle River Pharmacy for some cereal and paper towels, but she was also heading home with a frozen pizza she didn’t really need and a most-unexpected surprise. Along with some life advice from Chris.

“You told me something similar,” she reminded him, “the first time I ran into Alex in your store. So it’s still true, then? Whatever it is?”

“Yep. Nothing’s changed. And it won’t.” Chris retreated to the curb. “I’d better get back inside and help Janet, or she’s going to want me to rake the entire lawn on my own, too. Just think about it, OK?”

Kate promised she would. And as she got behind Bertha’s wheel and turned toward home, she hoped she could find the courage to face whatever Alex had been keeping from her.

19

The antique wagon was a welcome change, Kate decided. It was a simple, rustic piece, the sort that would have transported a load of corn, or taken the family into town for their Saturday shopping.

Lacking any hint of gleaming brass or bright paint, the wagon's simple varnish and clean lines were the perfect backdrop for the garlands of synthetic apple blossoms now tacked to its sides.

"There. It's perfect." Stacy gave her approval as she adjusted the last swag. "You know, this is truly authentic. I think I like it better than the fancy one they've used in recent years. Because way back, when this tradition started, no one around here would have had one of those show wagons, anyway."

While Dylan had convinced his dad to continue the auction barn's role in the May Day celebration, the Wheelers had had a change of heart when it came to their traditional partners for the procession.

The Binghams were nowhere to be found on this bright, warm May Day. This simple wagon would be pulled by a pair of Belgian draft horses owned by a family over by Swanton.

Bev carefully navigated the metal step on the back of the wagon, then dropped to the ground with a small sigh of relief.

"Mercy, I'm not used to that. But those high-school girls are much more nimble than I am. Even while wearing long dresses."

"I'm glad you added those towels to the benches," Stacy told Bev. "Rustic elegance is fine and all, but we don't need anyone getting a nasty splinter."

Stacy reached for her phone and began to type. "Hmm. 'Rustic elegance.' I like the sound of that."

Kate and Bev just waited. Stacy had only three months until her own big show, and she'd been grappling with table-favor options for weeks.

"I bet she goes with Mason-jar candles wrapped with gingham ribbon," Kate whispered to Bev.

"A likely suspect, to be sure," Bev said. "However, mini lanterns draped with herb sprigs cannot be ruled out."

Bev had offered to help Stacy and Kate get the wagon, and also the dancers, ready for the festival, but that wasn't Bev's only reason for being at the auction barn this afternoon.

It would be a great opportunity to wander around, she had reminded Kate, and get another look at some of the people who might be involved in the embezzlement case. There wasn't a sale today, but the lot still buzzed with activity as crew members cleaned up after yesterday's auction and prepped for Friday's cattle sale.

As for the vandalism that had taken place on the lot, there was nothing left to see. Employees had moved at lightning speed to replace the busted-out windows and repair the rest of the damage, as the Wheelers had been as eager to remove any visible signs of their troubles as they'd been to restore their historic building.

While Bev hoped for something that could be of use, such as overhearing a possible lead in a conversation or two, Kate had her doubts that today's visit would give them anything productive on that front.

Or maybe, it was just that she'd already stumbled across

something so significant, so astonishing, that she couldn't imagine what she might discover today that would top it.

Even so, she tried to keep an open mind. Because if she could uncover something else, something she would be free to share with Bev, it would go a long way toward easing the guilt she was carrying.

And while Kate was fairly certain Vernon was the mastermind behind this complex series of crimes, he certainly wasn't working alone.

"The girls should be here soon," Stacy said. "Some of them are carpooling from the high school, and a few are coming on the bus with the marching band."

Kate unzipped her fleece jacket. The weather, for once, was just about perfect. "Betsy said the dancers can have the entire front women's restroom to get ready. Maybe we should head inside."

Stacy's grin stretched from ear to ear as she opened her car trunk. "Ladies, I think this celebration is going to go off without a hitch! I know the girls said they'd bring their own styling stuff, but I wanted to be prepared."

Her arms loaded down with three bulging tote bags filled with curling irons, makeup, and whatever else might be needed during a fashion emergency, Stacy hustled for the auction barn's front entrance. Kate and Bev lagged several steps behind.

"I'm a little leery about what we might uncover here today," Bev admitted. "If it's just more sleazy gossip, like what we heard at the co-op, I'm not sure I want to know."

A school bus had just turned into the drive, and dozens of teenagers dressed in blue, white, and black marching-band uniforms soon spilled out onto the parking lot. Their polished instruments gleamed in the bright afternoon sun.

"Maybe we'll spot someone wandering around with a bag of cash in their hands." Kate kept her tone light. After all, it was a beautiful day. "A girl can hope, I guess."

Bev laughed. "Can we ask all the auction crew guys to empty their pockets for us? Just in case one of them is carrying around an unencrypted thumb drive of stolen account information?"

"I wish." Kate rolled her eyes. "How about you give it a try? What about those guys over there?"

She gestured at two burly men transferring fifty-pound bags of oats from a large metal pallet to a cart pulled by a small tractor. They tossed the sacks with an impressive lack of effort, and still had enough stamina to keep up a rambling conversation as they worked.

"No thanks," Bev said. "I wouldn't want to make any demands on their time, much less get into a tussle with the likes of them."

Kate gave the two men a closer look as she passed by. One of them might have been Chuck, who'd confronted Dylan at the bar that night, but she couldn't be sure.

Was there a possibility either, or both, of these guys had been at the same party as Brody? Unfortunately, "ball caps and hoodies" wasn't much of a description to go on.

As she and Bev entered the lobby, Kate decided the people on the inside of this case were too smart to draw attention to themselves while so many strangers were present. And, given the web of silence that had surrounded the scandal for several weeks, they probably felt confident they were getting away with ... well, whatever it was they were up to.

"Oh, there's Pete." Bev pointed out Dylan's dad, who was chatting with Ben Dvorak outside the main office. "Let's go say hello."

Pete Wheeler's face was creased with worry lines, but Kate noted a hint of cheerfulness in his blue eyes today. He even laughed heartily at something Ben said, and patted Bev on the shoulder when she offered him a greeting.

"Well, hello there! Good to see you, Bev. And Kate." Pete extended his hand, and Kate was pleased to find his grip was firm. "We're just about ready to go, I think."

Kate didn't know what Dylan had said to his father, how exactly he'd convinced his dad to keep this May Day tradition alive. But whatever it was, Dylan had worked some sort of miracle. Because it seemed like the showman of this auction house might be ready to take a few tentative steps back into the ring.

"The wagon's all decorated," Kate told Pete and Ben. "The band is here, and Stacy's helping the dancers get ready."

"Pete's going to drive the team," Ben said with a grin. "The owner was willing to do it, but ..."

"I sure am! It's been several years since I've done the honors myself." Pete's grin faltered slightly. "More recently, we've always let the horses' owners take the reins."

"Well, that's exciting," Bev was quick to fill the silence. "You're back in the saddle, then."

The lobby of the auction barn was filled with people this afternoon. Kate suspected many of them were longtime friends and patrons of the Wheelers who'd stopped in on their way to find places along the procession's route.

Marvin and Vivian, Dylan's grandparents, were holding court over by the main entrance to the show ring. They were in their eighties and, while Marvin was casually dressed, his plaid shirt and jeans were immaculate. He seemed to lean heavily on his cane, but that didn't stop him from chatting up everyone who passed by.

Vivian was as petite as her husband was tall, and her white hair was perfectly curled. She sported a floral dress along with bright-red lipstick, and the massive diamond ring on her left hand winked in the light.

As Kate looked around, she realized Andrea and Elton Bingham weren't the only familiar faces absent that day. She'd yet to catch even a glimpse of Dylan's Uncle Bill. He might be in the office, or in the back of the barn, but Kate would have expected Bill to be out here with Pete and Ben.

Pete Wheeler said he was driving the team this afternoon. Would he be the only one?

Whatever was going on between Bill Kirkland and Andrea Bingham, if anything, Kate decided the Wheelers had made a smart move to switch teams for today's celebration. Perhaps the family was starting to cut ties, or at least loosen them, with some of their associates in an attempt to squash the rumors and get to the bottom of the criminal activity.

"You'll do just fine," Ben was telling Pete. "Why don't you check in with Ed? I'm sure he's getting the boys ready to be harnessed up."

With another wave to Kate and Bev, Pete started toward the back of the auction barn. Ben gave the ladies a triumphant grin.

"Well!" Bev nodded her approval. "You and Dylan have worked wonders with him. I'm so glad he's going to take part today."

"Me, too," Kate said, "and not just because the festival's court doesn't have to ride on a fire engine."

Ben laughed. "We could have made that work, sure. I would have just put on my other hat." He snapped his fingers. "Easy-peasy. Seriously, though; this is tradition, and it's really important to keep it going. Once Dylan and I got Pete on board, it gave him something to look forward to."

"But you have to wonder," Bev said, "if the Wheelers sell this place, would the new owners even want to participate? Especially if some big corporation were to buy the company. That's about the only people who would have the collateral to invest in it, these days."

"Oh, that's not going to happen." Ben's confidence was as noteworthy as the way he'd just lowered his voice. "You're right, the cost to acquire such an established business would be significant. But, no ... the Wheelers are no longer looking to sell."

"Are you sure?" Kate matched Ben's quiet tone. "They

can't do it right now, of course, not with all this going on. But if they can get this cleared up ..."

"Oh, sure, no one would want to buy it today. But once this problem is solved, it would be a different story." He paused to greet a few passing farmers, then turned back to Kate and Bev.

"But I think the family has realized what a special thing they have here. They knew it before, especially the old guard. But if anything good has come from this mess, it's that the younger generations have decided they are game to keep this going far into the future."

Dylan and Nate were determined to step up, Ben said, with the support and blessing of their older relatives. Dylan's children were still very young, but Nate's oldest was already a teenager, and he was showing interest in the family business. At the very least, any sale of Wheeler Auction Company had likely been delayed by a decade or two.

Kate was elated to hear this news, and relieved by what it meant for her hometown. "It sounds like you think these crimes are going to be solved. I hope that means there's some light at the end of the barn aisle, so to speak?"

Ben grinned. "Well, I'd like to think so. I don't know any details," he added hastily. "It's complicated, with many layers to it. I don't know how, or when, this will get sorted out. But I have to hope it will be sooner, rather than later."

And then he laughed. "I mean, it's May, right? Look at all that sunshine out there! Who could be a pessimist on such a beautiful afternoon?"

* * *

Since Stacy had everything under control, Bev and Kate were free to find a spot along the processional route. Kate hopped in Bev's truck, and they turned south on Main Street.

Chief Calcott was directing traffic at the foot of the bridge, where Main shared stoplights with the county highway. The intersection would only close long enough to let the marching band and the girls' wagon pass through, but this was the closest Eagle River would come to a traffic jam until the sweet corn festival in late summer. The police chief flashed Kate and Bev a grin as he waved them forward.

"What a blowhard," Bev told Kate as they gave Calcott big smiles and even-bigger waves. "He might as well trade in his uniform for a chicken costume. That way, he could fluff up his feathers with pride. As if he has anything more pressing to do this afternoon."

Kate laughed. "I don't think he's going to have to make too many vehicles wait for the procession. Given how crowded the sidewalks are, I'd say most of this town is already lined up along the parade route."

Bev parked on a side street near the elementary school, so they'd have a quick walk to the festival site once the procession had passed.

As they lingered near the corner, Kate listened in on the conversations that swirled around them. She was pleased to notice none of those chats seemed to include words such as "embezzlement," "theft," or "crimes."

The scandal had thrown a dark cloud over the Wheelers, and the rest of Eagle River, for weeks now. But maybe, just for today, tradition and celebration had the upper hand.

Bev's thoughts were apparently running along similar lines. "I'm glad to see such a great turnout. The weather helps, of course, but you have to wonder how many people are here to get a glimpse of the *circus* rather than the girls and the horses, if you know what I mean."

Kate did. If Melinda were here, she'd put on her marketing hat and say this was the perfect moment for one of Eagle River's highest-profile families to rebrand itself.

The Wheelers knew it, too. They weren't hiding in the shadows today, staying out of sight while malicious rumors clocked their every move. Instead, Pete Wheeler was attempting to restore his family's good standing by literally parading through the heart of town.

Up and down the sidewalk, people slipped off their jackets and adjusted their sunglasses. The marching band was still two blocks away, but their rousing tunes preceded them on the warm breeze.

"You know," Bev said, "one year when I was a girl, there was a sort-of concerted effort to squash this whole show. Some people thought it made us look like a bunch of hicks, that Eagle River wasn't modern, progressive. The flower crowns, the flowing dresses, the ribbon dances ... Sure, the girls look like wood nymphs out of some fairy tale, but so what? I'm glad we still do it."

"Me, too." Kate's grin stretched from ear to ear. "It was fun to be a part of it again, if only in a different way. Even better, this means all I have to do for Stacy's wedding is put on my dress, show up, and enjoy myself."

"Good thinking," Bev muttered. "Many women end up petticoat-over-heels when it's time to plan their big day, but she takes the cake. You're smart to be out of the way."

In more ways than one, Kate thought but didn't say to Bev. *And, as hard as it is sometimes, I'm going to keep you out of that other mess, too.*

Kate anxiously scanned the faces around her, then felt a wave of relief when she didn't spot Vernon Millard anywhere in the crowd. Of course, the co-op was on the far southern edge of town; if Vernon had closed the shop long enough to enjoy the short procession, he was more likely to be posted right on Main Street.

Pete Wheeler had already made a big step forward by agreeing to personally take part in this parade. Kate could only hope Dylan's dad would keep his focus on the horses and their path, rather than the crowds that lined the streets.

But then, Vernon would never do or say anything to give himself away to Pete Wheeler, or anyone else. He would be applauding and waving with the rest, full of smiles, good cheer, and gratitude for the beautiful day and the start of another growing season.

Kate just hoped the wily old fox's complicated scheme would be snuffed out long before this year's harvest.

It was highly unlikely that Pete, Dylan, Ben, and the rest of the auction barn staff had any idea the authorities were looking at Vernon, unless they had their own reasons to suspect their longtime co-op rep was up to no good. But Pete's change of heart about today's festival, and Ben's surprisingly optimistic assessment of the situation, told Kate something had changed recently, and for the better.

Charges had yet to be filed against anyone regarding the vandalism at the auction barn, but she suspected authorities had that part of the case well in hand. Law-enforcement officials often pressured suspects to give up their co-conspirators in exchange for lesser charges for themselves. Defense attorneys did the same.

Perhaps the vandalism was leading authorities toward whoever was involved in the embezzlement case from inside Wheeler Auction Company. Kate really, really hoped that was true. Because she'd been working this case from the outside, and she was done.

While Vernon's role in all this was stunning in its magnitude, it still fell under the umbrella of white-collar crime. Even if he was charged with vandalism, too, it wouldn't be enough to keep him in jail until his case went to trial.

Sure, he'd lose his job. But that would just give him more time to pace around at home, fret and fume about his scheme coming to an end. Enough time to attempt to figure out who'd ratted him out, and seek revenge.

If Vernon was indeed the mastermind behind all the stolen cash, then Kate's hunch had been correct. But it wouldn't be safe for her to take any of the credit.

So be it. Her safety, and that of her friends and family,

was far-more important than having her day in the sun for helping save an important part of Eagle River's past and present ... and now, what looked to be its future.

"Here they come!" a little boy shouted to his parents. "I see the band!"

Two members of the high school's cheerleading squad took the lead, carrying the band's competition banner. Cheers erupted along the route as the teenage musicians began a rousing rendition of an old English folk tune.

While many of the area's initial settlers had arrived from Germany, they had been joined by a sizable number of English and Irish immigrants. And, quite frankly, those songs were much easier for the crowds along the parade route to remember and sing.

Kate found herself holding her breath as the band marched past. The team and wagon were right behind the musicians, and just about to turn this last corner. What kind of reaction would they get from this final section of the crowd?

But she gasped with surprise and delight when she saw three members of the Wheeler family sharing the front seat of the wagon.

Dylan was in the middle, driving the team. His dad sat on his left, and Nate was on his cousin's right. Just as Ben had promised, two members of a younger generation were indeed taking the reins at Wheeler Auction Company.

A few handclaps echoed from the packed sidewalks as the wagon approached. The applause then swelled into a polite show of appreciation for the dancers waving from the bed of the wagon. Soon, a happy whistle came from somewhere along the route, followed by another, and cheers quickly erupted in the crowd.

Nate started to wave back as all three of the Wheelers' faces broke into grins. By the time the wagon made it another half block, the people lining the street were cheering for the men with all their might. Dylan nudged his dad, and Pete was soon waving, too.

"Way to go, boys!" someone shouted.

A man next to Kate let out a loud hoot of appreciation. "That'll show 'em! No one can keep the Wheelers down!"

"The law will get them yet!" another man called out. "People ought to know better than to mess with folks from Eagle River!"

Encouraged by the adulation, the sleek draft horses held their heads even higher, and tossed their beribboned manes with pride as the wagon continued down the street.

"Will you look at that?" Bev wiped away a few happy tears. "It's better than I ever could have expected. Oh, I'm so happy for them!"

Kate felt the same. "I think Ben's right to have a little bit of hope. With this kind of support from the community, maybe the Wheelers can push on and see justice delivered."

Kate didn't know which pieces of the puzzle were still missing. But as she took in the throngs of revelers along the procession's route, she wondered who might have the information the authorities needed to bring this case to a close. In a crowd as large as this one, it was very likely that someone, or more than one person along the route, knew something. She thought of Brody, and how reticent he'd been to get involved.

"Say something," Kate whispered as the revelers started to make their way over to the elementary school. The maypole, in all its vibrant, beribboned glory, waited on the front lawn.

"Please say something. Not just for the Wheelers, but for the rest of us, too."

20

Just as promised, Alex's truck was the only vehicle at Paul's Place when Kate pulled up. They'd texted, then talked; but Alex had insisted this was a conversation they needed to have in person.

"I don't know if that's good or bad," Kate muttered as she made her way around the side of the old building, which was backed by the river. The new grass was thick, and so were the dandelions. "I guess I'm going to find out."

It had been more than two weeks since they'd run into each other at the pharmacy. A few days ago, after much reflection, Kate had decided to take Alex up on his offer to come clean.

Part of it was sheer curiosity; as close as she'd gotten to Alex, there always seemed to be something he was holding back from her. The sleuth in Kate was eager to find out exactly what that was.

But there was more at stake, of course. Once Kate uncovered Alex's secret, she could unpack it as she had the time, and maybe the courage, to do so. And then, one way or another, it might help her decide if she was going to let this man be as close to her as he'd been before.

As she came around the bar's back corner, Kate spotted two familiar faces waiting for her by the picnic table. Moose jumped up from the boards with a meow of greeting and, his tail held high, rushed to meet Kate halfway.

"Hey, buddy!" The big cat tried to climb the leg of Kate's jeans, and she picked him up. "Wow, you have packed on a few pounds, just like I'd heard."

"It's the truth." Alex said with a grin. "I wouldn't lie about my favorite cat in the whole wide world."

But what would you lie about? Kate thought but didn't say.

She was here for answers, not a confrontation. It was best to let this meeting unfold at its own speed. Alex seemed nervous, if glad to see her. Kate decided she wasn't the only one relieved that Moose was hanging around, providing an easy opener along with lots of purrs.

"Be careful," Alex warned Kate. "He really gets those paws going when he's happy, and his claws are sharp. What's that called, again? Making cookies, or something?"

Kate chuckled. "Making biscuits! Biscuits ... like kneading dough."

She was glad to have Moose in her arms, as it solved the question of how to greet Alex.

She wasn't about to go in for a hug, or anything else; but a handshake seemed out of place, too. Because Kate didn't know where she stood with this man, as they lingered by the bar's back door.

"Want a beer?" Alex asked. "We don't have a patio permit but, well, I don't think anyone's going to see us back here. Or care, for that matter."

"Sure." Kate sat down at the picnic table, and Moose stretched out on its top. She thought the big cat might linger there, enjoying the sun's warm rays on his fur. But by the time Alex returned with two frosty bottles, Moose had run off into the nearby woods.

Alex only shrugged when Kate shared this news.

"He likes to come to work with me, sometimes. At first, I

thought maybe he was going to leave. You know, run off again and not come back."

A shadow crossed Alex's handsome face before he smiled.

"But I think he just likes to roam around in his old stomping grounds along the river, especially at night. Long before I'm ready to lock up and go home, he's either out here by the back stoop; or out front, waiting in the bed of the truck."

"Does he still beg for food?"

"Always." Alex rolled his eyes. "Nobody can catch a break out here at break time. I don't feed him French fries at home, but some of the staff have admitted they do. Maybe that's why he tags along. Who knows?"

He pushed up the sleeves of his sweatshirt, then gave a big sigh. "Well, we're not here to talk about Moose."

Kate nodded. "Yeah. I don't even know where to start."

Alex leaned back, just a bit, and pulled down the bill of his faded ball cap. "What do you want to know, exactly?"

"Everything."

As soon as she said it, Kate realized she truly meant it. She'd been right to come here today. She needed answers, and as many of them as she could get. "Everything you can, and are willing, to tell me."

Alex nodded, and stared at the table for a moment. "You know I'm from Austin." The city was not far north of the Iowa-Minnesota line.

"Yes."

"And I've been in Eagle River for five years, I have a sister and a brother, and my parents now live outside of Lake Mills. And obviously, my cousin's the police chief in this town, and my widowed aunt Helen lives here, too."

"Yes."

Alex took a deep breath. Kate felt a twinge in her stomach, and it wasn't from the fermentation of the beer. She'd never seen Alex at a loss for words. Reflective, sure.

Carefully considering what he said before he said it, nearly always. But this ...

"I guess I'll start at the beginning." He picked at one corner of his bottle's label. "Or, I mean, when everything started to go wrong."

"Take your time," she urged him. "Go back and forth, if you need to. Just explain it as best as you can."

Alex looked up, and Kate saw sadness and regret in his eyes. "I haven't always been a bartender. I had a different career, very different." He closed his eyes for a moment. "Kate, my cousin's not the only cop in my family. I mean, he is now, but ..."

She raised her eyebrows.

"I used to be one, too."

Kate's mind shifted this way and that, tried to piece together what she knew about Alex and what he was telling her now. She could see it: His insatiable curiosity, and the way he sized up a room in an instant. How in public spaces, he liked to sit so he could see the door. How there always seemed to be so much more going on inside him than what he'd let on.

Alex Walsh was a complicated person; Kate already knew that. Despite his quick wit and knack for easy conversation, he was as deep as the river behind this bar when it swelled with snowmelt and rain in the spring.

But what was lurking in those depths? Maybe, finally, she was about to find out.

"So what happened?" She reached for his hand. Alex didn't hesitate to meet her halfway, and Kate's heart ached over how good it was to feel his touch again. He squeezed her hand, as if he couldn't bear to let it go, and Kate held fast.

"I loved my job, it meant everything to me. And then, I messed up." Alex choked back a sob, and took a swig from his beer. "And then ... I was just done. I couldn't do it anymore. I tried, but I couldn't do it."

He'd been on the Austin force for three years when it all happened, he told Kate. There was a bank robbery in progress, and he and his partner were the first police car on the scene.

Todd took the lead when they came through the front doors of the bank. Eleven customers were flat on their faces on the floor of the lobby, their hands over their heads. Two tellers were behind the front counter.

"The one woman was silent," Alex told Kate. "But the other was sobbing. 'They're in the vault,' she told us. 'They have Veronica.'"

The officers turned down a hallway, one that was so narrow they had to proceed single file. In seconds, they saw two men in face masks. The first had a still-empty canvas bag in one hand, and a gun in the other. The second robber's gun was pointed at Veronica's temple as he dragged her toward the vault.

Veronica grasped a chain crowded with master keys, and her hands were shaking so badly that the *cling-clang* of metal on metal rang through the otherwise-silent bank.

"We didn't make a sound, of course," Alex told Kate. "But even though the carpet muted our steps, they sensed we were behind them. Everything happened so fast."

The man with the bag pointed his gun at the officers. They both fired, and the robber did, too. One of the officers' bullets hit the shooter in the chest, but it was too late. Todd was down with a shot in his neck.

The second man let Veronica go, and ran out of the bank. Other officers caught him in the parking lot as medics rushed inside. They applied pressure to Todd's wound, but the bullet had nicked an artery.

"It just missed his vest. There was blood everywhere. He faded so fast. He ... he was gone by the time they got him to the hospital." Alex put his face in his hands. "I should have gone first. It should have been me."

Kate shook her head. “You couldn’t have known how it ...”

“No.” Alex was adamant. “No. You don’t understand. They had three little girls. I had my dog, Buster. Otherwise, it was just me.” He laughed bitterly. “I didn’t even have a scratch on me, for God’s sake! But Todd ...” He shook his head again.

“If I’d fired sooner, I might have been able to stop it. Took that guy down before he could even get a round off. But I was in the rear; my sight line wasn’t good, and I ... I failed my best friend.”

The wind whispered through the trees along the river, and a crow called out. Somewhere, out in the fast-flowing water, something splashed to the surface then dived down again.

Kate went around the table, and sat next to Alex. His head was on her shoulder before she could even think of anything to say. So she just put her arms around him, and held on.

It took several hours of surgery, but the shooter survived. There was a funeral procession where the streets were crowded with mourners from around the city. And a graveside service will full honors that Alex said he couldn’t, or maybe didn’t want to, remember.

The state handled the investigation of the incident, and Alex had spent days telling and retelling what had happened.

“No one blamed me, but it didn’t matter. Even worse, the chief kept calling me a hero because none of the bystanders had been hurt. Like it was somehow OK that Todd was dead, if everyone else got out alive.”

Alex was put on desk duty for a while, set up with a counselor. Eventually he was back on the streets, with a different partner, but it just wasn’t the same.

Or in some ways, it was. Because every call that potentially involved weapons made his heart race and his hands sweat.

He transferred to the traffic investigations department in a bid to make a fresh start, but that came with mounds of extra paperwork and countless fatalities that only reminded him of his dead friend.

The drinking started to get out of control. Buster got cancer and passed away. Alex's girlfriend said she couldn't take his mood swings anymore. More and more often, he'd wake up shouting and shaking, reeling from the trauma-fueled nightmares that stalked him in his sleep.

"And then, Ray called. He'd been here, oh, a couple of years. He said the old guy who'd run this bar forever wanted to retire, was looking for someone to buy him out. I was looking for a *way* out, by then. So, I took it."

He'd moved in with Aunt Helen while he got the bar up and running, helped her with odd jobs around her place, until he found his fixer-upper for sale.

Alex discovered that small-town life suited him. Away from the day-to-day reminders of what had happened, he was able to clear his head. Eventually, he was able to trade too-much drinking for long runs on the trails around Eagle River.

"So that's me," Alex said simply. "Well, one of my big secrets, at least."

"Do many people know? Around here?"

"Yeah, a few do." That made Kate think of Chris Everton. "Most others don't, and that suits me just fine." He wiped his eyes with the back of his hand, and took a sip of his beer.

"But the other thing I wanted to tell you ... that's a different story. You have to promise not to say a word, not to anyone. For your own good, as well as mine."

The anguish in Alex's eyes was gone, but the quick flash of fear in them made Kate very uneasy.

What could be worse, be harder, than what she'd just learned? Even as she reminded herself that she'd come here for answers, Kate wondered how much more she could process in one afternoon.

"Do I really need to know?"

"Well, if we're going to ... pick up where we left off. And I want to, I really do." He squeezed her hand. "Then I think you should."

"OK." She steadied herself, and glanced around. They were still alone, except for the fat crow who now perched on the lid of the Dumpster and watched them with keen, dark eyes. "Yes. I promise."

"I'm no longer a cop; I no longer wear a badge. But this bar?" He gestured to it with his beer bottle. "Lots of people roam in and out of it, day and night. Lots of interesting information does, too."

Alex gave Kate a sideways glance. "And sometimes, I pass along things I've heard. Or things I suspect. To people who have a right to know."

Kate's mouth fell open. This wasn't what she'd suspected. But in a way, it was a huge relief. Alex wasn't mixed up in anything criminal; but he obviously knew about things that were.

"And sometimes," she said as she picked up the thread of the conversation, "you feel the need to spring out of bed, in the middle of the night, and make a phone call or two."

Alex allowed himself a small chuckle. He already seemed more at ease, having shared such a heavy burden. But it was one that Kate felt settling on her own shoulders.

"Yeah, well, emails and texts can be problematic with this sort of thing. Verbal conversations, as long as they are discreet, are always better." He shrugged. "It feels good, you know? I can still seek justice for those who deserve it."

Then his face darkened with worry. "But that's also why it is so very important that you don't tell anyone about this."

Kate nodded emphatically. There were always going to be some secrets between her and Alex, then. But those secrets would keep her safe.

She wanted the same for him. Wanted to do what she could to be there for him, for this complicated man who had captured her affection and, if she'd admit it, most of her heart. This wasn't going to be easy. And there was always the chance that, in a few weeks or a few months, Kate would decide all of this was too much for her to bear. But for now, she was going to dare to give this another chance.

"Alex Walsh," she whispered as he wrapped his arms around her. "I promise to let you slink around in the shadows now and then. I promise to understand when you're having a tough day, and need to talk. Or, not to talk."

He kissed her, and everything else melted away. Kate leaned in, slipped her hands around his neck, and felt the heat rise in her body. Exactly how long had it been since they'd been this way? Kate couldn't remember; she couldn't remember much of anything right now, other than it was so, so good to have him back.

"And I promise to keep you in the dark," Alex said. "But only when I must. And to never again let anything, or anyone, interfere with *this*."

"Sounds like a plan." The sun had shifted, just a bit, and it was time for Kate to head home.

"I have to close tonight," Alex said as they got up from the picnic table. "But I'm off tomorrow night."

He didn't ask her a question, yet Kate answered him with a nod. As it so often had been between them, nothing more needed to be said.

* 21 *

Kate had known this day would arrive. But she was still a bit surprised, and a little disappointed, to come downstairs Wednesday morning the following week to find Patches yowling on the top basement step behind the still-closed door.

Because this time, the calico had four accomplices. Her gray-tabby boy, Hamlet, the biggest and most adventurous of the bunch, was right next to her. Juliet, Ophelia, and Romeo lingered only a few steps up from the bottom, where they batted at each other and their own fluffy tails while they added their meows to their mother's demands.

"So, you want to take them outside, huh?" Kate sighed with resignation as she gently held Hazel back. "I knew you wouldn't want to stay down there forever, much less keep Charlie and Hazel company in the house. Charlie wouldn't allow it, anyway."

Kate gazed out the window over the sink, and took in the gentle glow of the late-May morning. The lawn was at last green and thick, and the lilac trees along the driveway had already burst into bloom. Even so, Patches' brood was only five weeks old.

"I'm sorry, but I have to veto your proposal," she told the calico. "They need to stay down there for a few more weeks.

But when the time is right, I'll move you and the kids, and all your gear, out to the shed."

Brave little Hamlet had followed Patches into the kitchen, and stared about with saucer-sized eyes. Hazel, at least, was familiar, and the boy scampered over to lean against the dog's leg. He got a sizable lick on the face in return.

Kate laughed as she picked up the gray kitten. "Mama is going out for her morning break, and she's going alone. All of you spending more time in here will also give me a chance to figure out how to give you your own space out there. The Three Mouseketeers will need to size you up, from a safe distance, before I'll let you kids roam around."

As she headed out into the sunshine with a bucket of cat food over one arm and a small tote of birdseed in her other hand, Kate reflected on how everything always changes.

She really needed to clear off the rest of the garden and turn the soil, as the weather was finally warm enough for planting vegetables. This would be her first full year with her own plot, and she was looking forward to fresh-from-the-dirt tomatoes and peppers, maybe even sweet corn.

"There will be plenty of weeds, too," she reminded herself as she entered the machine shed to feed the outdoor cats their breakfast. "I'd better not plant more than I can realistically take care of. I also need to figure out those prairie plants in the pasture."

Patches was right behind her, and the calico butted into the civilized fray around the dishes. Maggie gave Patches an annoyed glare, but kept her opinions to herself.

"Just wait," Kate told Scout as she gave the big tuxedo cat a gentle pet. "Patches is going to move back in eventually, along with her kids. Don't let their cultured, elegant names fool you; they're going to turn your world inside out. But you'll get your peace and serenity back once the kittens find their forever homes."

Kate was showered, dressed, and washing out her cereal

bowl when her phone buzzed on the counter. "Alex Walsh" flashed on the screen, and she smiled.

"Well, good morning! How's it ..."

"You work today, right?" There was an odd tension in Alex's voice.

"Um, yeah. I'm getting ready to leave." She paused, dish towel in hand. "What's going on? Are you OK?"

"I'm fine, thanks. Just ... when you get to town, go straight to the post office. Don't stop for gas, or hit The Daily Grind for coffee. Oh, no, don't do that."

Kate tossed the towel aside. "What's going on?"

"I can't tell you, I'm sorry. Text me when you get to the post office, let me know you made it."

"Sure. Look, I don't know what the deal is, but I want you to be careful."

"I will; I promise. Oh, and leave Hazel at home today. I know you sometimes take her along."

"Should I lock her in the house?"

"Yes." The certainty in his voice made Kate cringe. "Lock her in before you leave. Lock your sheds, if you can. And go straight to the post office."

"Got it."

Alex hung up. Kate stared at her phone, bewildered, as if waiting for something to flash across its screen that would tell her what was happening. She was signed up to get all the emergency alerts from Hartland County, and Eagle River's municipal messages, too. But there were no new texts or emails from either of those sources.

As she hurried out to the porch to usher Hazel and Patches back into the house, Kate was filled with dread. Was there a fugitive on the loose, or something? Why else would Alex be so concerned about her whereabouts, and tell her to lock her outbuildings before she left home?

Roberta hadn't called or texted. Kate almost reached out, but glanced at the clock and realized there wasn't time. If she needed to lock down her little farm before getting behind Bertha's wheel, she had to keep moving or she'd be late.

* * *

All along the way into Eagle River, Kate watched for any sign that something was wrong on this beautiful morning. But all she saw were fields lined with young rows of corn and beans, and greening pastures dotted with grazing cows and sheep.

"But something must be happening. Alex wouldn't call with that kind of warning if it wasn't."

Just before Eagle River came into view, Kate's phone chirped. She steered Bertha to the shoulder, and snatched her device from her purse.

It was a text alert from the sheriff's office. Authorities had attempted to take Brent Carlson, 28, into custody this morning on the north end of Eagle River. Carlson had eluded law enforcement and was now missing. He was considered armed and dangerous, and had last been spotted along the river's west bank.

"No wonder Alex was so concerned." Kate was very aware of her surroundings as she passed over the bridge on the east side of town. "This guy would have to come out into the open to cross the river here. Otherwise, he'd need to be an amazing swimmer, with the current like it is. I bet he's hiding in the woods."

Kate peered north as she passed the corner that led to Paul's Place, but didn't see Alex's truck, or any other sign of life, in the bar's parking lot. And then, just as she reached Eagle River's main intersection, she spotted flashing red and blue lights off to the south.

They were several blocks away, on the opposite end of the business district. Wait; what was *that*?

A massive, rectangular vehicle with thick tires had just entered Main from a side street, and headed south toward the flashing lights. It was dark gray, and looked like the sort of transportation used by the military.

"A Humvee?" Kate gasped in disbelief as she waited at the red light. "No, that's not right. But it's similar. What is it doing down there? Because I highly doubt this Carlson guy could run all the way through town and not get caught."

As she turned right to go over the main highway's bridge, Kate got a better look at the scene on the south edge of Eagle River. There were several emergency vehicles, and countless people milling about.

And all the commotion, from what Kate could now see, looked to be happening right in front of the Eagle River Farmers Cooperative.

"That's a tactical team in that truck! Is this about Vernon? It has to be!"

Before she turned into the post office's back lot, Kate spotted more flashing emergency lights on the north end of Main Street. She doubted this second batch of first responders was enjoying from-scratch pancakes at Peabody's. They had to be at Wheeler Auction Company, which was right across the street.

The text alert hadn't referenced the auction barn, although Kate was now fairly certain that was where authorities had tried to take Carlson into custody. The short stretch of pasture behind its back lot met up with the woods along the river.

There had been no mention of what was happening at the co-op. Although from what Kate had just witnessed, she wondered when her phone might light up again.

It had been three weeks since the May Day festival. And, aside from Ben Dvorak's comments that afternoon, even longer than that since Kate had heard anything new about the case. Whatever investigators had discovered, they'd decided today was the day to take action.

Four of the other carriers' vehicles were already in the lot;

Kate was grateful she wasn't the first to arrive. She was anxious to get inside, but she took a moment to steady herself before she got out of the car.

While she was eager to find out more, she reminded herself that the flow of information had to be a one-way street. Everything she knew, and everything else she suspected? She couldn't say a word. She could show her fears, and express her worries and concerns. But that was all. Even with Roberta. And, especially, with Bev.

Kate closed her eyes and took a few deep breaths. Although she'd danced in the May Day festival for three years running in high school, Kate didn't consider herself to be much of an actress. But today, she'd need to put on a performance worthy of an Academy Award.

She made sure Bertha was locked before she hustled toward the post office's back entrance. The outside door flew open just as Kate reached for its handle.

"Get in here!" Jack ordered before he locked the exterior door behind her. Kate had never seen him this rattled. "I'll watch for the others. Roberta's keeping us here until they catch this guy."

Bev, Roberta, and Allison were huddled around one of the back tables. Before Kate could share what she'd just witnessed, Allison offered her own update.

"Betsy's been told to not come into work today." Allison scrolled her phone's screen. "Jean called her, said a whole team of investigators is swarming the auction barn."

Then Allison frowned. "It sounds like Jean is at the office, right now. She never goes in this early, none of them do. Betsy thinks Jean knew this was going to happen."

"They must not suspect Jean, then," Bev offered. "If they did, she wouldn't have been told anything about what was going on."

Allison nodded, then tossed a triumphant glance toward Jack, who was still hovering by the back window.

There was a knock, and Jack went into the vestibule to let Randy and Aaron inside.

"The co-op is surrounded," Randy reported as he set his coffee thermos on the nearest counter. "I was lucky they let me through. They're setting up barricades. Main's blocked off now, both ways, on the south side of town."

"I saw them," Kate said as her co-workers tried to process what Randy had just said. "I saw the tactical team's truck heading toward the co-op."

Jack couldn't resist following Randy to the huddle to hear the latest. "I get the thing at the auction barn; this Carlson guy is obviously wanted as part of that. But why the co-op? What's that got to do with any of it?"

Kate stared at her phone. It gave her something to do with her hands, as they'd started to shake. And it kept her from having to look any of her co-workers in the eye just now.

"I doubt Carlson's at the co-op," Bev said. "But maybe there's another auction barn employee they're looking for? It's early; someone could have gone down for a load of feed and bedding. There's a big sale tomorrow, since there won't be a Saturday sale due to Memorial Day weekend. Some of the farmers will bring in their livestock this afternoon, already."

Jack wasn't sure about that theory. "But that would be someone from the barn staff, in the back. Not any of the office folks." Allison looked about to say something, and Jack hurried on. "I mean, it just doesn't make any sense."

"Unless it's one of the Wheelers, themselves," Roberta put in. "I'd wonder if Pete or Dylan, someone like that, does those co-op runs."

"How many people are involved in this thing?" Randy asked. "There must be two, if not more. I have to say, this is the right way to catch those crooks. Move in early, when there aren't many people milling around town."

Jack nodded his approval. "And you'd want to nab them

when they're not together, then keep them separated. They're more likely to squeal on each other."

"Where's Mae?" Roberta was worried. "I know she has to drop off the kids, but ..."

"She's probably stuck behind a barricade, somewhere," Randy said. "Just running a little late, that's all."

Aaron had wandered over to his locker while the rest of the group debated the latest developments. Except for Kate, who noticed the way her younger co-worker grasped his locker door for support while he took a phone call.

"It's Vernon Millard," Aaron told the group when he returned to the table. "Jared says Vernon's holed up in the co-op's office. He's armed, and he refuses to come out."

Jared, who was off today, was a member of the volunteer fire department. He wasn't at the scene, but he would be hearing from people in the know.

The carriers stared at each other in disbelief. Jack was the first to speak. "This is like something out of one of those cop shows. I can't believe this is happening!"

Kate couldn't, either. But she hadn't forgotten Auggie's pointed assessment of Vernon: *He's like a snake in the grass, waiting to strike.*

Someone, whether it was Eagle River police, or Sheriff Preston's crew, or state and federal investigators, had poked Vernon Millard with a sharp stick this morning. And apparently, he wasn't about to come out of his den without a fight.

Roberta had her phone to her ear. "I've been trying to get Ward, he's not ..."

A few seconds later, the postmaster gave her crew a thumbs-up.

"What in the devil is going on?" Roberta nearly shouted at the mayor. She peeled away from the counter, and started to pace back and forth. Then she stopped.

"Oh, no. That's terrible!" She nodded once, twice. "Yes, I

see. No, we'll stay put, as long as it takes."

Roberta blinked away a few tears. "Let's hope it doesn't come to that. This is so, so scary. Let me know as soon as you hear anything more."

It wasn't a request. Roberta snapped off her phone.

Bev gave Kate's arm a squeeze. Allison had her hands clasped in prayer.

"I can't believe I'm saying this," the postmaster said, "but Vernon Millard is wanted in connection with the embezzlement case. He is threatening to harm himself, and anyone who tries to come in. He's also claiming he has explosives stashed on the property."

"*What*?" Randy beat Jack to it. "You can't be ..."

"In *two* places. In the back room of the co-op's office, and in the grain tower on the west edge of the lot." Roberta closed her eyes for a second and took a deep breath. "Which, as we all know, is right next to the secondary-school campus."

"What are we supposed to do?" Jack wanted to know. "Just sit here, and wait him out?"

He gestured at the cartons of letters, and then the piles of parcels waiting in one corner. "'The mail always goes through,' isn't that what they say?"

"Not today." Roberta shook her head. "No one leaves this post office. The front door stays locked, as well as the back. I don't want any of you risking your safety. Ward says there's another alert coming out in the next few minutes. Everyone is being told to shelter in place, and that is exactly what we are going to do."

Bev was distraught. "I've known Vernon and Martha for years. I can't imagine him doing something like this; what they're saying he's done, and especially what's going on, right now."

"You really think he's going to blow that place up?" Aaron asked no one in particular as all their phones began to chime. "How unhinged is he, anyway?"

Randy shook his head in awe.

"If he's the mastermind behind the whole mess, who knows what he might do? And given the show he's putting on in this town, right now, embezzlement won't be the worst of the charges he's going to face."

Jack crossed his arms. "Obstruction of justice, harassment of law-enforcement officials, the list will go on and on. Maybe he thinks he doesn't have anything left to live for."

Allison had brought in blueberry muffins, and they still waited on the far counter next to the cartons of unsorted mail. Their presence was a jarring reminder of how this morning offered some small hints of normalcy, yet was completely bizarre at the same time.

Bev saw Aaron eyeing the muffins, and gave a shrug and a wry smile. "We might as well enjoy them, I guess."

Allison quickly looked up from her phone, as if she'd forgotten about the treats. "Help yourselves. It sounds like we'll be here for a while."

Updates continued to pour in. Between the fugitive on the loose and the standoff at the co-op, school had been canceled for the day. While the middle and high schools were directly behind the co-op, the elementary building was only a few blocks to the east.

The few children who'd arrived early would remain inside the district's buildings. The bus drivers, who were partway through their rural morning routes, had been instructed to turn around and take those students home.

Mae soon texted Roberta to let her know she was scrambling for child care; Randy reported his grandchildren were on their way to Grandma and Grandpa's house.

Main Street was now closed on both ends of town, which left the east-west blacktop as the only way to get in and out of Eagle River.

Police officers were posted at the stoplight, stopping

incoming cars to explain the situation and directing them to take alternate routes.

K-9 units had been spotted at both the co-op and the auction barn. Several people were sheltering in place at the coffee shop and Eagle River's lone gas station, which were both close to the co-op.

Grandpa Wayne soon called Kate to say he and the breakfast gang were at Peabody's, and everyone was gathered at the front windows.

Along with a swarm of uniformed officers, Grandpa Wayne reported seeing "lots of guys in dress shirts and ties." White plastic totes were being carried out of the auction barn and loaded into an unmarked van.

He'd also spotted a younger man being marched out of the auction barn in handcuffs. Grandpa didn't recognize the guy, which meant he definitely wasn't part of the Wheeler family's immediate circle.

Grandpa Wayne also noted the number of people apparently connected to the embezzlement case now stood at three. And it was likely to rise, he said, given the gossip buzzing around the restaurant. How many more were there?

"I have no idea." This time, Kate was telling the whole truth. "This thing is making my head spin."

After she hung up, Kate took a bite of her blueberry muffin and washed it down with a bracing gulp of coffee. She had been unusually quiet that morning; but all of her co-workers, including Bev, had been too distracted to notice.

Kate started for the bathroom as fast as she could without drawing attention to herself. She bolted the door, and pulled up Auggie's number on her phone. She stared at it for a moment, then put her device back in her pocket.

As much as she wanted to talk this over with Auggie, this definitely wasn't the right time. And, given what was happening in her hometown this morning, there might never be one.

The ramifications of what she'd possibly set into motion made Kate lightheaded, and she leaned against the bathroom's cinder-block wall and closed her eyes.

"Maybe they already knew," she whispered. "Maybe Auggie and I just reinforced what someone already suspected about Vernon." That idea didn't give Kate much comfort, but she'd take it where she could find it today.

Make hay while the sun shines may have been the embezzlement crew's motto, but it certainly didn't fit what was happening now.

Unless you were a member of law enforcement.

Maybe another old saying was more fitting for this dark day in Eagle River, Kate decided. *You reap what you sow.*

* 22 *

Vernon ultimately surrendered to authorities, but the residents of Eagle River were subjected to four long, anxious hours before the standoff finally came to an end.

While various law-enforcement officers and mental-health counselors had worked diligently to keep the lines of communication open during that tense time, it was the pleas made by Vernon's son that seemed to sway him in the end. The grandchildren were afraid their lives were in danger, Vernon's son told him, and they wanted to go back to school and be reunited with their teachers and friends.

Randy and Jack had been right about the long list of crimes Vernon could face.

Along with embezzlement, fraud, and theft, authorities had added charges of terrorism, harassment, and interference with official acts, as well as two counts of assault on a peace officer after Vernon fought back against the agents determined to get him in handcuffs and out of the co-op.

Officers confiscated the rifle Vernon legally had in his possession that morning, and they found a crude, homemade bomb hidden in the co-op's office.

Despite hours spent searching every corner of every structure on the lot, investigators finally determined Vernon had lied about the second explosive device. That threat had been just one more way the co-op manager had tried to intimidate law enforcement and the community.

It was the terrorism charges that had Vernon cooling his heels in the Hartland County Jail. At his initial court appearance on Thursday, a judge declared Vernon dangerous to society, and upheld law enforcement's request that he be denied bail.

"I still can't believe Vernon's behind bars," Kate told Scout Friday morning when she found the big tuxedo cat in front of the garage after breakfast. "And that he might stay there until his trial, which is likely months away. Everyone thinks his attorney will try again to get him released; I hope that plan fails."

Kate was out the door earlier than usual today. She was eager to collect a coffee treat, along with more information on the still-unfolding case, at The Daily Grind before she headed to the post office. A surprising amount of details had spread through the community in less than two days, and Kate wondered how many people had harbored suspicions that they now felt they could safely share.

Determined to support the area's farmers and spread the message that "the show must go on," the Wheelers had refused to cancel yesterday's sale. That event had also provided people with another chance to gather, refine their theories about the situation, and hear new tidbits offered by friends and strangers alike.

While some of the rumors might turn out to be false, Kate suspected many of them carried a ring of truth. Because while Vernon had pleaded "not guilty" to all his charges, his crafty accomplice had been eager to spill all their secrets to investigators, as well as his own family and friends, as soon as he'd been taken into custody.

"I knew this case had to be complicated, but I still can hardly believe how many layers it has." Kate sighed as she waited for a passing tractor before she pulled out onto the blacktop. "This is why you should never jump to conclusions. As it turns out, Brent Carlson was only a minor player in this production."

The dubious honor of being hand-picked as a partner in Vernon's embezzlement enterprise went to Caleb McBride, another barn hand at Wheeler Auction Company.

"Vernon's too proud, or maybe too stupid, to cooperate in any way. But Caleb? He didn't put up a fight when investigators nabbed him at the auction barn Wednesday morning. He knew it was in his best interests to come clean."

Between cooperating with authorities, and not threatening to blow up Eagle River, Caleb was out on bail while Vernon was stuck in jail. While it was too early to know exactly how things would shake out, it was a good bet Caleb would see his own charges and punishments reduced for exposing all the duo's secrets.

"Vernon and Caleb kept their scam going for seven years." Kate shook her head in amazement as the outskirts of Eagle River came into view. "But that's not even the half of it."

Kate had been right about how the whole mess had started. Many years ago, Vernon began overcharging Wheeler Auction Company for their co-op orders of feed and bedding. He'd entered the regular rates in his registers, and pocketed the difference. Word was he'd deposited his ill-gotten gains in an account he'd opened at a bank in Mason City.

Vernon had increased the discrepancies slowly over time and, given that the cost of everything seemed to only go up, the Wheelers didn't question the changes. Besides, no one at the auction barn would have wanted the public drama of severing those ties.

Vernon was content with this solo scheme for a long time; but when he discovered a potential accomplice working in the barn area of Wheeler Auction Company, greed motivated him to grasp for more.

Caleb McBride was a Swanton native who'd moved away

after college to launch a tech career in Silicon Valley. But he soon grew tired of California's fast-paced lifestyle, and quit the rat race eight years ago to return to his small-town roots.

At least, that's the story he'd told his family and friends. And he'd repeated that tall tale to Pete Wheeler before Pete hired him to be a livestock hand at the auction barn.

The real deal? Caleb had quietly quit his tech job after being accused of fraud and system tampering.

Pete had only checked the personal references Caleb had provided, and hadn't bothered to talk to the young man's former bosses. Beyond making Caleb the obvious choice for the barn hand who added the co-op's invoices to the system, his computer skills were of no interest to the Wheelers. But they were certainly useful to Vernon Millard.

No one was sure exactly how Vernon had uncovered Caleb's past, or how he'd approached the Wheelers' barn hand about a dubious partnership. But even though Caleb was thirty years his junior, and as sophisticated as Vernon was small-town neighborly, Vernon had found his perfect partner in crime.

Caleb had apparently bragged that it was relatively easy to hack into the auction barn's antiquated accounting software, which allowed him to see how money flowed in and out of the business. And then, just as Vernon had done with the co-op invoices, Caleb started small. He made minor changes, both positive and negative, to some customers' accounts. When it became clear those were going undetected, he started to swipe money from the auction barn's system.

This scheme accomplished much more than allowing Caleb and Vernon to steal greater amounts of money from the auction barn. It created a pattern of errors that, if ever discovered, would point the finger at the Wheelers' office staff. To further cover his tracks, Caleb admitted, he'd also altered some transactions that predated his employment at the business.

The official word was that Caleb and Vernon had taken at least $80,000 from the auction company. However, that figure only scratched the surface of what Vernon had likely stolen from the Wheelers' business during his decades as the co-op's manager. That haul could be hundreds of thousands of dollars, gossip noted, and it could take weeks, even months, before the scope of that much-larger scheme might be known.

As their financial gains increased, the duo's web of holding accounts had expanded, too. Money was transferred to several banks in Wisconsin and Minnesota, and others as far away as Idaho and Montana. Caleb had even converted some of their ill-gotten gains into cryptocurrency.

That made many in Eagle River wonder if Vernon and Caleb had escape plans in place. But Kate felt certain she knew why they'd stayed in town.

People left Eagle River all the time, for many reasons; she had done the same. But no one simply disappeared. And Vernon in particular, with both a decades-long marriage and career, and a brood of children and grandchildren, would have only drawn scrutiny if he'd tried to flee.

Instead, Vernon and Caleb had stayed ... and instigated a rash of vandalism to threaten those determined to smoke them out.

That part of the plan was outsourced to a handful of other back-of-the-barn employees.

The gang had included Brent Carlson as well as Sam Hatfield, one of the guys who had squared off with Dylan Wheeler at the bar the night of the big basketball game. Both now faced charges of vandalism and harassment in connection with the damage at the auction barn and the Wellingtons' home.

Kate had no way to confirm the identities of the three guys Brody had observed at that party, so she didn't assume that Caleb, Brent, and Sam made up that trio. Brody had thought one of the guys was named Mitch or Mike; and officials had announced that more arrests might be made in the coming days.

Once she reached the south end of Main Street, Kate kept an eye out for a parking spot. The Daily Grind was always bustling at this hour of the morning, and the back lot would already be full.

"You have to wonder what Sam and Brent knew, and when," Kate mused as she scored a parking spot near the coffee shop's front door. "Did they put two and two together, come up with a crime, and threaten to squeal? That would have been enough for Caleb to deal them into this game. Or maybe, they just jumped at the chance to create a little chaos and make some easy money."

Like Caleb, Sam had been smart enough to let the cops take him into custody. But since Brent took off running, he'd been charged with resisting arrest, as well.

"That unregistered handgun isn't helping his case. And he could have hidden in the woods along the river until dark; but instead, he called his girlfriend to come pick him up." Kate laughed as she reached for her purse. "I bet he was surprised when she dropped him off at the police station."

* * *

Barricades still encircled the co-op's main lot, which was separated from The Daily Grind by only a side street and the corner's empty storefront. Kate had heard those barriers would be removed today, and the shop would reopen tomorrow morning.

It may have been the start of a holiday weekend, but the area's farmers needed supplies. While Vernon and Caleb's futures remained uncertain, it was time for the rest of Eagle River to return to normal.

Kate removed her sunglasses as soon as she stepped inside the coffee shop, but it still took her eyes a moment to adjust to the interior of the old building. While the bank of front windows let in a great deal of natural light, the rest of the long and narrow space consisted of weathered-brick walls crowned with track lighting just below the high ceiling.

Most of the tables were occupied, and a half-dozen people were in line at the counter. While Kate waited her turn, she listened in on the conversations swirling around her.

Many of them focused on the embezzlement case: Where people were when they got the first alert, their reactions to the tense situation, and how it had affected not just their routines but their sense of safety in this small town.

When it was Kate's turn at the counter, she got the lowdown on The Daily Grind's front-row seat to the chaos.

"It was *crazy*," Austin Freitag, the shop's owner, said as he wrote down her order. "We had over a dozen people trapped in here for all those hours."

"I'd wondered how you were doing." Kate wasn't able to resist the plate of chocolate-chip scones that winked at her from behind the showcase's glass front. "All of us carriers were stuck inside the post office, of course. With such a late start on our routes, it made for a very, very long day."

"But that order from the feds was a nice bonus, I guess," Austin said as he started Kate's coffee confection. "I mean, it's not every day someone from the FBI calls in an order for pickup. They certainly tip well."

Federal officials had requested two carafes of coffee, one each of decaf and regular; three dozen assorted pastries; and disposable cups and plates. They sent two well-armed, uniformed officers up the street to meet Cordelia, Austin's assistant manager, at the shop's temporarily unlocked door.

Kate laughed. "What's the saying? 'An army crawls on its stomach?' I suppose it's the same during a standoff."

Austin motioned for Cordelia to help the next person in line, then leaned over the counter toward Kate again.

"You'll never guess who showed up here yesterday

afternoon," Austin said in a low voice. "Donald Wellington came in with his wife, looking surprisingly well-rested. He's the only person I've seen around here with a nice tan, by the way."

Kate was relieved. "Some folks get spring fever, you know? They like to get out of town, now and then."

"Donald handles our taxes. It's amazing what one can do through the internet these days," Austin said as he plated Kate's scone. "And as president of our little chamber of commerce, I'm usually encouraged when I see folks moving back to the area."

He gave Kate a knowing look. "But apparently, there are some shady characters out there."

"You don't have to worry about me," Kate promised. "I think I'll stick with delivering the mail. The pay's not the greatest, but the benefits are amazing."

Kate found a small table toward the back of the coffee shop, and settled in with her treat. She only had about fifteen minutes to spare, and hoped it would be enough. She wasn't disappointed.

Two teenagers across the way, likely a guy and his girlfriend, were finishing their breakfast sandwiches before they left for class.

"Do you think that story is real?" the wide-eyed girl asked as she twirled her long, brown hair around one finger. "The buried suitcase, I mean."

Kate set down her scone, determined not to miss one second of this exchange.

"Dunno." The boy raised an eyebrow. "Adam says it is. And he would know. His grandpa's been Vernon's neighbor for thirty years."

Caleb and Vernon had used the latest technology to move money across state lines, but apparently some of Eagle River's younger residents believed Vernon had buried some of his loot. It was deep in Vernon's backyard, according to one of the theories Kate now heard, maybe under a hydrangea on the edge of the garden. Or it was in the woods, down by the river. The girl thought it was next to a certain oak tree, but her boyfriend was sure the haul was hidden near the pilings of the east bridge.

"Here's what I think." The guy took his girl's hand and smiled. "There's a full moon next week. Let's sneak out some night, go down there, and see if we can find it."

Kate smiled as she sipped her coffee. Regardless of what he really believed about Vernon's money, this boy was looking to score in another way if he could.

It wasn't long before a conversation at the next table also caught her attention.

"I heard Vernon's now going to try a defense of insanity," one middle-aged man told his buddies. "He'd better start cooperating, either way. Especially because Caleb's saying plenty; those other two are, as well. And the co-op board held that emergency meeting yesterday so they could fire him."

"Maybe Martha talked some sense into him," his friend said. "She's filing for divorce next week, my wife says. And the house goes on the market soon after that."

"Sounds like she had her ducks in a row," the third man said with an approving nod. "Makes you wonder what her life's been like all these years. Do you think she had a clue?"

The first guy shook his head. "I doubt it. I always liked Vernon well enough. But he seemed, I don't know ... too good to be true? And he might as well plead insanity. I mean, he threatened to *blow himself up*."

The others laughed. "It's like that crazy fool in those old Saturday-morning cartoons," one of the men said. "You know, the one that carried around the dynamite. I don't think it was Elmer, he always had a gun in his hands. Was it the coyote? Or the dude from the spaceship?"

"I'm not sure." The third man took a sip of his coffee. "But old Vernon's nuttier than all of them put together."

23

As Kate turned up her parents' driveway that evening, she let out a sigh of relief when she saw an extra truck parked by the house. And then, she laughed.

"Of course he's here! He promised he would be." She glanced in the rearview mirror to where Hazel lounged on the back seat.

"You get to see your buddy again! And I'm talking about Alex; you already expected to see Waylon and the barn kitties."

The bar's assistant manager had opened Paul's Place on his own, even though it was a Friday night and happy hour was always packed, so Alex could fit time with the Duncan clan into his schedule. But Kate and Alex had decided to drive separately so he could leave when he needed to, and Kate and Hazel could stay as long as they wanted.

Kate just hoped Alex didn't come up with some excuse to leave earlier than expected. He was eager to meet her family, but he was also nervous. Incredibly nervous.

And sure enough, he was still lingering by his truck, waiting for her arrival to head inside. He was happily complying with Waylon's demands for attention, but Kate noticed a bit of uneasiness in Alex's brown eyes when she reached him, and reached for his hand.

"It's going to be fine," she promised. "You'll dazzle them all with a few great stories about the bar. Just remember: Dad is a Cubs fan, and Bryan is a Royals fan."

"Got it." Alex nodded. "And the way in with your mom is to ask her about her garden. She planted twice as many tomato plants as last year, but not the cherry ones. And she can't wait to be a full-time grandma this summer. Prosper's elementary kids get out of school on Wednesday, the office closes Thursday afternoon, and then she's free until August."

Kate raised her eyebrows. "Very good."

"Did you think I'd show up unprepared?" Alex pretended to be offended as they watched Hazel and Waylon dash off around the garage. Two barn cats were close behind, determined not to miss out on the fun.

"I mean, you do remember that I used to be ..."

Kate put her arm around him. "I haven't told them about that. And I won't bring it up. We don't need to talk about it tonight. That's a discussion for later, and one you'll drive the bus for."

"Thanks," he whispered. Then he grinned. "Is that a pie there, on the front seat?"

"It sure is. I'll get it, if you can get the door."

Kate took another deep breath as they made their way into the kitchen. But this one came from gratitude, not nerves. So much had happened in the past few months, but this house? It never changed.

That was true not only of its somewhat-dated look, but of the love and support that were always available there.

Kate knew her family would extend the same to Alex. She just hoped he would let his guard down far enough to let it in.

"Anna texted, they're running late," Charlotte called over her shoulder as she dried her hands on a dishtowel. "Bryan had to wrap up a few things, then they had to do chores."

She hurried over to where Alex still lingered by the back door.

"Well, am I glad to finally meet you!" Charlotte went for the hug.

Kate had expected that, but Alex probably hadn't. Even so, his face lit up when he met Kate's mom halfway.

"You know," Charlotte said, "we were starting to wonder if she'd made you up out of thin air!"

Because Kate had told her parents hardly anything about Alex, she hadn't said a word to them about their estrangement. That had worked out perfectly.

There was something to be said for not having to answer too many prying questions.

Alex laughed. "Oh, I'm real."

He studied his surroundings. "I like this kitchen. It feels so comfortable, and homey."

"You're welcome here, anytime." The oven beeped, and Charlotte hurried over to it. "We're ready to go, looks like."

Kate set her purse, and the apple pie, on the kitchen table. "Once we get the pizzas in the oven, do you need help with the salad?"

Charlotte waved away her daughter's offer. "No, no, it's fine. Just the garlic bread, later. Why don't you give Alex the grand tour, instead? Your dad will be in from chores soon, and he'll be eager to meet our guest of honor."

Kate showed Alex the living and dining rooms, and the office that took up a small, former bedroom on the northeast corner of the first floor. They made a stop at the generously sized open front porch, which gazed down a slight slope toward the road.

Alex shook his head in awe. "Look at that view! This must be the perfect place to hang out on a summer night."

"Bryan and Anna live in the original farmhouse, just up the road. It's been remodeled several times, but the rooms are still small and sort-of closed off." Kate shrugged. "It's full of history, but I think I'm partial to this place."

"You grew up here. Of course you are."

With their first-floor tour complete, they went upstairs. They peeked into this room and that one; and then, Kate paused at the last door. "This used to be my room, growing up. But it's all set up for little Ethan now."

The peach-colored walls had come in handy when it was time to decorate the new nursery. While peach-and-cream gingham curtains still hugged the windows, Kate's old bed had been dismantled and put into storage, and the drawer fronts on her former dresser were now painted a rainbow of pastel hues.

A crib and changing table had been added, and a vintage family rocking chair rested by the south window. There was just enough space for a toddler bed to be brought in someday, while saving room for a younger sibling to also stay with Grandma and Grandpa.

Alex was drawn to the farm-themed mobile over the crib. "Oh, I like this. Cows, pigs, sheep, cats, dogs ... everyone is here."

Then he laughed. "Get Ethan interested early; maybe he'll be the next generation to farm this land. Which one would that be?"

"The sixth," Kate said with pride. "But Bryan and Anna have already decided, they aren't going to push their kids into that profession. Little Ethan, and any future siblings, will get to make their own choices when the time comes."

She paused at the east window, and gazed out over the fields just beyond the garden. The young, delicate corn plants looked like green stitches in a brown blanket that rolled off toward the windbreak of trees that marked Bryan and Anna's farm.

It was a scene that had comforted Kate for so many years. No matter what was happening in her life, she had always known what she'd find out this window, season after season.

She looked around her old bedroom, and shook her head in awe.

"It's amazing how this space has changed so much, but it feels the same."

"My parents don't live in my childhood home anymore, as you know." There was a note of wistfulness in Alex's voice. "But I still think of my old room sometimes. Those hold so much meaning for us, even all these years later."

The rich finish of the wooden crib and changing table glowed in the evening light. And Alex was right about the mobile. Ethan had everything he could possibly want, or need.

Even so, tears sprang into Kate's eyes.

"Hey," Alex whispered as he wrapped his arms around her. "It's OK. No wonder you're feeling so sentimental; this room has to bring back so many memories. I hope most of them are good ones."

Kate wiped her cheeks with the back of one hand. "Oh, they are."

But that wasn't where the tears were coming from. For a moment, Kate almost said something, opened her heart a little wider to Alex. Told him about all the years of frustration and disappointment, the long-held hope that she would have been the one to choose a crib for this room and staff it with stuffies.

It was one of the reasons her marriage had fallen apart. While it wasn't the biggest one, and certainly not the final blow, Kate still carried that hurt around with her. Most days, it didn't bother her at all, but sometimes ...

Alex was watching her closely, as he often did. But this wasn't the right time to tell him; it was still too soon. However, Kate sensed that day was likely to come. She'd be content to wait for it.

That night when they'd argued in his kitchen, he had reminded her that everyone has secrets.

He had many, even after all the ones he'd shared with her in the past few weeks.

She had hers, too. And this one? She'd keep it to herself a little while longer.

The back door opened and closed downstairs, and a rush of chatter and laughter rose up the stairwell. Next came the gurgling cry of a happy little baby who was eager to be passed into the arms of all the people who loved him.

"Kate!" Charlotte called up the stairs. "They're here! And it's time to start the bread."

While Kate pulled the nursery door closed behind her, Alex lingered in the hallway. "You told me garlic bread was part of the pizza-night tradition. I think I can get behind that."

"I have a top-secret recipe." She winked at him, then gestured toward the stairs. "It's classified, but I'll show you how it's done."

Kate's adventures will continue
in Book 5 of the "Mailbox Mysteries" series!
If you aren't already on the email list,
go to the "connect" tab at fremontcreekpress.com
and sign up to receive news about future books.

ABOUT THE BOOKS

Don't miss any of the titles in these heartwarming rural fiction series

THE GROWING SEASON SERIES

Melinda is at a crossroads when the “for rent” sign beckons her down a dusty gravel lane. Facing forty, single and downsized from her stellar career at a big-city ad agency, she’s struggling to start over when a phone call brings her home to Iowa.

She moves to the country, takes on a rundown farm and its headstrong animals, and lands behind the counter of her family’s hardware store in the community of Prosper, whose motto is “The Great Little Town That Didn’t.” And just like the sprawling garden she tends under the summer sun, Melinda begins to thrive. But when storm clouds arrive on her horizon, can she hold on to the new life she’s worked so hard to create?

Filled with memorable characters, from a big-hearted farm dog to the weather-obsessed owner of the local co-op, “Growing Season” celebrates the twists and turns of small-town life. Discover the heartwarming series that’s filled with new friends, fresh starts and second chances.

FOR DETAILS ON ALL THE TITLES
VISIT FREMONTCREEKPRESS.COM

THE MAILBOX MYSTERIES SERIES

It's been a rough year for Kate Duncan, both on and off the job. Being a mail carrier puts her in close proximity to her customers, with consequences that can't always be foreseen. So when a position opens at her hometown post office, she decides to leave Chicago in her rearview mirror.

Kate and her cat settle into a charming apartment above Eagle River's historic Main Street, but she dreams of a different home to call her own. And as she drives the back roads around Eagle River, Kate begins to take a personal interest in the people on her route.

So when an elderly resident goes missing, she feels compelled to help track him down. It's a quest marked not by miles of gravel, but matters of the heart: friendship, family, and the small connections that add up to a well-lived life.

A TIN TRAIN CHRISTMAS

The toy train was everything two boys could want: colorful, shiny, and the perfect vehicle for their imaginations. But was it meant to be theirs? Revisit Horace's childhood for this special holiday short story inspired by the "Growing Season" series!

Made in the USA
Las Vegas, NV
18 February 2025

18336157R00171